COLD RUN

Michael Dault

2Sox Publishing Pack

U.S.A.

Second Edition, 2026

ISBN: 9781952439193

Library of Congress LCCN: 2021919429

Copyright 2021 by Michael Dault

This book is a work of fiction. Names, characters, businesses, places, events, conversations, opinions, and incidents are either products of the author's imagination or are used fictitiously. Any resemblance to actual events, locales, conversations, opinions, business establishments, or persons, living or dead, is entirely coincidental and unintended.

All rights reserved. No part of this book may be reproduced in whole or in part without written permission from the publisher except by reviewers who may quote brief excerpts in connection with a review in a newspaper, magazine, or electronic publication; nor may any part of this book be reproduced, stored in a retrieval system, or transmitted in any form or by any means electronic, mechanical, photocopying, recording or any other means, without written permission from the publisher.

Cover courtesy of the author; interior design by Moonshine Cove staff.

For Mickey and Mays

About the Author

Michael was born in the state of Virginia and raised in the beauty of Michigan's Upper Peninsula. After a short stint in professional  baseball, he began his media career working for television and radio. Later, he transitioned into online and print sports journalism. In 2006, he founded his own film and television production company TipToe Productions, which he presently owns and operates. This has led to collaborating on award-winning projects and various producing, directing, screenwriting, and acting roles. In 2017, *The Sons of Summer* was Michael's first published novel. *Cold Run* is the first book in a forthcoming series.

www.MichaelDault.com

MEET THE MAN WITH NO NAME. WHEN THE SNOW FALLS, HE'S RUNNING.

By all appearances, Cy Ford is no more than a quiet loner living in Michigan's Upper Peninsula. He works as a conservation officer and prefers the company of his sled dogs. What nobody suspects is that Ford's past is a fractured one, and all of it, down to his name, is a lie. During the winter months, Ford moonlights as a drug-running dog sled musher, a lucrative sideline that's allowed him to amass a small fortune. With Christmas around the corner, Ford has decided to get out of the game, but it won't be that easy. When a turf war breaks out between his Canadian employer and a Detroit-based mobster, he finds himself forced into one last run he and his team may never reach the end of.

What People are Saying about Cold Run

"I read every piece of fiction and non-fiction about sled dogs that I can get my hands on, and no author or poet better captures the Klondike culture — at least no one since Jack London and Robert W. Service. The poet Service was right when he wrote that strange things are done in the midnight sun. Michael Dault proves it with his exquisite novel *Cold Run*." —**Del Jones, author of** *The Cremation of Sam McGee*

"A bold, unique and intriguing approach to action-adventure fiction." —**Suzanne Parrott, Author, Publisher, Speaker**

"I'm always prepared for a journey when reading Dault's work. His stories move you, tug at your heart, open your eyes in ways that life doesn't let you. A master storyteller that takes you on a ride every time, *Cold Run* had me captivated on every turn of the page." —**Kevin Interdonato, Actor/Producer: *City on a Hill, Sopranos, Bad Frank***

"As you embark on this *Cold Run*, the story will take you on a powerful, exciting, and emotional ride, filled with twists and turns to a gripping conclusion. Dault is masterful at bringing all the characters in the book to life." —**Kenyon Kemnitz, Sports Announcer**

Excerpt

The look on Ford's face had long showed that he was ready, reminiscent of an athlete before an important game. When the morning's sun was at its highest, Ford clicked his tongue twice and he was off to the races. His lead dog North led the sled with command and grace as Ford steered by yelling "Speed" when he wanted them to run faster or "Slow" when he wanted them to slow their pace. "Whoa" when he wanted them to stop. For right turns, he yelled "Gee" and for left turns he yelled "Haw." On quick turns, he'd lean his body any which way and kicked his foot behind the sled to use it as a rudder.

Trail-to-trail the team pivoted and sprinted that afternoon as they ran the same planned routes they've taken so many times in the past. There was something beautiful about the way the sled glided along the changing terrain. Almost as if they were poetry in motion, the dogs ran and ran, slowing and speeding in unison, whatever Ford desired. They were never winded, giving evidence to his claim that dog power was more reliable than any auto's horsepower. Most trails they rode were heavily used by snowmobiles, but over the last decade or so, dog sleds were increasingly becoming a staple of winter travel in more rural communities across the northern frontier.

COLD RUN

There was a peculiar smell. An eye-pinching aroma that hung in the air and its intensity grew with the seconds. A pair of lifeless, soot-covered hands were draped above broad metal. One of them twitched. Then the other. They began to awaken and scraped for something, anything to hold onto. A haggard man hung upside down in the passenger seat of an apple red F-150 truck that lay on its roof from an apparent accident. His seat belt was the only saving grace, securing him from falling completely onto the cab's inside roof. Streams of sweat and blood ran from his face wounds under his dark and mangled beard that flowed past his Adam's apple. His hazel eyes stung when they pooled in his sockets. Somewhere behind that wild tame of facial hair and blood, there was a hitchhiker in his mid-thirties, simply caught in the wrong place, wrong time.

The world around him felt as it looked. Cloudy.

Confused, he gradually gathered his bearings. When he turned his head to the side, he saw the male driver of the rig, of the same age, was in even worse shape. A bloody mess of what was once a dark-featured, smooth-talking Texan. His pearl white cowboy hat was crumpled over his face, and it was smeared with red. Unlike the haggard man, he hadn't worn a seat belt, but was still positioned in the same manner as his passenger. The only reason he wasn't completely thrown from the vehicle was because the dashboard had crushed into his chest, pinning him.

When the haggard man tried to reach to shake the driver to see if he was alive, he felt intense heat that beamed off his clothes. He then glanced through the cracked windshield to find heaps of flames spitting and crackling on the outside as if they were taunting them. He figured they originated from the engine block. It was only when he shifted his eyes at the driver's gator-skin boots melting that he realized the entire cab was ablaze.

Panic set in. He had to free himself and do it quickly.

His seat belt wouldn't give an inch, though. It was jammed. Smoke billowed into the cab from under the driver's side footboard and stole the air. The haggard man coughed and choked when more seeped in. There wasn't time to formulate a plan. If he were to escape, he had to do it now. He tried to reach for his nylon backpack on the floor. There was a knife inside it he could use to cut himself free. Over and over, he stretched his arms as far as they humanly could to no avail. His backpack was too far under the seat for his reach. His thoughts quickly set in on the windshield again and he thrusted his foot forward to kick it, in hopes he could smash it entirely to release as much smoke in the cab as he could. When his foot wasn't doing the trick, he used both feet and busted a hole that caught his right boot's laces and refused to let him go. Awkwardly, he hung there. The more he twisted his body to try to extricate the boot the more stuck it became.

He released a frustrated scream from the hollows of his smoke-filled lungs and tried to use his other foot to break his stuck one out. As he did, his ears perked to a soft whimper followed by painful groans from the driver next to him. The driver's cowboy hat slid aside, revealing his deformed face to the haggard man's horror. His nose was ripped from his face, and it hung by a strand of skin on his cheek. One eye protruded from his skull, and the other was gone.

"Hey!" the haggard man yelled to him with his craggy voice as if the rust shook from his larynx.

He saw the driver's head move slightly and then he choked a cough.

"Hey," the haggard man yelled to him again. "Can you hear me? Hey!"

Through the coughing, the driver still didn't answer, but at least the haggard man knew he was still alive. He felt useless. There wasn't a thing he could do to assist the helpless driver, unless he could free himself first.

Panic turned to anger, which fueled his adrenaline, and he used his elbow to try to break his passenger side window. He slammed it with everything he had. The window bowed past its frame but declined to crack. Repeatedly he kept at it, every effort harder than the last. With a final elbow-shattering blow he broke through the window, and the blackest smoke he had ever seen in his life filtered out following shards of glass.

His baby blue denim shirt was torn, leaving the deepest of gashes on his forearm. He didn't pay the wounds any mind and grabbed a sharp shard that was on the door's armrest. Threads from the waist part of his seat belt started to give as he sawed the shard along it in an up and down manner. With every painful cough the driver next to him hacked, it kept the fight alive in the haggard man to keep cutting at his belt.

Faster and faster, the threads broke with whip sound snaps.

Groans turned into screams when the driver further entered consciousness. By now the fire had caught above his waist. His torturous howls stung the haggard man's ears, who tried to block them out, and focus on the task at hand as best he could. It appeared the driver couldn't move his arms or even his legs. He was presumably paralyzed, unbeknownst to the haggard man.

By the time the haggard man completely cut through his belt, its release helped dislodge his boot from the windshield, and he plunged on the inside of the cab's roof. He felt like sizzling bacon on the metal that was now as hot as a greasy pan on a stove. Any exposed skin he covered with his clothes to prevent serious burns. With his hands balled inside the sleeves of his shirt, he crawled from the truck's cab, rolling feet away into the brown grass. Fresh air hit his lungs and he coughed and rolled back on all fours. He gagged and heaved black mucus onto the ground underneath him, willing himself and clawing the grass to a stand.

There he stood, man versus inferno. Rest wasn't an option, regardless of how exhausted he felt. To him, in this critical juncture, rest was for the weak. Surveying the spot, he saw the entire truck was in a ditch on the side of the highway they'd rode on mere minutes prior. Hard to believe that one moment he was listening to George Jones play on the radio as background music to the driver's rambling, the next he was staring mortality in the face. The rig he considered lay halfway in the thick woods that surrounded the desolate area, and the other end of it was on the incline of the ditch. He scanned the wreck for any other opening he could enter the cab from that was easiest, as well as safest, to extract the driver. He scurried around to the driver's side; the door was crushed and sunk into the earth. There wasn't a sliver of freedom. Prying it open wasn't an option. Damn near impossible. Back to the passenger side he went. Before he could even make a move to return, the engine exploded, blowing out the windshield completely. Flames poured into the cab like running water. The haggard man covered his head from what debris rained on the spot. Still, though, he could hear the driver's screams. They pierced his ears, louder than ever before.

"Come on you stupid son of a bitch," the haggard man whispered to himself as he tried to gather the courage to enter what was surely a death trap.

His legs shook. He pumped the fingers on both hands into his palms, each pump tossing aside the fear. His fingers formed a fist and he bolted back inside the cab.

II
YEARS LATER

Gray skies above provided a calm morning. A ghostly calm that seemed as if the sound was stolen from the world. Snow was visible for miles across a frozen lake. A lone ice shanty sat in the middle of it; a brown speck in the tundra of cold white. Beyond, a dog sled approached from a distance. After a while, it pulled to a stop twenty or so paces away from the shanty. A mysterious driver dismounted. Like some mix of Johnny Cash and Wyatt Earp, he stood fully draped in black. A LawPro classic bomber jacket with a black sheep shearling collar, slender Carhartt snow bibs, Baffin boots, and knit cap — the whole nine yards. An Upper Peninsula of Michigan Conservation officer's badge was clearly identified on his right breast, with the last name *"Ford"* etched in white. He ambled to his lead dog North, the name burnt deep in the leather of his collar, and stroked the pooch's face gently with his gloved hand.

    North had a very distinct appearance to him for a Siberian Husky and Akita mix. His coat was a sleek gray and black, with touches of white, and he had pointed ears that folded slightly at their tips. His paws were white to the shin as if he were wearing socks. And his tail was curly like an Arby's fry. From his all-black face, his golden eyes were absolutely striking, forcing one to look into them, rather than at them.

    Strapped in behind North in twos were the swing dogs, Kaya, a female, and Elmer, a male. These two helped set the pace from the leader's and provided the horsepower of the team. Essentially, they were the heart. Both were Chinook breeds. Both dogs were light brown and white and were the most playful of the group. They were also the youngest at two-years-old, which, in the pecking order of packs when together, took the most shit, ate last, and bowed before the dominant.

    The pair behind them were the wheel dogs, which were considered the strongest. Astro, a male, and Maisey, a female. Astro was a mostly white with hints of black Siberian Husky and he was twelve-years-old — the eldest of the pack. There was a time when he was the leader of this sled team, before Ford made the call to alternate him to the wheel position, a position that suited the group best, since he was becoming slower.

By the time North had joined the department dogs three years ago, it was clear from the very first day that he was the alpha, and no longer Astro. North was the right dog to lead this special pack.

Maisey was a gray and white Alaskan Malamute. She was the only rescue dog of them and had a hard time trusting new people, which naturally made her stubborn personality a difficult task to break in order to train her. Ford eventually had enough luck to break her though, and that in turn developed a trust between the two that she never had with any other human.

"Stay on my six, North," Ford told his lead dog.

North licked the palm of his hand then sat in place. The rest of the pack followed suit after their alpha. Ford then crouched near his brown sled to observe a set of boot prints that led to the shanty. Right next to them he floated his impassive hazel eyes to another set as well that merged into the same place. An ominous conclusion hit him, and then he pulled down his black neck gaiter around his scruffy face, revealing him as the haggard man from years before. Now he appeared as sure as ever. He was a profound man of strength and confidence. What little life he had that time ago, prisoner to an endless and aimless journey, was gone. Here, trading warmth for cold, this man named Ford seemed like someone else. Someone else with a purpose.

From the ice shanty, a meek, elderly man in his seventies, who was short in stature with white hair poking from under his bright orange hunter's cap, exited with an ice auger in hand. He placed it against the shanty's thin wall.

Ford noticed from the get that he hesitated to face him. Observing his careful actions, he saw the frozen breaths from the fisherman puff from his white-bearded face with a certain rapidness. Maybe from nervousness, Ford considered. The elderly man finally regained his composure and turned about-face to fake the best greeting he could for the officer.

"Ford," the elderly man said in his soft-spoken voice. "Fine morning for poking some holes in the ice, ain't it?"

Ford didn't answer him at first, instead, he just examined his surroundings with obvious caution.

"It is, Vernon," Ford finally responded with a slight nod.

"There's something therapeutic about coming way out here," Vernon said to Ford, while he nervously moved his cooler closer to his other belongings that lay near the shanty.

"Catch anything?"

"Unfortunately, no. My luck near Christmas."

Vernon cleared his throat and continued to aimlessly move gear around his fishing post, without any real purpose.

"To what do I owe the honor?" he asked Ford, while he dug into his Dickies coveralls for his fishing license. "My fishing license is current."

"We've got a problem. Your boy is on the run again. Broke outta Marquette County Prison days back."

"Yeah. Yeah, I heard about that. Damn shame. Trouble just has a way of finding him, I guess."

"Seems that way."

Ford's cold ways made Vernon keep his gaze to the ground and he warily kicked the snow beneath him.

In almost an unsure whisper, he told Ford, "Already spoke to Sheriff Anson and told him the same thing. I haven't heard from Henry. Nothing's changed. Now, I don't mean any disrespect, but why is this any concern of the DNR?"

"Escapees flee on the lands. State boys don't know the terrain, so it's on my department if these things occur."

Vernon stood there, not knowing what else he could say to the suspecting officer. Ford knew his intense stare made him increasingly anxious. The more this continued, the more he chipped away the kind-hearted man's guile.

Vernon was a blue-collar citizen of the area. He had spent most of his life working at the sawmill and taking care of his wife, who died of breast cancer a while back.

Nowadays, there wasn't an ounce of happiness left in him anymore. Loneliness was his cross to bear.

"I've got some time today," Ford told him. "Like you said, it's a good day to fish. What do you say you and I see what we can catch for lunch?"

Vernon swallowed the hardest of lumps in his throat. His eyeballs fluttered and blinked about as if the wind blew directly in them.

"Well, I— I'd like that, you know. But…you sorta caught me at a bad time. See, I was just gathering my things."

Without reason, he turned around to find something else he could move around. A transparent act to appear as if he were busy. This made Ford casually remove his gloves and drop them onto the ice in preparation for the tension that began to rise.

"Calling it a day already, huh?" Ford said, unsnapping the single strap on his holstered service Sig Sauer P226, and he draped his hand over the side piece.

Vernon noticed the gloves on the ground. "Mmm, that's— that's right…"

Ford kept his hardened sights on him and nothing else.

He was tired of the old man's bullshit games. Then he flickered his eyes to the shanty without warning.

"Henry," Ford shouted. "Come on out of there now."

Vernon exhaled, defeated, and plopped his ass on his cooler, his forehead in his meaty hands. Everything went still. Not a single movement or sound.

"Let's move!" Ford called out again, louder.

Nothing.

"I miss fishing with my boy," Vernon said with a certain peace. "You ever fish with your old man?"

Ford ignored him; his sights glued to the shanty instead.

"Those are moments you never forget as a father," Vernon said. "As a son."

"Either he exits on his own, or I'm dragging him from there."

Vernon's lids brimmed with tears, his voice strained, "Ford... He ain't going back to prison..."

The shanty's door suddenly and violently swung open. A bony man in his early thirties with a patchy beard and rotted teeth appeared with a hunting rifle swung to Ford, and he pulled the trigger. Ford dodged it, sliding like a base stealer in the snow. He planted his left foot on a rough patch of ice to stop himself, quickly drew his Sig from his holster, and fired two into the young man's chest before he could rack a second shot.

The echoed gunshots startled the sled dogs, as they pounced in place and yelped some. But North held his team strong, digging his paws into the ice and snow like daggers, and kept his body straight, without give, to trickle them to a calm.

Henry's body flopped onto the ice, where he lay halfway in the shanty's door. His father rushed to his side, picked up his head, and rested it on his lap. Blood pooled on his leg from his son's mouth.

"My boy! Oh, God! No..."

Ford arose from his firing position, expressionless. He holstered his piece, still observing his kill, and grabbed his two-way radio that was clipped to his utility belt. There was a second he thought he should say something to ease Vernon's pain, but he knew it was inappropriate. Instead, he just brought the radio to his mouth to call in the incident.

* * *

What appeared as a ground-level rustic log cabin from simpler times sat in the thick of the wild, made up of bare trees and pine trees with a touch of serenity, entirely undetected from the main paved roads.

Anyone could miss it if they weren't looking for it. This was seemingly the last law enforcement post of an era forgotten. Here, in the outskirts of the village of Newberry, which was a part of Luce County, was one of nearly one hundred Department of Natural Resources posts that were stationed in Northern Michigan's Upper Peninsula.

Near the back of the cabin, Ford caged his sled team and fed them dry Alpo food in a kennel that looked like a tiny canine village. It was large and in the open, surrounded by wire fencing. The middle ground of the kennel, where the dogs convened, was covered with snow, mud, hay, and feces. It was quite the chore to clean the space, which Ford had to do at least twice a week. Each dog had their own heated cage that led into a tiny wooden house.

A perfect living space for the teams, which Ford and his co-workers considered family, not just partners.

For the first time that tragic day, Ford smiled. It was a warm smile. A hidden expression to those who didn't know him. There was a sense of self-comfort caring for these sled dogs. Unlike the people he'd come across in his travels, dogs weren't full of hate, resentment, or judgment. They never wanted anything from him. They were just loyal. Loyalty was a quality he rarely saw in people. But for dogs, it was literally their code from birth. A straightforward code that Ford understood and could get behind.

Above each cage, the dogs' names were carved on wooden tags and painted in yellow. Across from the cages, on the other side of the kennel, another set of five cages were filled with a second team of Siberian Huskies and Malamutes. Ford walked to the corner of the kennel to a cage on the same side that was built apart from the others. Above it, the name Lucy was carved into the wood. The Siberian Husky inside the cage was of tan and white color and had an inviting face, with the only blemish being a scarred snout from a vicious bear attack from when she was two. Ford unhooked the dog's cage door to an open and caressed her head and back to relax her as best he could. She whimpered and lay on her side, panting heavily. Her belly protruded, which was the cause of the stress. She was pregnant, and uncomfortably so.

North was the father of the oncoming litter, so the department assumed they'd come from good stock, no less.

The officers could train them to become the future of their mush teams, especially since a few dogs among the two squads, such as Astro, were getting older and weary, nearing retirement.

Not long after, Ford entered through the backdoor of the post, peeling his winter layers onto his oak wood desk near the front windows. The desk was full of papers and had a police scanner on top of them, a mess he never managed much. Around the inside of the post, the entire place was decorated for the holiday, from red and green streamers drooping from the ceiling to a ceramic nativity scene near the coffee pot, right down to the plastic tree that was stuffed in the corner. Nat King Cole's genteel singing soothed the room's mood on a radio somewhere to set the ambiance. The department never shied away from the Christmas spirit.

"There he is," a male voice projected from behind Ford when he sat.

There, at the other desk staggered behind his in the same office space, his shift partner Jett Prevo slouched in his desk chair with a giant dip of Skoal packed in his lower lip. Occasionally, he spat into an empty plastic water bottle. He was in his mid-twenties with dark features and shaggy, almost black, hair. Jett was a fidgety type. A high-energy individual. Couldn't stand any sort of silence and couldn't sit still for very long. He was a local kid who never left the area after high school as most around did.

From adolescence, he knew he was a lifer.

He was proud of where he came from. He was a fine outdoorsman too. So much so that he decided to pursue a career in it, and became one of the youngest officers to ever join the Michigan DNR.

"Christ, seems you had most of the fun today, bud," Jett said to Ford in his thick Upper Peninsula accent, or 'Yooper English' as it was widely referred to. "I maybe gave, what, three fines on snowmobile trails? Still writing up this stupid shit."

Ford paid no attention and continued his routine of filling and organizing paperwork, while Jett rambled on.

"And don't get me started on the mounds of paperwork. You know, I swear that's half the job."

Restless, he rose from his desk and walked over to lean against Ford's.

"Quit talking so much, eh," Jett jabbed with a nudge. "Think you talk more to them dogs than you do most people."

"Cuz they don't talk back," Ford said.

"Fuckin-A."

Ford carried on with his work as if it were any normal day. It was his calmness that nagged at Jett, though. He couldn't grasp, nor could Ford himself explain, how he was able to stay so calm after the incident that had transpired earlier in the day.

"Vernon's kin, eh?" Jett asked.

Ford stopped his writing.

"Ya want me to do the run today?" Jett asked, hinting a smirk.

Almost annoyed by Jett's perceived, maybe even joking, notion that he had a touch of weakness, Ford ignored him.

"If your head's not in—"

"I'll be fine."

"Right on, bud..." Jett backed away and then sat back down in his chair, sighed, and scratched his temple before he dove back into his paperwork.

Soon, motor revs from outside caught Ford's attention. Through his half-shade-drawn window, he saw a neon purple and black Yamaha snowmobile parked in front of the post, next to a department truck and two other personal-owned trucks that had plows attached to their fronts. One of those trucks belonged to Ford — a blue and silver 1998 Dodge Ram, the other truck Jett's — a burgundy 2016 Chevy Silverado.

Avery Kinnomen dismounted from the snowmobile and removed

her neon graffiti-designed helmet. Her long, ginger red hair unfurled out of it to reveal her true beauty. She was a few years younger than Ford and could be described as someone between Agent Scully of *X-Files* and Thelma of *Thelma and Louise*. She appeared gentle and wholesome, but was most certainly a tomboy, having been raised like a son by her late father — a former DNR officer himself.

If she had any special ability considered as a superpower, it was those green eyes. Those gems could hypnotize anyone — male or female — and they had definitely broken some hearts.

When she walked inside and closed the door with her elbow, Ford dove back into his work, so he wouldn't get caught watching her. Entering the main office space, she took off her leather riding gloves and placed her helmet on the corner of Jett's desk. She reached into her jacket pocket and removed several scratch-off lottery tickets; some she had previously played and others that didn't have a single mark on them yet.

"Have a good weekend, Avery?" Jett asked.

"Sure did," she replied with mocking enthusiasm. "I went to the casino over there in Bark River and won big finally."

"Really?" Jett asked.

"Pssh, no, I lost my ass. So, yeah, the weekend could've been a touch better."

Ford's lips tightened, holding back a smile. Avery caught it and grinned coyly at him.

"Ford got Vernon's boy," Jett said, breaking the flirtatious moment between his co-workers.

"I heard. God, that must've been crazy. How are you holding up?"

"What I did could bring unwanted attention our way," Ford remarked with all seriousness.

"True, but it was him or you, right?" Jett asked.

Ford sat on the question before he tried to change the awkwardness of the whole discussion, "Lucy is pretty close to having her pups."

"She is," Avery said without skipping a beat. "Hopefully we have enough for another team from this litter. Lucy and Astro aren't getting any younger."

"They still have some good runs left in them," Jett said.

Ford shrugged in agreement and thanked Avery with his eyes for her help in redirecting the conversation.

III

There was once a city that was stripped of its identity.

What was left were remnants of the auto industry that attracted new business. With new business came corruption. Corruption that fostered violence and spread like a disease. Here was the new Wild West. A feral environment that manufactured the mean. It rewarded those who could work the hustle and punished those who resisted. Its streets were nothing but dingy, forsaken slums of dirty snow with little life. Welcome to the Motor City. Detroit.

If there was a single person considered to have the most power of Detroit's streets — a king perhaps — it was Oscar Easter. Oscar long held court in Detroit since the mid-nineties. From his beginnings as a crack dealer on the corner of Mack Avenue, to taking on a more entrepreneurial path by buying abandoned and foreclosed real estate and land, Oscar saw the city's hardships as opportunities.

Most saw the city's fall from economic grace as a plague. To Oscar, there was always money to make from any misfortune.

In the former General Motors building he bought and renovated as his headquarters and home, Oscar was seated at his glass desk in his over-the-top Motown-themed office.

Sitting there in deep thought with a sort of admiration, he just stared at a large-framed picture of legendary R&B singer Ellis Easter that hung behind him. A Marvin Gaye vinyl played on his Linn LP 12 record player, amid the soulful atmosphere of his gaudy lion's den.

Oscar had soft features and a thin mustache. He rocked a flattop, mostly because he was losing hair on the roof, and it was the only style that didn't expose his age. He opted for sweaters and dress slacks as his chosen attire, instead of the suits he required his crew to wear. To him, in order to conduct any sort of business, there must be a certain class and aesthetic sense to maintain respect from your peers, even your adversary. His strong voice soothed others, and he spoke with an educated diction. His contagious passion for what he pitched closed more deals than any violence ever did. Still, though, violence was always in his back pocket.

Beyond the conference table in the middle of the room, the entrance doors opened. In walked Oscar's only child Ray Easter. With him was his best friend and right-hand man, who everyone simply referred to as Judge. Ray was a giant of a man in his mid-thirties.

He stood somewhere between seven-foot and seven-foot-two. His navy-blue Gucci suit was tight and fit perfectly on his Olympian body, and he had flashy diamond earrings, rings on each hand, two necklaces, and a twenty-thousand-dollar platinum watch to complete his ridiculous ensemble of wealth.

Ray was new to Detroit, in a sense. At one time he was a five-star basketball recruit straight out of high school, before injuries forced his NBA aspirations into playing overseas instead. A decade went by when Ray realized that he was a journeyman basketball player at best, and he wasn't going to earn the kind of bread he could earn as part of his family's business. His less than desired fate left a permanent chip on his shoulder because he wanted to provide for himself. At a very young age, he was uncomfortable with the idea of being privileged. He fought against presumed nepotism. An earned piece of his own he could be proud of was what he sought most. Getting into his father's line of work was something he'd desperately tried to avoid for years, before it eventually sucked him in. And in turn, his prior neglect of his birthright put him at odds with his father for as long as he could remember. So much in fact that Oscar never even attended a single game of his after high school. Never even visited him in Europe, China, and Australia, anywhere he played. Oscar made it clear that Ray was on his own if he turned his back on the business.

And, boy, did Ray feel the cold.

Hidden underneath his long dreadlocks that covered the majority of his mug, Judge always had a scowl, which fit his morose expressions. A trait someone would find from post-war vets who were in the shit. He wasn't much for talking either, unless it was necessary. Though he and Ray were both raised in the city, Judge's adolescence was in chaotic contrast to his friend's. While Ray had financial entitlement, opportunities, and was well-known as a local star athlete, Judge grew up on the polluted streets among addicts, swindlers, and savage scum of the earth. Same as Oscar had.

Judge was raised by prostitutes much of his youth, while his mother killed herself day in and day out, getting her fix on Michigan meth in abandoned houses along Livernois Avenue. He could remember a specific winter when his mother finally succumbed to the drug and never woke up again.

"Pop," Ray said to his father, not looking up from his iPhone. "Mr. Krowchuck has arrived from Canada."

"How many guns he bring?" Oscar asked, his attention still on Ellis Easter's portrait.

When he didn't get an immediate answer from his son, he turned to find him texting on his cell.

"Ray," he said to get his attention.

"About a dozen men," Ray responded without looking up.

Oscar cleared his throat to get his son's attention again, "Well, lead the Canucks in then."

Ray paused his texting fury for a minute, then slid his cell in his blazer's pocket, letting out a quick, "Right. Okay."

Oscar's brow line dropped in annoyance, and he exhaled an exaggerated sigh that hissed like a deflated ball.

When the clock hit ten that morning, the earlier empty conference table was filled with the biggest and baddest men from Michigan and Canada. Having orchestrated the meeting, Oscar sat at the head of the table. Ray, Judge, and a squad of three guards from Oscar's security team were seated on the left side of it, one of them being Oscar's very own right-hand man, known by all as Diz.

Diz was a mute fellow. Much like Judge, his silence made him even more intimidating than the mythical number of contracted hits he was notoriously known for among Easter's circle, and even rival mafia families. He was a follower of the Nation of Islam. Fittingly so, he wore a blood-red bowtie and was dressed in a blue corduroy suit that fit even smaller on his lean body, as if it had shrunk in the dryer. But it was his bulgy, shark eyes through those thick, black-framed glasses that drew the fear in people. They were hard to miss. For his victims, they were the last horrific sight they saw. Amid everyone's initial, tense stare down, he didn't bat a lash and opted to clean his glasses on his sleeve. *Business as usual*, he thought. Let's get on with it then.

Seated at the other end of the table was an ambitious and charismatic youngster by the name of Niko Krowchuck. He was nineteen, almost twenty. Possibly the youngest person to ever sit at this marble table that was filled with years of history of political conversations and deals, discussed hits, campaigns of racketeering, and endless strategies of greed.

His dirty blonde hair was blown out on top and slicked back with American Crew pomade, and the sides were shaved close to his scalp. He had a well-groomed, wispy mustache that was more Tony Stark than Ron Burgundy. It was most certainly the only facial hair he could grow on his baby face, and he took advantage of it too. Much like everyone else in the room, which could be confused as a GQ photoshoot of some wild American-Canadian theme, the kid was nicely and flashily dressed in a tight-fitted white, gray, and black plaid Zara suit jacket and pants. His pants rose well above his ankles when he sat, showing his Louis Vuitton loafers, and under the suit jacket he wore a black Ralph Lauren polo shirt that was buttoned to his throat. Overall, Niko was somewhere between a hipster and a late-life Bowie.

His team of security sat on his left side, mostly consisting of crooked Canadian Border Patrol officers. All of whom appeared as fancy as their boss. They wore the whole gamut of Banana Republic turtlenecks and Paul Smith sweaters to Ralph Lauren Peacoats and leather gloves. A stylish bunch of gangsters, nonetheless.

Sitting next to Niko was his main guy, Calvin Witter. He, too, was a part of the Canadian Border Patrol squad. He was in his thirties, and unlike his facial-hair-friendly comrades, he opted for more of a clean-cut appearance. Most of the men in this room were tall, but Calvin was short. And he wasn't as laid back as Niko was, rather, he was always on alert and fancied himself as a human lie detector — a skill the kid boss admired most about him.

"On behalf of my family, Merry Christmas," Oscar greeted Niko. "Welcome to Detroit."

Niko's Android cell vibrated. He checked it before he turned it off and stuffed it in his blazer again.

"We love it here," Niko said. "The casinos and the Red Wings are worth sneaking into the country for. Not better than my Maple Leafs, but close enough."

Oscar politely smiled, "Well then, I don't want to keep you boys, so we'll jump right into it."

Niko leaned forward to intensely listen to Oscar cut to the chase, instead of the tormented small talk, something he was always uncomfortable with anyway.

"Normally, we don't care about what the Canadians do," Oscar said. "To each their own, I say. However, it has recently come to my attention that the northern territory of my state, which I believed to be unclaimed, has been conducting methamphetamine trafficking operations. From what I hear, impressive."

Niko gave a long nod followed by a complacent look before he wondered where the conversation was headed, "Sure."

"I assume you don't have children, so this might be hard for you to understand," Oscar said as he reached over next to him and gripped his son's shoulder as if he was grabbing a mountain's peak. "My boy Ray has returned from being away for...many years. I would like nothing more than to have my only child take over what I have built someday."

Oscar looked to his son again, "Someday." Then released his grip as if it were some sort of rehearsed act for Niko's benefit. "I built everything I have right here in the toughest city in the goddamn world. Our time to penetrate the far north has long been evident. A territory I want to give my son. A territory you control."

Niko stared at him to try to gauge how this meeting would develop. Oscar waited for his response with a slightly forced but calm smile. The Canadian kid just eyed Oscar's men, then Ray, and finally his own crew as if he were expecting more of a speech from the slick Detroit gangster.

"Mr. Easter—"

"Call me Oscar."

"Fine. Oscar. I get it. I've come across plenty of men like you before. My late father was the same. I suppose it's generational. A generation that craves more money. More power. More control. More everything. Now you want my gold mine, Mr. Redd— Oscar."

He shed a snide smile before continuing, "I'm not greedy. That's not my thing. My brand is much more important to me. See, Yooper meth is the best meth around. I dare you to find better. It is my touch that has made it Canada's most sought-after black-market import. No one can run it better than me. Nobody."

"Your perception is something," Oscar said, not expecting his adversary's interesting position. "Are you aware of who I am, son?"

"Oh, I've heard the stories."

"Have you heard everything?"

"Enough."

Oscar stood and paced around the den before he leaned on his throne as the room watched his every movement.

He then projected with copious animation, "Anything worth a damn is started from the ground. Your father hustled the same way, I imagine. Myself, I am the illegitimate son of a famous musician. The late Ellis Easter."

He presented the picture behind his desk across the room as if he was introducing a headlining act.

"Unlike him, I couldn't carry a fuckin' tune, so I needed to develop a different skill. The business you and I are in, that's my skill."

"Then we both can agree that I can't just hand over a business my father established," Niko explained.

"No, of course not. That's why I want you to name a price."

"There isn't an amount high enough."

Oscar chuckled a little, "In all my years, I've never let anyone name a price. Son, now I'm showing you respect here. Real respect. Take that into consideration when I say again... Name a price."

"Thanks, but I'm going to have to pass," Niko replied almost too hastily, took his cell from his pocket to check it, and then rose from his chair.

This abruptly ended the meeting. His men stood with him, and they strutted to the doors together.

"Many counties I've come across, they also had their little operations," Oscar said, to which halted Niko, making his men turn to face the kingpin once more. "A story behind all of them. Drugs, chops shops, gun-running. Whatever. I never asked for a cut. I never offered a partnership. I just took it, my way. That's my generation."

"Are you threatening me?" asked Niko with a smirk.

"Just trying to enlighten you on who it is you're talking to. Because from where I'm standing, you have no idea, son."

Silence hit the room like a stack of bricks.

"Again, thanks for having us, Mr. Easter, This was...something."

He then exited with his men, leaving Oscar to retire to his chair behind his desk.

Furious with the meeting's result, Ray stomped to the front windows near the desk. Judge lingered in behind.

"Say the word, Pops," he said with his fists clenched as he watched the Canadians enter their Humvees on the street below the building. "Judge and I will drop that wannabe Bowie motherfucker!"

His threat made Oscar glance at him, then to Judge behind.

"Fish in a barrel," Ray added, as he pretended to shoot the Canadians with his long finger. "Let's just take care of 'em already."

Oscar stepped in front of Ray and slapped him hard across the face. Judge backed away, trying not to get involved.

"Use your head, boy!" Oscar yelled.

His giant son dropped his head in shame, standing over his father as if he were an adolescent again. One could frame a picture in a collage throughout Ray's life of this same pose — son disappointing his father.

"You promised me no more fuck ups when you returned," Oscar said. "This isn't a game anymore. You're an Easter. Start acting like one."

Ray watched his disgruntled father storm through the doors of his office. He then glimpsed through the window again to see the Humvees pull away. Judge inched to his side again in concern and kept his focus on his friend, instead of the nefarious competition leaving the premises.

IV

Timbers, just outside the town of Marquette, was the loudest bar establishment around in these parts. DNR officers from posts across the Upper Peninsula filled the spot for their annual Christmas party. On occasion, the officers would run into each other throughout the year, mostly on the job, but hardly ever. The holiday party was the only chance they could come together and share stories and celebrate over drinks and various homemade dishes. Timbers' doors were endlessly revolving from the smokers that would come and go as well as those who grabbed more money from the ATM outside, because it was a cash bar only.

Ford stood alone in the corner of the bar, almost hidden by the ridiculous amounts of silver-and-gold-colored tinsel that dangled from the ceiling like Spanish moss. He nursed a glass of spiked eggnog, which by now was lukewarm.

Normally, he'd find a seat at the bar or a table and just fixate on a college basketball or hockey game on the televisions around, but the place was so packed with co-workers that he couldn't find a spot. Not that he wanted to ask anyone to scoot either. He didn't mind. Where he stood provided a straight-line view of the Karaoke section that Avery made her domain for most of the night. Watching her perform pop hits from Kelly Clarkson to the classics of Billy Joel amused him to no end. She was an okay singer, not great, but her excitement and dedication to legitimate dance moves made her an enjoyable watch. If it wasn't for her, Ford wouldn't dare make an appearance at the party. She was truly the only reason he ever attended these things, regardless of his perpetual resistance. Small talk and conversing with strangers, even if they worked within the same department, was never really his thing. His low profile proceeded him, which prevented other officers from approaching him to talk, or simply forget he was even at the event.

Didn't matter to Ford anyway. He was more of an observer than a talker.

"Next round's on me!" Jett's voice carried clear across the other side of the bar.

Ford got a front-row seat to witness Jett's high motor in a public setting. He watched the charismatic Yooper work the room in his usual loud and boisterous manner. Pats on the back when he passed by, blathering with this person and that person on his way to the bar for another round. It never ended.

Constant fist bumps and high-fives around and over groups of others on his way to the pisser, there wasn't a single person he didn't know and didn't chatter with. Everyone felt his presence. It was hard to miss him. Compared to the rest, who wore nice sweaters and dressier outfits for tonight, Jett came to the event as he would any other day at the bar on the weekend. He wore faded blue jeans that had holes in the knees with his winter work boots, and a red, black, and white plaid long sleeve. His rabbit fur trapper hat he kept on always, with the ears down, unlike everyone else who had removed their hats upon entry. He was a gregarious drunk, and the more beverages he consumed, the more Ford saw him transform into the life of the DNR holiday party.

Regardless of how tired his antics or constant rambling made Ford, he envied the young man a little. Jett had this innate ability to charm the pants off people, regardless of how he did it. Everyone knew him and gravitated towards him. But what was most compelling to Ford was that Jett was never alone. Friends, family, acquaintances, he constantly had them around. Ford could only imagine how nice of a feeling it was to have that company on the regular. It was out of his depth to comprehend.

"Yo, Ford," Jett called to him when he spotted him through the crowd across the horseshoe-shaped bar. "Wanna take a shot with me?"

Ford graciously refused with a slight shake of his head.

"Come on. Just a shot."

Ford mouthed *no* and rose his drink hand to show he still had a drink he was working on.

"Later then," Jett said. "Me and you, bud."

And he spun back around to the small group of officers he bought the round for. They held their shot glasses of Jägermeister high in the air.

"Midnight Rider!" a short, bald officer cheered to Jett.

Each drunk officer in the group shouted the same name to him and Jett roared a laugh from deep and threw back his shot with the rest.

Ford apathetically watched them from across the room as he sipped his warm eggnog. He had heard the nickname before and never was fond of it. Jett always shrugged it off and explained to him the nickname was something that just caught on around town because of how he could last longer in the night than most when he drank. Ford never bought that for a second, but like tonight, always kept a close watch on the kid in case.

A rise of celebratory cheers erupted without warning from the furthest end of the muggy watering hole. It became louder in a wave that overwhelmed around Ford before his last swallow. By now, the majority of the crowd had gathered on the dirty and sticky dance floor, facing the karaoke machine on the folding table. "Oops I Did it Again" by Britney Spears evoked the room and the volume rose with the beat of the bass. Avery held the mic in her hand below her waist, her eyes down.

She was stuck in a straight statue pose, anticipating her cue to sing the first lyrics. Her body then morphed with a kick outward, then a quick spin when the first words on the karaoke monitor were highlighted. She busted into a choreographed number that won the crowd's attention from the start.

Ford grinned. Seeing Avery in her element was different than her stiff, by the book work presence. Her voice was good enough for the song, but was overshadowed by her stunning dance moves, which were timed perfectly to the beat. Even Britney Spears would be proud. Ford practically fell into a trance, a spotlight on Avery in an empty room in his vision. To him, she was perfect. She was everything he never found in a woman before. She was the only person that ever made him feel shy. He had always questioned how to approach her and dissected any conversation they had immediately after they spoke. Conversations that left him feeling embarrassed, or stupid, even though Avery wasn't to blame. A first for him.

In the closing parts of the song, she shook her hip to the side and punched the air, freezing in that same pose when the song ended. Everyone jumped with their hands up, cheering and whistling and clapping at her performance. Her smirk broke into a wide smile, and she blew the bangs from her face in a single puff. Beyond the crowd, she scanned the room for Ford, but he had vanished — the bar's front door shut behind him.

Temperatures outdoors had dropped below zero when it turned dark. Ford zipped his jacket and placed his knit winter cap on his head. He cupped his hands to a hollow fist around his mouth and filled them with his warm breath.

Smokers poured from the bar's doors, raving to each other of Avery's performance. Some were discussing what songs they wanted to sing next, and there were others that were already talking about heading home. By now, most were inebriated and sobering themselves before they called it a night. As Ford dug his gloves from his pockets, Avery made her way through the smokers, partially draping her coat around her shoulders as if it were a cape. A lit cigarette dangled from her lips. When she laid her sights on Ford, she planted herself on his side, unbeknownst to him.

"Bailing?" she asked to get his attention.

"Yeah. It's getting late."

"Geez, thanks for saying goodbye."

"Oh. I— I didn't mean—"

Avery chuckled, "Ford, I'm fucking with you."

Ford's confused expression transformed into a grin. Both just looked into the single lamp-lit street. Not a word between them for a good minute.

"You did really good in there," Ford said.

"You think so?"

"Yes. I remember you said you used to dance. Vegas, right?"

Avery took a drag from her cigarette and released a long exhale of smoke. "Forever ago, yeah. Ventured there after college to become one of them showgirls. Well, exactly one of them. You know, the feathers, glitter, legs for miles, headlining acts. That sort of thing."

Ford smiled.

"My legs ain't that long, though," she snorted a light laugh. "No, but it was nothing but a pipe dream. Fantasy, whatever."

Ford sensed the topic was sore for her. The silence crept to them again and Avery continued to take quick drags from her cigarette, deep in thought of her previous life.

Ford could hear the chatter of her teeth in the quiet. He grabbed a side of her coat, and when she realized what he was doing, she slid her arms into each sleeve to fully put it on for him. She stumbled back a bit after, a drink too many.

Ford held her by her shoulders then pulled up the zipper on her coat. He felt her eyes following his and he gazed into them after.

"You got a ride home?" he quickly asked.

"Sure do. Jill from the Marquette post. Woman's about as fun as a turtle. You know, I think she spent most of the night smoking out here. She gave me a ride to the party, so—"

"Okay."

Avery felt her coat pockets. "Shit," she said. "Shit!"

"What?"

"Damn money. I must've forgotten it at home. I still have a tab inside."

"I can help you with that."

"Really? Are you sure? I'm so sorry."

"Don't be. It's not a problem."

"You're sweet, Ford, you know you are." She then leaned her head on his shoulder. "And warm. I'm staying right here."

Ford wrapped his arm around her far shoulder to keep her close and led her inside so he could pay her tab.

"You're kind of a softy, you know that?"

"Right," he said, trying not to grin.

* * *

Avery swept away the hay and dirt inside Lucy's cage the following Monday to reveal a secret door underneath that she opened. Stacked neatly on a pallet packaged in plastic-type bricks were fifty pounds of methamphetamine. She stared at the crystal treasure with a sort of anxious curiosity or even anticipation, as if it was a lottery jackpot of some kind. Ford and Jett appeared in the kennel and commenced to load the hidden meth onto Ford's traditional full-size racing sled that was built by Jett's father.

Mr. Prevo helped create and customize many things for the DNR as a contracted craftsman. This was a family business of sorts.

The sleds he built for his son, Ford, and Avery were light and made from titanium, Kevlar, and wood, with rubber mat footboards, a double claw brake system, and a drag mat that helped slow the sled — especially when riding downhill — to keep it agile around sharp turns. It was also built with a wedge-shaped brush bow and a U-shaped handlebar to maximize its durability.

While the men prepared the sled, Avery handled Ford's dogs, attaching them to it with leather harnesses. When the meth was loaded, strapped, and secured, Ford placed a backpack of supplies and a Serbu Super Shorty shotgun on top. He referred to the particular hidden piece as his "last resort" in case he was ever disarmed of any of his other weapons. Once the innards of the precious cargo were in place, he covered his entire sled with a brown canvas tarp that was also strapped under numerous bungee cords. He then holstered his service Sig Sauer handgun on the right side of his utility belt, and a gray hatchet on the other. To finish his preparation, he slid a four-inch Kershaw knife into a sheath, concealed inside his boot. Ford kept his same DNR attire on with his badge, as he always did, in case he ever ran into a fellow conservation officer, or God forbid — even though it had happened in the past — a cop. Not a single officer had ever suspected anything foul of Ford, Jett, or Avery when they spotted them on the trails with their sleds. Most brushed it off as them doing their daily jobs. If they were ever stopped, it was to make small talk and catch up.

Surely, no one would ever suspect a law-abiding DNR officer of smuggling drugs. Especially someone like Jett or Avery, whose families were well-known and respected among law enforcement and DNR officials alike, across the Upper Peninsula.

Avery handed cheap burner flip cells to Ford and Jett.

"Fresh from Wisconsin," Avery said. "Paid in cash. No receipts."

She kept a phone for herself.

"Did y'all get rid of the other ones?" she asked.

Ford nodded.

"Yup," said Jett.

"Good boys. Got new batteries in your two-way?"

Ford nodded.

"You're ready to run," Avery said.

The look on Ford's face had long shown that he was ready, reminiscent of an athlete before an important game. When the morning's sun was at its highest, Ford clicked his tongue twice and he was off to the races. His lead dog North led the sled with command and grace as Ford steered by yelling "Speed" when he wanted them to run faster or "Slow" when he wanted them to slow their pace. "Whoa" when he wanted them to stop. For right turns, he yelled "Gee" and for left turns, he yelled "Haw." On quick turns, he'd lean his body any which way and kicked his foot behind the sled to use it as a rudder.

Trail-to-trail the team pivoted and sprinted that afternoon as they ran the same planned routes they've taken so many times in the past. There was something beautiful about the way the sled glided along the changing terrain. Almost as if they were poetry in motion, the dogs ran and ran, slowing and speeding in unison, whatever Ford desired. They were never winded, giving evidence to his claim that dog power was more reliable than any auto's horsepower. Most trails they rode were heavily used by snowmobiles, but over the last decade or so, dog sleds were increasingly becoming a staple of winter travel in more rural communities across the northern frontier.

An hour and a half went by. Through an endless row of Jack Pine trees along an eastbound trail, Ford spotted flashes of a street in the outskirts of the small town of Soo Junction. A lone Michigan State Police cruiser rode the street at the same speed as his sled. A middle-aged female officer was driving. She didn't notice the sled. There were only a few people around the street. Curious about law activity in the area, Ford called the only numbers Avery inserted in his cell — hers and Jett's.

"Staties in the Blue Zone," Ford said. "Anything going on?"

Back at the DNR post, Jett was seated at a corner desk, in front of radio equipment they used for the DNR portion of their job, and a giant map of the Upper Peninsula was pinned on a large corkboard right behind it.

To his side was a police scanner that was within earshot, to which he listened closely. At the time, he was bored. He played with anything around him to keep his mind busy before his burner cell on his desk started ringing to the tone of the *Back to the Future* theme song.

Avery, who was slicing pieces of an apple with a knife, stopped playing an online poker game on her computer in her own office when she heard Jett's cell. She joined Jett in the main room, just as he answered the call.

"All clear, bud," Jett relayed to Ford.

"Okay," Ford said.

Avery lingered in behind Jett. She cut a fresh slice of apple and shoved it in her mouth.

"Fun fact," Jett said to Ford. "Best lay I ever had was in Soo

Junction."

"Christ, Jett," Avery said, shaking her head at him with disgust.

On the trails, Ford tried not to laugh at Jett's crude comment, but the remark did bring a smirk to his face. As he glided into a clearing, where the row of pines ended, he glanced back at the cruiser, and this time he saw the officer staring right at him. Ford gradually brought up a hand and waved at her. The officer took a second before she returned the gesture. Ford shifted his focus back to the trail and mushed with constant clicks to boost their pace.

When they reached an elongated stretch of ground he yelled, "Speed!" and the team dug in and picked up the pace, flinging waves of snow that split to the sides of Ford as if he were Moses parting the Red Sea.

An hour or so later, atop the Chippewa County hillsides that overlooked breathtaking land of frozen farm fields, amid low rolling hills below, Ford stood at its peak and took a piss. So did his dogs. Beyond them, the view unfolded for miles and miles. This specific area was a good spot for them to take a break. Nobody ventured up the hill that far. He was hidden from any snowmobiles, which in these parts, didn't travel the hills, as the snow and ice movements were too unpredictable. It was thick in some areas and too thin in others. There were constant slide-offs, and trails always changed for the worse with the weather. It was almost as if the hill was alive and transformed itself whenever it woke from its summer-long sleep.

Last winter, three local teenagers got drunk and rode the hills with their machines, only to disappear into thin air one brisk day. It took search parties almost an entire week to find them. When they did, they discovered the teens on the north end of the hillside, where they were thought to have rolled off. If they didn't succumb to the crash, they most certainly did in the frigid temperatures during the night. A fierce winter storm that came in covered their tracks and made it near impossible for anyone to locate them straight away.

Ford remembered the teens vividly; his DNR crew was a part of the search party that recovered them. As he gazed across the overwhelming sights and took in what was left of the day's warm sun, he thought of those boys. He thought of their families and the agony they must've suffered through. Lives that were taken too soon. What he remembered most about that incident was how the communities pulled together to help find them. Even to people that didn't know them, it'd felt like one of their own kids went missing.

Never in his life had Ford come across such selflessness. It gave him a satisfying feeling to be a part of something like that. Though the result wasn't a happy ending, it felt rewarding to help people and become a part of a community.

With a few hours left of light, Ford arrived on Drummond Island by way of the narrow St. Mary's River, a three-mile trek that was completely frozen over. Drummond Island was the eastern-most landmass of the state of Michigan. The area around it was entirely frozen solid as well. If someone went more east or further south, within a couple of miles, they'd be swimming in the bone-chilling waters of Lake Huron. But north of Drummond was a fifteen-mile stretch of thick, thick ice that connected the United States to Canada.

Right here, ahead of Ford and his team, was the famous ice bridge. Drummond Island would only open the bridge when the ice was at least five inches thick. Since Michigan winters were unpredictable, the opening could float anytime between November to January.

Recreational snowmobilers and cross-country skiers loved the ice bridge, because of the freedom it gave them. As for contraband-running, it was ridiculously profitable, depending on the length of a season, so it was obvious that the players in the drug trafficking industry might've loved the ice bridge even more than most.

Ford pressed his drag mat between the footboards of his feet to idle the dogs, which eventually stopped his sled on the shore. Before him, on the shoreline, a sign protruded from a mound of snow that a plow had pushed against after the last big snowfall. It read: LEAVING MICHIGAN, USA. Ford reached for his burner cell from his coat. His senses tingled; the hair on the back of his neck stood. Something behind him caught his attention and he turned around to spot two snowmobilers about a hundred yards away, facing his direction. They were dressed in entirely black and silver snowsuits, including their racing-style helmets. Their brand-new midnight black Ski-Doo engines purred with a gentleness between their legs as they remained there just watching Ford's every move. Ford cleared his glove from his right hand and quickly sent a text, then mushed onto the ice bridge.

There was no time to waste. He was on a strict schedule. Ford was never late. Always on time. Always.

At the post, Jett's burner sounded off again. Lounging in his chair now, with his feet propped up on the desk, he leaned to his side to reach for it.

"Oooh Canadaaaa..." Jett sang the start of the country's national anthem when he read Ford's text.

Avery stepped behind his chair and sunk a red pushpin into the giant map on the wall to mark Ford's latest checkpoint. A rainbow of pushpins were lined behind those from Ford's earlier check-ins. Each pin was a different color in her coded system she'd created to mark important areas of communication between the runner and the post. Blue was for Soo Junction. Green was Seewhy. Yellow for Strongs. Brown was Rudyard. Orange for Pickford. Pink for DeTour. And red for Canada. Depending on the area, if there was any construction, known law presence from area events, or relevant incidents or accidents, they would talk in color code when explaining them on the cell phone, or in cases of bad reception on their radios.

As Ford rode on the ice bridge towards Canada, he took a glimpse back to find the same two snowmobilers that were watching him onshore were now following him.

Suspicious, he hovered his hand over his Sig Sauer. He didn't want to stop his team's momentum though, and stayed the course to the great white north, while he still trained an eye on the pair of snowmobilers every so often.

Coming directly at him from Canada, two more snowmobilers approached and passed. Each politely waved to him. They were dressed very differently than the following riders — most likely recreational. They didn't appear as a threat, so Ford nodded in return.

He then turned his head with the passing snowmobilers to find that the following riders in black and silver had since turned around to return to Michigan.

Ahead on St. Joseph Island's shore, eight Canadian Border Patrol officers huddled around an unmarked van and waited for Ford as he neared. A short man stepped forth from the mix with a pair of binoculars cupped in his hands. *"Witter"* glistened on his shiny badge.

"Right on time as usual, eh," Calvin Witter said with a thick Canadian accent, lowering his binoculars.

Within the hour, Ford had reached the shore. When he pulled down his neck gaiter, he saw that the group of border patrol surrounded him almost immediately from the moment he had touched Canadian snow. He dismounted his sled and squatted to his dog team's level to praise them and thank them for a successful trip, while the patrol checked his entire sled. He could care less. His disregard to acknowledge the patrol irked them occasionally. Typical of Ford; they were used to it. He, Avery, and even Jett, who got along with just about everyone, cared about Niko's hired guns as much as they cared about them. Business was all it ever was.

"Spread 'em," Calvin demanded of Ford as he approached.

When he went to frisk Ford, he stood and handed him his side piece from his holster, his hatchet from the other, but neglected to show him his concealed knife. Ford never informed them he had it on him.

Witter then removed Ford's shorty shotgun on the sled and handed the weapons over to another patrol officer.

"Niko wants to see you," said Calvin.

"Why?" Ford asked.

Calvin ignored his question and had him follow him to the van, where the meth from his sled was currently in the process of being loaded.

* * *

Niko Krowchuck strolled through clusters of maple trees checking taps buried in the trunks and the sap they produced into old metal buckets. He kept his hands cuffed behind his back, and he wore dark rectangle shades, even though it was overcast. He seemed at peace in this element.

Ford and Calvin arrived at that moment. They stepped around hose lines connected to taps that extended to other maples that made them appear as telephone lines in the woods.

Niko took his sweet time before acknowledging the pair, as he snapped selfies of himself next to his maples and shared them on Instagram with the hashtags #instacanada and #Krowchuckdrizzle. It was that irrepressible swagger he worked hard branding for himself and his company that he carried over to his drug business. His efforts had catapulted him to cult-hero status in Ontario among dealers, buyers, distributors, and wannabes. It was a big reason why people admired his unique methods of running an empire, which was very different than his parents. He built a generation of followers in the Information Age, which continued to grow daily, and he used this to help sell his infamous product.

"Mr. Ford," Niko greeted as he turned and strolled toward them.

Ford looked to Calvin, unsure. Calvin nodded him to follow his boss, and he did, staying a step behind him the entire time, while he continued to check taps.

"I come to this spot to reset my mind from the stress," Niko said. "These were the first taps my father put in when he was a young man starting in the syrup industry. I still keep them up, even though we have far better rigs on our property. They're a reminder. They remind me of the hard work that comes with any business. They also remind me of him."

Ford just listened as they walked from tap to tap.

"He was a man of pride and grit, my father. He never wanted to take my grandfather's money to start this venture. I guess that's why he dipped his toes into the drug business. He paid back my grandfather's loan ten times over. Drugs and syrup, it has been quite a juggling act, to say the least. That's how I see it."

Niko dipped his pinky in the sap of a metal bucket and approved its texture with a smile.

"I like to imagine my father standing in this very spot. What did he think about? What strategies ruminated in his genius mind? The nostalgia of it all really inspires me, Mr. Ford."

Niko closed his eyes as if he was absorbing his father's memory to inspire his own future, while Ford thought it was odd theatrics here and now. Niko then opened his eyes, faced Ford, motioned him to follow again, and they moved on.

"You know what I love about dog sleds?" Niko asked Ford. "The quiet. They don't make any ruckus flying through trails or towns or lakes. They can go places most vehicles or snowmobiles can't. Law don't check them either. Even better, they don't break down. Completely under the radar. Nobody cares..."

He checked another tap and was pleased with its progress, then advanced to another, Ford still on his heels.

"We're growing faster than I had anticipated," Niko said. "That being said, I'd like to increase our monthly runs from four to six going forward."

"That's not possible," Ford grunted behind his hesitation. "Too many—"

Niko interrupted him, bringing a full mason jar of syrup from his gray peacoat to Ford's face. Ford flinched back and read the *KROWCHUCK SYRUP* label.

"Taste," Niko offered to him.

Ford reluctantly did, twisting the top and poked his finger in the famous sweetness, then to his tongue.

"Raspberry?"

"Good, right?"

"Yes."

"Ha. I think I met your approval for the first time. Mark it down... Go on, taste. It's our new flavor. We believe it's going to catch on."

He moved away again, leaving Ford to hold the opened jar he wanted to hand back.

"Recruit another musher," Niko nonchalantly responded of the original topic.

"What?" Ford asked, caught off guard. "That's too risky."

"We must build on our success now, my friend. It's imperative we keep up. From here I want to open more labs, hire more cooks, you get the idea."

Ford thwarted his attempt to follow Niko. He didn't dig his plan from the start.

"We're in mid-season already; it's too soon for all that. Better to aim for next winter instead."

"No. No, it has to be this winter," Niko urged in his return and then patted Ford's shoulder. "You're efficient, I'm sure the three of you will figure out something."

He then attempted to advance again, but Ford remained in the same spot.

"Seems you forgot our little deal from a while back," Ford reminded Niko. "I'm only working for you for so long. Remember, when I hit my dollar amount, I'm gone."

"Yes. I do remember," Niko replied and turned back to him. "Listen, Mr. Ford, now isn't a good time to lose runners. There must be something that will keep you on. Whatever it is, I—"

"I'll prep someone else before I leave. But after that our business concludes. Are we clear?"

Niko gave a hesitant but reassuring nod, then casually clasped his hands behind his back as they returned to Calvin.

"Sure there isn't anything I can do to change your mind?"

Ford shook his head, confident of his choice.

"Understood," Niko said.

Ford offered back the jar of syrup.

"Keep it," Niko told him. "Enjoy the latest load I'm sending back with you."

He returned to check the rest of his taps, while Calvin and Ford headed back to the unmarked van. Before Ford closed his door, he glanced at Niko, suspicious of his easygoing response to his refusal. Although he rarely spoke with him, the one thing Ford knew most about the kid was that he never gave an inch of democracy. Everything had to be his way, always.

* * *

Smoke from a hand-carved pipe danced in the rigid air above Tom Two Feathers. The thin and lanky Native American with lengthy black hair and hard features wore a headless hazmat suit, and he rocked on a wooden chair that creaked with every back-and-forth movement. The porch he sat on tilted a little downward into the ground because it was decades old, and it was attached to a shack of a house that was the sort of place a hermit would reside, complete with a cat population that put most cities to shame. Next to it was a rundown barn made of reclaimed wood. Most of which were on their last legs. It was big enough to house farm animals, which at a certain point it might've, considering the property and areas of abandoned and rusted farm equipment that were impeded in the ground with the earth growing around them.

A small spotlight in the dark caught Tom Two Feathers' peripheral. He rose from his chair and snagged his shotgun that leaned next to him on the dilapidated house.

When the spotlight neared and entered the porch light's perimeter, the Native American saw it was Ford and eased caution with his childlike toothless smile.

"Aye, my special drizzle under there, friend?" Tom asked Ford with his high-pitched, raspy voice.

He peeked under the tarp to spot three boxes of raspberry-flavored Krowchuck Syrup. Inside them were stacks of thousands of dollars wrapped in Saran wrap.

"Ooh, my favorite!" Tom exclaimed.

Ford texted Jett his final checkpoint location and let Tom retire the sled dogs to the barn.

"Let's get them pups kenneled for the night — come on," Tom said.

* * *

Sitting around a rickety, wooden card table, Ford and Tom Two Feathers played a close game of Cribbage, while they indulged in some cheap whiskey. Most likely homemade. Tom was a scientist with anything consumable that could impair judgment. Here, Ford stripped of his gear and a few layers of clothing, down to his long johns, seemed relaxed. Around them, scattered without purpose, were Tom's gas mask, an ounce of meth, ashtrays with endless cigarette butts, and a stack of money, which was Tom's cut from the latest successful run.

Like he was with Jett, Ford didn't mind Tom's company. The more runs he had under his belt, the more he got to know him. And Tom was a hard person to dislike. His demeanor was very innocuous and ingenuous, as if he didn't know he was the best meth cook around, working for the most criminal kid kingpin around. On the outside looking in, he seemed as if he were a character placed in the wrong story. Maybe even the wrong era. Suppose Tom went a different way, he could've possibly become more involved in his family's tribe as a veterinarian or an engineer. His people were proud Ojibwas.

Aside from his name, Tom could give a fuck less about his heritage, though. While they were mindful, or even aloof, of anyone who wasn't Native American, Tom was different. And it maddened them. He was inviting of all people and all things. Not a mean bone in his gaunt body. A lover of animals, he took in every stray cat he found, leaving him with nearly a couple hundred in and around his house. Littered on his floor were endless Tupperware dishes of cat food and water, and around them inhabited every kind of cat species there was.

From calicos to snowshoe, to three-legged, and aged and kitten, Tom brought in every single feline as his own personal family.

The rusty doorknob to the shack jiggled, sparking Ford to jerk upright from his metal chair. He held his hand above his holstered Sig Sauer, still on his hip. He was ready to throw down if the occasion called for it.

Tom Two Feathers stood and put his hand out to Ford, "Whoa, whoa, friend. Wait."

He went and carefully cracked open the door to full. A pale man entered, cradling a Winchester 94 Deluxe rifle with a dark brown leather gun stock cover in his left arm and a string full of nabbed partridges in his right. Ford checked the pale man over with a suspecting gaze.

He was also gaunt, like Tom Two Feathers, but his teeth were rotted and were destined for a pulling. When he removed his Stormy Kromer cap, his greasy hair fell flat over his chapped face and onto the shoulders of his blood-and-oil-stained blue 1980s snowmobile suit.

"My help," Tom told Ford, then introduced Ford to the man. "This is one of my musher friends, Cy Ford."

Ford lifted his hand from his gun and sat back at the table.

"Evening," the man mumbled and placed his rifle on the rack next to some rusted bear traps that were decorated on the wooden plank walls.

Ford watched him carefully as he placed the partridges in the deep sink at the other end of the kitchen to prepare them.

"Found him a couple weeks ago, near death on some street in Rudyard," Tom said. "Crystal about done the poor bastard in. I took a chance on him, cleaned him up best I could. I don't know where he hails from, but he's a hell of a cook and a damn fine hunter. Sharpshooter, aren't ya?"

The man let loose a grin from his scruffy jaw and walked over to the two. Tom poured him some whiskey, then filled more into Ford's mason jar he was using to drink.

"Best security I ever had," Tom said.

"Got a name?" Ford asked the unknown man.

The man threw back his whiskey with Tom, not even wincing the bite, and just returned to preparing what he hunted, pretending as if he didn't hear the question.

Tom chuckled some, "Good luck getting it outta him. I'm still trying. I just call him Drifter. That's what he is, so fuck it."

He fell back into his own chair to continue the Cribbage match he had going against Ford.

"He's okay to me, though," he added. "A real hard worker."

Ford's interest locked in on the enigmatic drifter as he kept a constant watch on him throughout.

"Niko's talking about adding more runs," Ford said to Tom, refocusing on the game.

"Hear that?" Tom said as he hooked his head back and spoke to Drifter. "Might need to keep you on full-time, eh?"

From Drifter, Tom's head repositioned to the cloudy white crystal on his side of the table and asked with his eyes if he minded. Drifter shrugged the go-ahead, which caught Ford's suspicions further. Tom crushed the crystals with the butt of his hunting knife, then snorted the crumble. His face floated upward and back, and it popped with instant climax.

"Best stuff anywhere," Tom said.

He offered a taste to Ford after, who declined, while Drifter paid no mind, keeping to himself, purposely avoiding the drug use happening in front of him completely. The fact that Drifter, just like Ford, carried a secretive aura, increased Ford's curiosity about him.

Who is this man I've never met before? Everyone wants something. What does he want?

V

Avery waited next to the twelve-foot swing gate that led around to the back of the post and into the kennels when the sun rose. Right on time, she thought, when she saw Ford appear from the post's exit trail. He steered his sled inside the gate, and she followed him, swinging it shut behind them.

Ford and Jett peeled off the tarp and loaded the new batch of packaged meth from Tom Two Feathers in the space under Lucy's cage, where they kept the last batch hidden.

Inside the post, they stacked sixty-thousand dollars cash onto Avery's desk. Each took separate stacks and began to count their take in chairs around her. They stayed alert on the door and windows throughout, their day job duties still in mind.

"Might be nothing, but I might've had some eyes on me," Ford said.

Jett and Avery grew concerned by the news as soon as the words rolled from his tongue.

"There was two of 'em on some lead-sleds. Thought they were following me when I hit the ice bridge, but I'm not sure."

"Well, how far they follow you for?" Avery asked.

"Halfway to the red zone... It's probably a good idea to start planning an exit here..."

"Exit?" Jett asked, confused, money fanned in his mitts. "Thinking of going straight or something?"

Ford shrugged.

"We've got a good thing here," Jett said. "I ain't going back to just living on state salaries. That's shitty if you ask me."

Avery nodded, even though she took Ford's words to heart. She trusted whenever he spoke in such away that there was always a good reason behind his words.

"Old rule," Ford said to them both. "Nothing good lasts forever."

He continued to split the cash, leaving his co-workers with his final thought.

* * *

Following his shift, Ford entered his rundown house that was located in a lower-middle-class neighborhood, the oldest in the county. His work duffel of secrets was clung tight in his fist. If only his neighbors realized who they were living next to. He was the mysterious neighbor, as described by the others there. None of them knew anything about him.

Never letting anyone close was a personal rule Ford had set for himself for God knows how long. As mundane as this area was, if his neighbors discovered a drug runner that moonlighted as a DNR officer lived among them, that would surely be a highlight story worth passing down for the generations.

Ford's house was empty. There wasn't much furniture, or life, for that matter. Just the bare essentials for living. As boring as the grass grew, it was his domain. He took two stacks of bills worth twenty-thousand from the duffel and went about trying to find hiding places. In the kitchen, he opened the false bottom of a counter's framing and saw this spot already had money he had stored from a previous run. In the living room, he separated a brick from inside the fireplace and noticed this location was also full of money. In his bedroom, he opened the floor's register to find it chocked-full too. He sighed, annoyed he was exhausting places to hide his take. He went to the basement next and checked the group of paint cans on a shelf. As he expected, they were also full. An empty can in the shadows at the end of the shelf caught his attention. He slid it aside and determined, at last, it was empty. He stuffed only two stacks in the can and positioned it back on the shelf to blend in with the rest.

He shoveled some beef stroganoff he cooked, or tried to cook, into his mouth. The noodles were semi-soft and the sauce bland and runny. He didn't care. It was food and he needed to eat, whether he was hungry or not. His arm was wrapped around his plate on the kitchen table as if he were guarding it, and he just stared at nothing, while thoughts plagued his mind in his normal lonely state.

Before bed, he took a shower and decided to clean his arsenal of guns, while he watched a Detroit Red Wings versus New York Rangers hockey game on the small television, since there wasn't much else that needed to be done before he crashed. He laid the guns on the bed, one after another, very carefully. An array of semi-automatic pistols, a few Smith & Wesson revolvers, an AK-47, various hunting rifles, some with scopes, some without, and a few old shotguns. These were arms that he never kept in just a single spot on his property or at work. For every hiding place of loot, there was a weapon. Taped under his kitchen table where he ate, a weapon. In each cupboard's lining, a weapon. Under the lid of the toilet tank, a weapon. He prepared himself as if a fight to the death would arise at any given moment. Being overly prepared was what kept him alive to this point, he assumed. If it's not broke don't fix it was his mentality, regardless of how ridiculous it may sound.

Wrapped in only a bath towel, he sat on a frameless mattress on the floor and worked the gun oil from his rag onto a .357 Magnum revolver.

He wanted to give it that new shine, and secretly loved the distinct oily wood aroma it produced. Ford's body was covered in various scars. Some were old bullet wounds, others from blades and burns. They represented a mural of his cryptic past. There was a moment he caught a glance of himself in the mirror hung above his dresser. Something on the mirror made him halt his cleaning process routine. He stood and stepped to it, plucking a postcard that was lodged in its top corner. It had snow-covered mountains pictured in its background and a few grizzly bears pawing for fish in a choppy river on the forefront. Spread across it in big bold font was the word *ALASKA*. A special warmth circulated in him as he held the card. Flipping it over, it had various dollar amounts scribbled in pen. Written on the very bottom he read the inscription, *40 ACRES.*

* * *

Two bloated and headless deer carcasses lay in a ditch alongside a highway. Ford questioned a woman snowmobiler who reported them. She was older and her face was wind burnt, since she wore a helmet without a face shield. She was an avid rider, an old school retiree.

"Each morning I ride this same route and haven't come across anything of the sort before," she said with a shiver.

"Poachers," Ford mumbled.

"Excuse me?"

"Their heads. They're gone. Probably poachers."

A local sheriff's department truck rolled onto the scene. Ford lifted his gaze from his writing pad to the oncoming truck.

"Think I've got everything I need," Ford said to the woman. "Thank you, ma'am."

The older woman straddled her '98 Polaris XC 600 with racing stripes and rode across the highway, onto a trail, then vanished in a heartbeat with the cloud of snow.

Sheriff Oren Anson approached from the truck. He strolled somewhat hunched, which was due to a former football injury back in his college days. He rocked a bushy white beard that he kept year-round and wore a trooper department trapper hat with the ears buttoned on top.

He was a predictable man who hated change. Whatever had worked for him until now he stuck to. That included his routines and his outmoded methods. His wife had left him years before, so the job was what remained. Many close to him, including his own children, voiced their concerns for him to step down and retire. Anson scoffed at such a thing. He was the type to bow out on his terms when he was ready, and he wasn't.

"Never understood hunting for the trophy instead of the meat,"

Sheriff Anson commented in his deep, gruff tone that sounded like it hurt when he spoke. "Damn waste."

Ford barely paid attention to him; he just kept on filling out the rest of his report of the poached deer.

"You and I didn't really get a chance to talk the other day after the incident," Sheriff Anson said.

"Labeling it an incident, are we?" Ford asked.

"What do you think I should be labeling it then?"

"Wrong place, wrong time."

"Wrong place, wrong time?"

Ford finally looked up from his pad, "That's right."

"Could be. Could very well be. Then again, I'm reminded of the other wrong places, wrong times you seemed to have got yourself involved in. That trespasser last fall, remember him? Just a confused hunter doing some hunting on some private land, then went to the hospital with a broken jaw. Then there's the quad you shot the hell out of so a guy with priors couldn't use it anymore. There are others—"

"Don't tell me you came this way to share my job review. I have superiors for that, you know."

Anson put a hand to his upper lip to stroke his mustache, biting his tongue. He was keen on Ford's cocky ways.

"In my thirty-plus years in the department," Sheriff Anson said, "I've never met a DNR officer quite like you."

"Always a pleasure, Sheriff. Now if you don't mind, I need to get back to finding some poachers."

"All right then. Appreciate your time."

Anson closed his pad and returned to his Chevy. When he opened his door to enter, he lifted himself in the cab with a grunt, then hung halfway out to get a last word in.

"Oh. If you care to know, Vernon was found dead yesterday."

This made Ford turn to him.

"Hung himself in his boy's old room."

He shut his door and left Ford with that final, disturbing bit of information.

VI

A couple of weeks later, Ford, Avery, and Jett loaded the next batch on another dog sled in the kennels. The distinctive, sleek-built sled belonged to Jett, and he had it decorated with classic rock n' roll and Detroit Red Wings stickers. A loud appearance for a loud guy.

Once the batch was prepared and secured, Jett hopped on the footboards of his sled and Avery handed him his new burner phone.

"Please be careful," she told him with a concerned tone. "There's some potential flurries on their way tonight. We'll keep you updated on their movement."

"You're acting like my mother again," Jett replied.

"I just worry about you guys, that's all."

"No cowboy shit," Ford added in all seriousness.

Jett shook his head and followed with a smug grin as he put on his Oakley riding goggles over his trapper hat.

"Been riding these same trails since I was dick high," the young man announced. "Y'all can't be killing my fun now!"

He inserted some earbuds that were connected to his iPod and finished his preparation when he spat a long stream of tobacco juice onto the ground. He followed with a whistled tune of the beginning of "Love Me Do" by the Beatles, which triggered his sled to pull forward by the second team of dogs he and Avery shared. Fittingly, they had named them John, Paul, George, Ringo, and their lead dog, Sadie. Each dog was white with tinges of black on their tails and appeared as if they were a pack of ghosts floating above the snow in their sprint. Before Jett faded from sight into the cold wild, he gave Ford and Avery a rock-on sign and kept it as high in the air as he could.

Avery walked back into the post to man the communications. Ford, on the other hand, stood in the same spot and kept watching the path where Jett had disappeared. He could still hear the sprint of the sled dogs, mixed with their persistent yips and barks. Similar to their musher, they were a rambunctious bunch, complete opposites of Ford's team. Jett liked to rile his dogs at the start of his runs. He figured it was good for morale and good for their spirit. It invited the faster pace he craved.

As Ford stood there listening and watching, he kept thinking of how a partner like Jett Prevo made him nervous. He thought the kid to be sloppy. Reckless. He never agreed with Jett's decision to wait until close to nightfall before his trip. In fact, of their many disagreements, this topic was their most popular. The wilderness changes when darkness falls, he'd always argue to no result.

Yes, the young man was a fine outdoorsman and knew the land probably better than he did, but Ford told him countless times that it's hard to anticipate what you can't see in the dark. Drug smuggling 101. Jett was too often a risk-taker and these challenging night runs helped feed the ego of his self-proclaimed nickname Midnight Rider, after an Allman Brothers Band hit. Maybe that's why he continued to do it — to live up to the name, he thought. It also didn't help that he went about town vomiting the moniker every chance he could in every dive bar around, among his many groups of rowdies. He never shut his mouth.

While he hadn't let slip yet about his unlawful side gig, he did carry himself as anything but a DNR officer. Ford constantly worried if there were any nosey local or fellow DNR officers, or even a give-a-shit lawman who wanted to pry further into Jett's background, they wouldn't have a hard time doing so. And aside from these risks, he knew Jett's take was spent as fast as it was earned. Snowmobiles, quads, new boats, Jet Skis, grills, house improvements; he always bought frivolous gifts for himself and his family. But mostly his family. Ford constantly warned him of his careless ways, but it fell on deaf ears every time. For Jett, it was all about living in the moment. In his mind, these times were his moment, and he wasn't going to let it pass him by.

* * *

Jett rode the same routes as Ford and Avery. Starting westbound, he advanced across endless fields. He neared the town of Strongs as the sun commenced its dip, while listening to his music. The landscape glided by as if he were the star in a music video.

Unbeknownst to Jett, the two mysterious snowmobilers in black and silver had returned. Hidden behind the maze of trees, they stood straight, cradling their rides between their legs as they watched him. After he passed them, they revved their rides and steered toward his tracks, into the open.

The trail Jett rode on eventually became thick with paper birch and white pine trees that grew close together, barely enough to let any slats of moonlight peek through. Curving in behind him, the two snowmobilers followed at a safe distance. In the midst of him singing along with a song on his iPod, Jett glanced beyond his shoulder and noticed them. Their dark ensemble made them appear as ghostly silhouettes drifting at him. He squinted to hone in on the reality that was two riders tailing him.

"Speed!" he yelled to Sadie.

He looked past his shoulder again and, almost in a mocking way, the snowmobilers picked up their speed too. Then, one of them zoomed past Jett, almost knocking him from his sled.

"What the hell, man?!" Jett shouted.

The snowmobiler disappeared into the black ahead.

"Crazy bastard," Jett muttered.

The now lone rider trailing him didn't make any sudden moves whatsoever. Instead, this stranger remained behind, at a steady pace, slowing and accelerating in unison with the dog sled.

Jett decided to veer onto another trail he knew.

"Haw!"

Sadie and the dogs turned onto another path, and after a while, cut through untouched lands in Jett's hope he could shake his tail. He knew this wasn't the law. If it were, they wouldn't have followed him for such a lengthy period. They'd have forced a pullover from the beginning.

When Jett ventured on a third trail that was more fluff snow than packed hard, he took a glimpse back once more to spot the same rider following him. Struggling, but still pursuing. Jett figured he'd stay on this trail as long as he could, because any snowmobile couldn't endure this sort of terrain for much longer before it would eventually stall. For fifteen minutes he kept ahead of the rider. But the longer the chase dragged, the more increasingly paranoid he became.

"Speed! Speed, Sadie! Go!"

He mushed his dogs at full speed now. Much more of this and he knew they'd surely die of pure exhaustion.

Running in the thick snow made it worse. It might as well have been sand. Jett's only other option was to force a sharp right turn back to the original trail, in hopes the rider behind him would stall on the ninety-degree angle maneuver. *Fuck it*, he thought and went for it.

"Gee!"

He leaned his body low and hard to the right with Sadie's turn, keeping his right foot dangling and free to help steer the quick redirection, and his team veered onto the better trail.

They struggled to climb the powdered mound. So much so that Jett leaped from his footboards to lighten the load his team had to tow, and he helped their efforts by pushing the sled up onto the trail. When he did, he hopped back on his footboards in a single bounce and his team grabbed their second wind and went at it again, full speed. Their rapid pants puffed hard in the night's frozen air. Jett peeked over his shoulder again to see if he had lost his tail.

To his horror, he did not. Miraculously, the rider worked his way through the unreasonable powder and back onto the same trail.

"The fuck?" Jett said out loud.

When he turned his head forward again, he saw the same rider that had forged ahead of him earlier was now blocking the trail in the distance, with his machine directly facing him. Jett dug his cell from his navy-blue department jacket to make a distress call. Before he could hit call, a branch from a pine on the right side of the trail dropped from nowhere and clotheslined him clean off his sled. He hit the ground hard on his back and his fur hood fell over his face. He flipped his hood to his back and tried to catch his breath. From his ground view, he saw the blurry image of his dog team advancing his sled without him.

As his vision slowly began to return, Jett tried to gather himself and search for his cell in the frigid, dark abyss. It wasn't in sight. A thought hit him, and he reached into his coat for his iPod, remembering he could send texts from the device. A fist suddenly came across his face and the iPod sailed into yonder. A third man, without a snowmobile, also dressed in a black-and-silver snowsuit, but with a black ski mask on, stood above the dazed Jett. He shook his punching hand that stung in the bitter cold. The other two riders that tailed him from the onset approached on their machines and boxed the helpless drug runner in. On one of their helmets, the moon's glow bounced just right to where Jett could see his nose and lip were busted and bleeding from the hits he'd suffered.

"Wait, wait," he panted, putting forward his lacerated hand for them to hold on so he could stand. "Wait. Just—"

Each of the unknown riders brandished a semi-automatic rifle and aimed it at him. Jett could see on their helmets white skull and crossbones, like pirates. The man in the ski mask signaled with his gun for Jett to remove his side piece. Carefully and cautiously, he tossed it aside. He then partially raised his hands, surrendering to the trio. His heart beat a mile a minute.

They stood there, though, and examined Jett as if he owed them a move now. Thing was, he didn't have any more moves to make.

Locking in on each of them, he could observe their trigger fingers. One after another, each flicked the safety switch off on their weapons. Right then and there Jett came to the inevitable realization. He slowly began to lower his hands. Doing so, he spit some tobacco juice at the feet of the man in the ski mask.

"Let's get on with it, fellas," he said.

The gunmen lit him up where he stood in the cold, lonely night.

VII

At six in the morning, Ford stood on the snow-covered stairs to the entrance of the post, holding a steaming cup of coffee. Anxiously, he awaited Jett's return. Often, he'd check the time on his cell. Jett's routines were unorthodox, but that had never affected his punctuality. Every run he made was completed on time and up to the standards of their boss, the same as his co-workers.

Avery pulled in on her snowmobile and approached the building. She could sense the concern on Ford's face the second she touched the stairs. He didn't even need to say it. Jett had not returned yet.

"Guess we're all running late this morning," she said with optimism before she advanced past him into the post.

An hour went by, and still no sign of Jett. Ford and Avery decided to wait a little longer before they went to search for him. To keep his mind busy in the meantime, Ford fed and played with the dogs in the kennel.

He threw treats to each of them and even play-wrestled with the rowdy ones — Kaya and Elmer. Upon escaping the dog pile of slobber, he went to check on Lucy in her cage. She lay on her side — the only position that was comfortable for her this far into her pregnancy. She panted even heavier than before.

"Hanging in, old girl? Not much longer now."

Later, he checked his cell again while he waxed the runner skis of his sled. Nothing. Ford walked in from outside after he was done waxing, a job that wasn't nearly long enough to keep his concern in check. He saw Avery trying to call Jett on her cell at her desk.

"Still nothing?" Ford asked her.

"Goes right to voicemail. Calvin's too. No one's answering."

"Yesterday, when was his last check-in?"

"The yellow zone."

"Strongs."

"Yes."

Terrible silence hung. Neither of them wanted to be the first to say that they should initiate their search for him, because that would admit something bad had happened on his run.

"Maybe he let his phone die again?" Avery guessed, trying to bring some hope to the progressively dire situation. "Could be anything with him. You know how he is."

Ford nodded, unsure. He didn't want to panic Avery, but in his experience, these sorts of signs led to no good. If it didn't feel right, it wasn't right.

"Try Tom," Avery suggested.

Ford did so and put the call on speaker so he and Avery could both listen.

"Aye, friend, how ya doing?" Tom asked when he answered.

"Morning, Tom," Ford replied, holding the cell in his hand between him and Avery. "Listen, we haven't heard from Jett in a while. We were wondering how last night's handoff went on your end?"

"Well, it didn't. Kid never showed."

Avery leaned back in her seat, her hands thrown in the air in a mix of frustration and confusion.

"Is that right?" Ford asked.

"Yup. Had the next load ready and waiting with a new bottle of whiskey I brewed that I wanted him to try, but he never came by."

"Hmm..."

"What'd Canada say?"

"Can't reach 'em."

"Shit."

"Yeah. Shit."

"I assume this isn't good, right?"

"No, Tom, I don't think it is. Avery and I are going to gear up here and go look for him."

"All right. Maybe his sled broke down on the trails along the way. Could be he's camping somewheres."

"Hope so."

"I don't really like having a batch of mine somewhere out there, while sitting on another here, ya know?"

"I know."

"Kind of a double whammy there for me. For youse."

"We'll be sure to keep you updated on his whereabouts, Tom."

"All-righty then. I appreciate that, friend. If I see or hear anything, I'll give you a holler as well."

"Okay."

Ford disconnected the call.

"Should we go right now?" she asked, her apprehension obvious.

Ford checked the time on his cell. Eleven.

"Let's wait until noon, then I'll make the trip myself."

Avery nodded, "I'll get some feelers out to my contacts in the areas to see if anyone has seen or heard from him."

Ford nodded.

* * *

Noon neared. Ford stopped shoveling the excess snow around the entrance steps from last night's flurries and returned inside to his desk, where he tried to call Calvin Witter again. It went to voicemail.

For Jett not to answer was one thing, but not a word from Canada was a serious problem.

A vehicle's engine approached the post from the access road. It caught Ford's attention as he sat straight at his desk. It was the sheriff's truck, and from it stepped Sheriff Anson himself. In the covered bed of his truck were Jett and Avery's team of John, Paul, George, Ringo, and Sadie. The sheriff dawdled towards the post and entered even slower than he began. When he did, he removed his hat at the sight of Ford and held it on his belly. Avery wandered in from her back office when she heard the door ajar. She knew by the way Anson entered, calm and quiet, that it wasn't Jett.

"Sheriff," she said.

"Avery," Sheriff said, dipping his head in a ping of grief that appeared rehearsed. "There's no easy way to say this. Jett's body was found an hour and a half from here on a westbound trail, just outside the town of Strongs."

Ford sighed deeply and slumped back in his chair. A part of him had already known Jett wasn't coming back, although he tried hard not to admit it.

Upset, Avery crossed her arms, "Oh my God!"

"We're looking into it still, but, uh, it's safe to say it's a homicide. Coroner lost count of the bullet holes."

Avery cupped her hands over her mouth, her eyes brimming with tears. Sheriff Anson just shook his head in disgust.

Consoling, big or small, after delivering bad news, never came easy to him. As he stood there, he felt the pressure to make things better for them. It was a feeling he had always brought upon himself with anyone after giving them terrible news. This case wasn't any different.

"Excessive," Anson added. "Poor kid. I've known him since he was a child creating mischief up and down the streets of Newberry. He was kind-hearted, though. Respectful to his elders."

Anson stumbled for anything more he could add to memorialize the young man.

"The State Police's help is minimal with Christmas around the corner, but rest assured, we have the full support of my department on this, and we're doing everything we can to figure out what happened to him."

"Do his parents know yet?" Avery asked.

"I just left them."

"Our dogs are here," Avery mentioned when her sad sights caught them moving about in Anson's truck bed. "Were they with him?"

"We found them about a mile along the trail from his body. His sled was nowhere to be found, though. Only thing left were the harnesses the dogs were still in."

"Poor babies," Avery said, tears in her eyes.

Anson hesitated to ask, "Did Jett work yesterday? His normal shift?"

"Yes," she managed between her tears, trying to gather herself enough to answer his questions.

"Did he say anything about where he was going? Why was he using department dogs? Anything of the matter?"

"Not that I can recall. He told us he was going to the bar in town. We were going to join him after our shift."

Anson's head swept to Ford, who had remained composed and eerily silent during the entire conversation. He could tell the DNR officer's mind was elsewhere, which made him even more suspicious.

"Ford?" Anson said to pull his attention.

"Yup. That was the plan."

"Has he said anything recently about anything that might seem off?"

"Like what?"

"I don't know. Anything that seemed different from his normal, I suppose. Even anything small. Whatever seemed different from his daily routine on or away from the job."

"Jett is—was— kind of all over the place," Avery said. "We were never able to keep up with him."

"Taking the dogs," Anson said to Ford. "That a regular thing?"

There was an uncomfortable silence for long moments.

"Ford?"

Ford finally faced the sheriff, confused why *he* was asked the question. "Uh, no. Not that I can recall."

Anson nodded and stood there, studying Ford to detect any deception. During his time in law enforcement, he thought he was good at manipulating people to force the answers he needed from them. In interrogation rooms, he was known for being an absolute pitbull of an interrogator. Right at this moment wasn't a good time to dig further, he knew.

"Well, I sure appreciate you guys' time," he said, putting his hat back on his head. "If I have anything else, I'll know where to find you. Does someone want to help me unload the pooches?"

"Of course," Avery said.

She led Anson outside and wafted a knowing look at Ford in her exit. When Ford heard the front door shut, he began to clear everything important to him from his desk without hesitation. No doubt about it now, the heat was on.

* * *

Ford raced along the highway through the night in his pickup truck. It was quieter than usual. No other vehicles around. No birds or animals either. The light from his personal cell on his passenger seat kept illuminating his cab. Avery kept calling. Earlier on, he had broken and set his burner cell ablaze. She remained persistent and endlessly tried to reach Ford, whose mind was already ten steps ahead. Maybe even a time zone or two. Home first to grab his money and belongings, then hit the road. That was all that mattered to him right now.

With a closed fist on top of his glove box, it flipped open. Digging deep inside, he grabbed a wrinkled map and commenced planning his next relocation out of the state of Michigan. Over and over, his cell vibrated. With every buzz, his irritation increased.

He finally answered when his annoyance hit a breaking point, "Avery, meet me at my place. Now's as good a time as any to hit the road."

"That might be a problem," a deep, almost hypnotic male's voice answered on the other end of the line.

Ford slammed on his brakes and brought his truck to a skidding stop, just before it could slide into the ditch.

"Who's this?" Ford demanded.

"You'll find out soon enough."

"Where's Avery?"

"She's here. She's fine. Why don't you come meet me? Been dying to meet you. We have much to talk about... Officer Prevo for one."

Ford closed his eyes, sensing there was a shit storm in his future.

"Keep driving," the voice ordered. "First two-track on the right."

He hung up.

Ford reached under his bench seat and grabbed a side piece — a Colt 1911. It was a gun with a long history that landed in his possession during a truck stop meal gone wrong. A story for another time. He checked to make sure the piece had a full clip, then slammed it back in place and continued along the lone highway, until he found the two-track road the voice mentioned.

His hardened leer intensified the more he traveled this narrow path. He drove carefully over the uneven, bumpy road, so as not to bottom out.

A good mile in, headlights burst on everywhere around the truck. Beamed from the dark, full and many, the lights practically blinded him, and he braked hard. His old beater rattled to a halt. Through his windshield, he tried to squint past the group of lights several lengths in front of him.

Two black Escalades were parked in an arrow formation, touching front bumpers. Gathered around him like packs of wolves ready to pounce on prey were fifteen mercenaries on snowmobiles sprinkled throughout the trees. Their identities were hidden by their riding helmets, but he could easily detect the white skull and crossbones painted on them. Ford kept his gun close to his thigh. If things escalated, he was ready, even if the odds were against him here. *Think about how to live, not how to die.*

Silhouette figures blocked the front lights that shined directly at Ford. Clear as day, he could identify Judge behind Avery, who held her by her long red hair like she was his own dog on a leash. When he walked in direct sight of Ford, Judge forced her to her knees. Her hands were bound behind her back with zip ties, and by the looks of her bruises, she'd been struck by multiple blows.

Judge glanced back by the Escalades and waited. Someone was missing. Curious, he walked behind the vehicles to find Ray hunched and puking, not in sight of anyone else.

"Ray, you good?" Judge asked.

Ray gave a slight nod. Judge walked to him and rested his hand on the middle of his friend's back. When he did, Ray stood, straightening his long torso, towering high.

Embarrassment washed over him. His eyeballs fluttered, taking a second to sort himself, as if there was more vomit about to spill.

"Fuck, man," Ray said, his usual deep voice shriveled and meek sounding.

"Yo, it's cool," Judge reassured. "You got this. Remember who you are, bruh. You're a fuckin' Easter."

Judge then pulled a handkerchief from his puffy North Face jacket and wiped a bit of leftover vomit from the corner of his friend's mouth. Ray took the handkerchief to finish wiping himself. Both shared a fond but coy moment, looking at each other.

"Ready?" Judge asked.

Ray cracked a slight smile, and both emerged from behind the safe cover of the Escalades. He held Avery's phone he called Ford on.

Waiting inside his truck in anticipation, Ford eyed the giant of a man who appeared from the darkness.

His fascination for Ray's stature was almost instantly interrupted by five mercenaries fresh off their snowmobiles, who closed on his truck undetected with AR-15 rifles at the ready. They extracted him from his seat and made sure to swipe his gun from his hand before they patted him down for more weapons. After, they forced him to his knees in front of Avery.

Ford's gaze carefully swept over her to make sure she was okay. She didn't seem as panicked as he would've thought. She stayed tough, even though a trace of fear lingered. Ford then darted brief glances around, his head on a swivel, and noticed the excessive amount of firepower at every turn.

There wasn't a way he could figure an escape. His eyes went dead, and he floated them toward Ray again, who currently hovered above him and Avery.

"What do you want from us?" Avery asked Ray, her voice trembling.

"For starters, an introduction," Ray replied, then pointed at each. "I'm Ray. Ray Easter. And if my research is accurate, you're Officer Avery Kinnomen and you're Officer...Cyrus Ford."

Quiet remained. Quiet that gave Ray his answer. He grinned, impressed by the duo's fearlessness. Not anything he wasn't used to, though. Numerous times he saw his father and his men try to crack proud ones. These sorts took time, but they always cracked. Or died. Or both.

"Look at y'all," Ray said, admiring the officers.

"Figured you folks were country grunts or road construction or some shit. Corrupt cops go like peanut butter to jelly where I'm from. But possum cops? That's a first."

Ford kept his cold, brooding stare on him.

"Operations in these parts are switching hands," Ray went on. "Killing your partner was nothing personal, but shit, y'all ain't no strangers to how these things work. You chose this way of life. Honestly, I'd blame your boss. Real talk."

"What boss?" Avery asked.

"Nah, don't play that shit with me." Ray chuckled. "Y'all aren't as smooth as ya think. We've been up here a month now and know every trail you ride. How much crystal you run. Where you run it to. Right down to where you hide it and how much your take is after."

He stopped for effect. There was a thought that maybe the officers would converse or at the very least spit on him. He'd entertain any emotion here. No such luck, however. He knew he wasn't making any impact so far. They just kept quiet and let him say his peace. In a way, it kind of annoyed him.

"This whole territory has switched hands to me. Yeah, you'd like working for me. I'm a fuckin' dope boss."

"We're not running for you," Avery declared, her confidence peeking.

"Gotcha. A'right then. I guess you're defaulting to my next offer. Killing Niko Krowchuck."

Ford and Avery stole uncertain glances from each other.

"We're not doing that," Avery said.

"Good. Then you'll run for me."

"It's a suicide mission. Besides, we don't see Niko. Niko sees us."

Further annoyed, Ray motioned to Judge. His goon went to work and grabbed Avery by her hair again, this time pushing her face into the slushy snow. He then jammed his shiny Desert Eagle handgun in the back of her head. Didn't matter to him either way, he was ready to pull the trigger if Ray gave the word.

Ford jolted at Ray, rising from his spot to help, but he was promptly subdued by the others.

"Whoa," Ray said as he took a step back. "Feisty!"

Ford's jaw tightened. He was done fucking around. As far as he was concerned, he was staring at two dead men. By Judge's leer on Ford, the feeling was mutual.

"Let me put this in terms you dumbass Yoopers will understand," Ray bluntly said, more serious now. "Either you run for me, or you eliminate the kid boss. These are the only options on the table."

Both Ford and Avery remained unshakable, refusing to give him an answer or an inch. So, Judge took it upon himself to cock his gun and bury it in Avery's temple.

"For real?" Ray asked Ford, then turned to Judge. "Do it."

Ford stared at Avery's now fearful face. She released a horrific scream, knowing this was her end. Just before Judge squeezed his trigger fully, Ford broke his stance.

"Stop!" he yelled.

Everyone paused their actions.

"Fuck!" Ford yelled again. "Okay. We'll consider the offer. We just need time."

"The feisty possum cop finally speaks," Ray said.

He took a beat before he gestured to Judge, who uncocked his gun and tipped Avery upright, back to her shaking knees.

"Heavy shit, right?" Ray said with a sharp grin. "Sleep on it. I'll expect an answer before tomorrow night."

With a step backward in his long stride, he departed for the Escalade while Judge, whose keen desire to kill them was left unfulfilled, kept his terrorizing scowl on the two officers. Standing still above them, he hoped for either to make another threatening move so he could throw down. Ray returned and gently put his hand on his shoulder to release his friend's desire and led him back to the Escalade.

"Don't think about leaving town," Ray warned the runners. "We'll be watching. Always. Everywhere."

Even before Ford and Avery could let what happened sink in, Ray and his mercenaries were gone, leaving them behind to fend for themselves. Avery's seemingly resilient demeanor crumbled, and she spit blood onto the tire tracks that were left in the gangsters' wake. Ford rushed to free her restraints, and she fell into his arms to hug him tightly.

There, on their knees, alone among the bare oaks that creaked and swayed with the frigid wind, they held each other in the terror of darkness.

VIII

Inside the cab of Ford's parked truck on the shoulder of some back road, not far of a walk from where they met Ray, both Ford and Avery sat in silence. They were still reeling from what had happened. Ford could tell Avery was nervous by the way her hands shook uncontrollably when she lit a cigarette. She checked the bruises she'd incurred from Ray and his men in the mirror on the visor.

Ford just watched, somewhat trying to grasp the feeling of guilt he had. He knew she wasn't meant for this part of the criminal profession. Thing was, deep inside he always knew a day like this would come to their doorstep.

"Ever hear of Ellis Easter — the singer?" Ford asked, breaking the dispirited silence.

Avery thought to herself for a second, then nodded.

"Oscar Easter is his offspring, supposedly. That's the legend anyway. He heads a big outfit outta Detroit. And that giant son of a bitch we just met is his son. I recognized him. He was a popular basketball star at one time."

"We're so fucked," Avery said, taking a long drag of her cigarette before she flicked it through the crack of the window.

Ford reached for Avery's burner cell from the dash, called a number, and pushed the speaker button on.

"What?" Calvin Witter answered on the other end after a ring.

"Where the fuck were you?" Ford asked him. "Get Niko. Now."

Avery's face grew with apprehension.

"He'll have us killed," she whispered to Ford.

"If you're calling to bitch to him about Easter, he already knows," Calvin said.

To Ford, Avery mouthed a surprised, *What?*

"Niko received Oscar's message earlier today," Calvin added. "It was loud and clear. So, you're wasting your time."

"Get him on the fucking phone, Calvin!"

"Do yourself a favor and think about what you're going to do next here. The runs continue as scheduled, regardless of the issues at hand."

Ford's ears perked when he heard the subtle command.

"Goodnight, Ford."

With that, the call disconnected. A Michigan State Police cruiser rolled by them around the same time. It slowed to an idle, curious as to why any truck would be out that way at that time of night.

When the cruiser's brakes brightened the surrounding area with red, Avery and Ford knew they had to leave. Ford threw his truck in gear and turned the wheel hard to whip around in the opposite direction, away from the cruiser.

"Whoa, whoa!" Avery panicked, confused by Ford's actions.

Ford kept his acceleration at a safe speed while religiously checking the mirrors to see if the cruiser would follow.

"They're going to turn around after us. I know they will."

Ford didn't say anything and kept to the road, still with an eye on his mirror.

The cruiser's brake lights turned dark, and the cruiser continued its way forward, to the relief of both.

Within the half-hour, Ford pulled into Avery's driveway, alongside her house on the south side of town. It was an upscale neighborhood, much more modern than Ford's. Signs of children were everywhere. It was a neighborhood of young families and a sign of growth in this particular part of the town.

Avery jerked her body forward to leave the truck, but Ford softly grabbed her arm to have her wait so he could call Calvin again. Following many rings, the call was finally answered.

"Quit fucking around, Calvin, and get me Niko."

"Ask and you shall receive," Niko replied.

Avery held her breath. She never believed they'd get through to the boss.

"You know about the Easters?" Ford said. "Do you know we've been eating shit here on this side all day?"

"My apologies for being unreachable. I've been planning my next move."

"And?"

"And as Calvin told you, I feel very strongly that we should stick to our same run schedule. Leave me to worry about the Easters."

"Easy for you to say," Avery said. "You're not getting guns pointed in your face."

"Avery. Ford," Niko said with a relaxed tone. "These threats are beyond you. This is just an attempt to spook us. Mainly, to get my attention. They're trying to disrupt our flow. I need both of you to finish your next runs, do understand me? With Jett and his batch gone, we're still owed a batch."

"Owed?" Ford asked.

"Yes. Owed... Forgive me if I don't sound empathetic to what's going on in the trenches, but you must understand that business is business. The train always moves forward, even if there is something on the tracks. I'm not a hand-holder. Never have been."

Niko spoke from the safe confines of his luxurious childhood home.

Made from red cedar logs, it sat on close to a thousand acres of the boreal forests of Ontario. He stood in front of an impressive record collection he thumbed through, his stone fireplace as his backdrop. The likes of Lou Reed, Velvet Revolver, Radiohead, Modest Mouse, The Strokes, Postal Service, Iggy and the Stooges, and Big Star populated the many milk crates where he stored them. An object on top of the mantle of his fireplace kept his constant attention during the conversation. He then redirected to a Big Star record in the player and dropped the needle on the vinyl to have it play lightly to set his current mood.

"Losing more mushers is not something I'm ready for quite yet. There's plenty of season left. Plenty of money to make for us all. Production won't stop on account of Oscar Easter."

"That's not your call to make," Avery blurted with even more passion.

"Who do you think you work for?" Niko asked, his abrasiveness apparent. "Listen to me very carefully. I will handle the Easters. Me. Don't get fresh and start to rebel. Tempt me and I'll throw that prick sheriff a bone about two corrupt DNR officers right under his department's nose. I'm sure that won't look favorable for both of you, especially since Jett died working by your side. Get me?"

Ford and Avery didn't answer. Their backs were against the wall.

If anything was clear, it was Niko's rejection to have their back. Their safety meant as little to him as the addicts who bought his meth.

"Good. So, again, I want what's owed. Jett's lost batch. That's a whole lot of money to just vanish. And if after the season, either of you chooses to leave our partnership, I will allow it. No strings attached. However, before you do, I want new runners trained in your place. Much like you and your sled dogs, the master eats first. I know both of you can understand that."

"Motherfucker," Ford gritted through his teeth.

"Now, go get ready for the next run. Do what you two do best. Again, no hard feelings. Business is business."

Niko hung up before either of his mushers could get another word in. His attention drifted from a framed-family picture of himself, his mother, and his father. Happier times to him. Important times. Teaching times. Near a white velvet loveseat behind him, his mother Joëlle Krowchuck was sitting in a wheelchair, emotionless. Covered in sweaters with a quilt laid over her lap, she never twitched a muscle. A stroke had taken her speech and movement not long ago.

Niko turned around to face her and then knelt at her side with the framed picture in hand.

"This seems ages ago, mom," he said, showing it to her.

His mother, in her catatonic state, couldn't even flinch an expression toward the picture. Her mouth hung semi-open, and she had a blank stare at nothing.

"I miss him a lot... He'd want me to keep going with this. He wouldn't surrender to competition."

Those reflecting thoughts made him hug his mother, and then he grabbed her face with both of his manicured hands.

"We prepared for this obstacle. Don't worry, you and father taught me adequately. To take the family business — to take our name, and soar... I always promised I wouldn't disappoint either of you. I intend to uphold that very promise."

He stepped back to the fireplace's mantle and returned the picture next to the other object he was first observing. The object was Jett Prevo's bloody DNR badge that Ray had sent to him as a cryptic message. Niko grabbed it and tossed it in the fire below, where the flames swallowed it and grew. The young heir just stood in place, watching the badge burn, contemplating his next ploy.

* * *

Ford and Avery were at a loss for words following the call to Niko. They, too, were contemplating. Between their boss and their boss's rival, they were caught in the middle of two families' aspirations. Maybe even their fates.

"Listen, there's nothing here for us anymore," Ford said. "I've seen the way these things play over turf. It'll be a war soon enough."

"Ford—"

"Come with me."

"It's not that easy, okay? I imagine it wouldn't be for Jett either. We're not like you."

Ford knew she was right.

"When I was a little girl, I dreamed of being a DNR officer. Did I ever tell you that? Yeah. No shit. My father was one. His father the same. Some of my fondest memories were playing and exploring on my grandparents' land down a ways in Brevort. My grandpa built a cabin on that land, and we'd spend every summer there near Lake Michigan. Those memories are the world to me. Leaving here means leaving everything I cherish. The area I was raised in, the job I always wanted... Listen, I'm not stupid, I know that dream was compromised the moment I sold out for drug money. Never in my life would I have thought I would do anything like that. Now though, killing someone on top of leaving? I don't — I don't know if I could live with that sort of thing."

"If we don't kill Niko, believe me, we will be looking over our shoulders the rest of our lives. If we do it and run, there's no reason for the Easters to hunt for us, because they'll have what they wanted. The territory."

Avery reluctantly nodded that she understood Ford, albeit she wasn't fully on board with the dreadful idea. She then slid out of the cab of the truck to put the night in the books.

"He's just a kid, though..." she said after a thought.

There wasn't anything left to say. They both knew the plan was screwed up. No way to sugarcoat it.

She closed the truck's door and returned to her house. Ford watched her until she safely entered. The last thing he ever wanted was to involve Avery in the business of taking someone's life. Killing is an action no one can come back from, and Ford only knew two types of those kinds of people. Those who learn to live with it and those who let it consume them.

IX

Ray and Judge inhaled meat pies the locals called "pasties" at a booth in a tiny local joint named Dobson's. Dobson's was an eatery staple in Upper Michigan. It had franchises spread across the peninsulas. While there were many ways to make them, the traditional pasties were simply a baked pastry with meat and various vegetables inside. A favored treat for northerners, which was created by the early mining and forest workers in the region a century ago.

"Man, quit playin'," Judge joked with Ray, who was picking food from his plate with his plastic fork.

Their antics stopped when Judge reached for his Desert Eagle. His sights lifted beyond Ray's shoulder, which made Ray focus in on Ford and Avery entering the shop with purpose.

"Settle down," Ford told Judge, then looked at Ray. "We're in."

"For real?" Ray asked, still sensing a hint of doubt in them.

"We'll take care of him," Avery said. "After that, we're done. We won't owe anyone anything."

"Deal," Ray replied and wiped his mouth with a napkin close by. "Can't say I'd make the same choice."

"Give us two days to formulate a plan," Avery said.

"I'll need to see those plans when you're done."

Avery conceded with a nod and she and Ford began to leave.

"You ever try these pasty things?" Ray asked them in their exit. "Goddamn, these are dope!"

***

Two days went by faster than most weekdays for Ford and Avery. It was impossible to focus on work. By noon of the third day, they stood in front of the large map of Michigan's Upper Peninsula that they pinned on the wall in the office before every run. It was entirely marked in pencil, accompanied by their normal routes and plans. For this special mission, the routes they chose were somewhat unconventional. They stayed the normal course, sure, but the trip ahead was planned to extend a full day one way. Things had to change.

These new routes were inventive, with endless strokes of their pencils, each giving their own strategy to the secrets of the north country that unfurled abandoned and forgotten trails, some crudely blazed, others were old railroad tracks and logging roads from another time in history. Upon finishing, they both just studied their masterpiece of travel, if it was.

"I bet I could take someone's life," Avery said to Ford's surprise. "If I had to, I could."

Before Ford could respond to her statement, Ray and Judge entered the post from the front. Two Escalades full of their crew awaited behind in the lot.

"What kind of *Little House on the Prairie* bullshit is going on in here?" Ray said.

Ray practically owned the post the second he entered, while Judge stayed by the door, on the inside. He preferred hanging back so he could watch Ford and Avery from afar, whom he still didn't trust.

"It makes sense, this whole gig," Ray said about the runners' secret lives. "Under the radar this entire time. I get it. Genius, when you give it some thought."

"Can we focus here?" Avery said. "Let's get this over with already."

"Girl's got sass. Guess we know who wears the pants of this show."

Avery started to explain their planned mission by pointing at the map.

"As I'm sure you're aware, the majority of the westbound trails are currently under investigation since Jett's... We're going to have to work around these areas to avoid any heat."

"Good call," Ray said.

"Right," Avery said. "There's not much of a choice but to venture outside our normal trails. And since we're supposed to remain on schedule with our runs, we'll have to make a stop at Tom Two Feathers' place for a second batch."

"That's our master cook, yeah?" Ray asked.

"Yes."

"Right on."

"It's a bit of a trek from there 'til we make it inland to Drummond Island, so expect arrival times on our markers to be longer than usual. From Drummond, we take the ice bridge to Canada's border, where Ford and I will eliminate most of the patrol. We'll leave one, maybe two, patrol officers alive to take us to where Niko—"

"You and Ford?"

"Yes. We'll take—"

"Nah. Only one of you are doing the run. The other stays here with Judge and me."

"You can't expect just one person to kill that many onshore," Avery said. "Let alone once we make it on the Krowchuck property, who knows what we'll encounter."

"I know. That's why I'm lending you some of my crew, who'll meet you at Drummond to escort you to the border. We'd escort the whole way to Drummond, but as you implied, the heat right now is a bit much."

"That won't work," Ford said. "Niko's men have eyes on us within a few miles of their border. If they see you, then we'll have bigger problems on our hands."

"Well...," Ray said, studying the map while he thought. "Okay then. A single member of my crew will hide in the cargo on the sled after you reach Drummond. As soon as y'all are on their shore, you can carry out your ambush just as you had planned. Get on his property. Do the deed. Get in and dip. Dope fucking stealth attack."

"Why can't you have your men just eliminate Niko themselves?" Ford asked.

"Because this is my show. See, I ain't like my pops. I care about my crew enough not to use them as shields. We ain't bringing the war to them. This is gonna be a clean job. My strategy is simply to kill the king and let the dominos fall in place. We need a way to get to him, and you runners drew the short straw. You know y'all just bait. Feel me?"

"Then let Ford and I do our way. This is a two-person job. Also, don't forget, Niko is expecting back that batch he lost on Jett's run too. We'll need another runner to carry that."

"And risk y'all bailing on me? Nah. No chance. As for that second load, Niko ain't getting that shit back. You'll get through his patrol just fine with the single load. Besides, I promised my crew the previous batch is their little side take. Niko won't miss it anyway because he'll be dead."

With that, Ray brought up his iPhone and snapped a picture of the map.

"Got it," he said. "We got ourselves a fuckin' game plan. Tomorrow we execute. Until then, y'all get some sleep."

After he and Judge left the premises, Avery tossed the pencil on the desk as she leaned against it. She was incredibly uneasy about Ray's new plan, while she studied the map.

"Fuck if this ain't risky," she said.

"Mmhm," Ford said. "It's best if I do the run."

"I'm not going to act as if I should do it. You're clearly the better gunman. I'd be lying, though, if I said I wasn't worried for you. This mission, it's bleak, Ford. Damn bleak."

"I can handle bleak," he said with a smirk, trying to dab some humor on the grim situation.

Outside, positioned high on a ridge that overlooked the access road to the DNR post, Sheriff Anson was hunched on the hood of his truck. As if he were a shepherd with a herd, he diligently watched over the property through his 30-06 Winchester hunting rifle, which he steadied in true sniper form. Through his scope, he peered at Ray and his crew leaving the grounds. He didn't recognize any of them, but knew they were not from the area.

Appearances aside, there wasn't anybody who drove something as flashy as an Escalade in the winter in these parts. That was left for summer vacationers.

Little did Ford and Avery know Anson had been keeping surveillance on the post since Jett's murder. It was his only lead, and he chose to follow through on it by himself. He was nearing the end of his career and knew he didn't have time to sort through the red tape of the department, so he took it upon himself to investigate by his lonesome. Maybe it was his ego. Or maybe it was to bring some spice to a rather bland career. Up until this juncture, his tenure as sheriff was mundane and not much to write about. If it were a book, it'd be a ten-page short story of blah.

Sure, there was the occasional crazy standoff with some over-served head-case. Sometimes he nabbed some junkies or some pot growers in the middle of the year here and there, but nothing that would even make front-page headlines in the Mining Journal newspaper. When Anson retired, whenever that day came, he assumed he would quickly be forgotten. Forgotten and replaced by the next young, idealistic sheriff, who would probably lead the same destiny as him.

* * *

Ford lay on his bed wide awake that same night. How could he sleep? Tomorrow, everything would change. There was still that nagging guilt that remained inside him. The stakes had risen. No one was safe anymore.

As tough as Avery was, he knew her life was ultimately in his hands. If his run was unsuccessful, there wouldn't be a reason for Ray to keep her around any longer than he had to. She knew too much. And it wasn't like Ford hadn't thought about taking his money, getting Avery, and just escaping into the night. But that too came with its consequences. Say Ray's crew didn't have surveillance on their houses at the moment, which they probably did. He knew that. Fleeing the state would be a sheer miracle, at best. If they did succeed, then what? Live on the road, always looking over their shoulders for the Easters, Niko, or the law? *That's no way to live.* For himself, he could handle it for a while, maybe, but Avery? Not a chance. Doing that to her would kill him inside.

Before becoming a runner, Ford had settled into the fictitious lifestyle of a DNR officer. A career he thought, when he finally had the title, he maybe should've tried to work towards in his past. *Too late for a future. Far too late.*

He also believed he could've persuaded Jett and Avery not to accept the Krowchucks' offer from the beginning.

Certainly, he could've kept the offer for himself and trained other riders with less to lose. Some ruthless types fresh from a prison release, searching for money-making ventures that weren't exactly legal.

Or some ex-soldiers, yearning for that fix of the thrill they became addicted to during wartime. There were plenty of those around. These were scenarios he hadn't given a single thought to until right now.

At his core, Ford knew he was a man who never missed an opportunity. That was just how he'd always lived. It was a kind of living that led to hurting many people along the way. Avery, and Jett to some extent, were the first people to actually ignore his off-putting, unknown history, and trusted him — no questions asked. Ford presumed they were truly good-hearted people he helped turn corrupt. In the end, they'd all bitten off more than they could chew, and presently it seemed to have bitten them in the ass.

* * *

Six the following morning, Ford and Avery prepared the sled and attached Ford's team. As was his usual ritual, Ford placed his backpack of supplies and the shorty shotgun on top of the load, then covered and tied down the entire sled with a canvas tarp. He holstered his service gun on his right side and his hatchet on the other. Saving the best for last, he slid his Kershaw knife into the concealed sheath inside his boot. It had always blended in well with his ensemble.

While Ray and some of his crew gathered in front of the post to double-check the sled, Avery lingered behind Ford in the kennel.

He was just standing by Lucy's cage and staring at his Alaska postcard. He speculated how far that dream seemed now, and if he'd ever be able to fulfill it. Bringing the postcard with him was a reminder to keep fighting towards his goal. But the longer he stood there thinking it seemed silly to him, given the circumstances. When Avery reached him, she handed him his new burner phone, and as usual, she kept a phone for herself.

Ford quickly slipped the postcard into the inner pocket of his coat.

"Our department will take good care of her," Avery assured him, assuming he was watching Lucy instead.

"You know they won't just let us walk away after I kill Niko, right?" he said.

"Kinda figured."

"Listen... I stashed a gun under your desk this morning."

Avery had to do a double-take at his words.

"When I return, be prepared to use it, okay?"

She reluctantly nodded and said, "What if you don't return?"

Ford hesitated. He needed her ready to perform her task, without any hindering worries that could plague her actions. Actions that could potentially get them both killed.

"Then... Then you find a way to get to my house and take the cash I have stored in paint cans in my basement. You take my money, okay? You take what's in those paint cans and get the hell out of Michigan."

Her mouth opened with amazement, not quite comprehending what he revealed to her. She tried to mumble a response, but it sounded stuttered and awkward.

"You have to. You run and never look back, hear me?"

Avery accepted the possible reality with a hesitant nod.

"Time to go," Judge said when he stepped inside the kennel.

Both officers walked to the front of the post where Ford gave his sled and dog team a final once-over.

"My crew will meet you on Drummond Island," Ray told Ford. "Any trouble on the way, let us know. We'll be your muscle. Any fuckery from you possum cops, and, well, you know the rest of that story."

Ford's dog North continued to stare back at his human as if he was reassuring him of his and the team's readiness for their fateful journey. Ford took the sign and was just about to step on his footboards when Avery had a moment of reflection, stepped to him, and hugged him tightly.

He didn't hug back at first, because, like his rule with Avery, he didn't want to fill his mind with anything but the mission at hand. Ultimately, though, he gave in and hugged her back. Their hug eventually turned into a passionate kiss — initiated by Avery — that lasted for a few seconds but felt like forever to Ford. He hadn't kissed a woman for as long as he could remember.

"Please, Ford, be careful," Avery told him when she released her wet lip-lock. "You're all I've got left."

She knew Ford understood, and she let go of him when Judge took her by her shoulders to brush her back towards the stairs of the post.

"You hurt her, and I'll come back and kill every last one of you," Ford said to both Ray and Judge. "You have my word on that."

His threat clearly agitated Judge and he squared up at Ford with venomous distaste, his fists clenched at his sides. He wanted to pop him good. Ray, on the other hand, was more laid back. Overconfident. Ford's words didn't sink in as they had with Judge. He just stretched that big, megawatt white smile from ear to ear. The smile left a bitterness in Ford that fueled his own hate. It affected him more than any glare or verbal threat could.

Ford then clicked his tongue twice and his team advanced onto the trail. Less than an hour went by before they hopped the main route, then veered into another more downhill path, which transformed into a creek bed. He halted his team and sent the first check-in text to Avery: *Clear westbound.*

Roger that. Nothing happening ahead of you, Avery texted back.

Ford clicked his tongue again and the dogs proceeded.

At the post, Avery slinked back her police scanner headphones from her ears to her neck.

"He won't check in for a little while yet," she told Ray.

"Better get comfortable then," Ray replied.

"You guys aren't fixin' to hang around the whole time, are you?"

Ray chuckled.

"It's best if you don't," Avery said. "You being here is bound to bring unwanted attention from anyone in the area. Remember, I still must keep up with my daily work. I can pawn some of it to the other nearby posts but not everything."

Ray took a moment to think about it, then rose from his seat. "Fine. Judge will stay here with you while I take the boys to get us something to eat."

Judge walked with Ray outside of the post to talk with him. Avery leaned back in her chair to try to listen to the conversation. Discreetly, she feathered her feet on the floor to push her chair into a quiet roll closer to the front door.

"How long y'all gonna be?" Judge asked Ray.

"Shouldn't be no more than an hour. If anybody shows up here, just take care of it."

Judge watched the rest of the crew climb in the Escalades and leave the DNR post. Before he went back inside, he relieved himself just offside the corner of the steps while Avery made her way back to her desk to feel under it for the hidden gun. Ford made sure to load the small snub nose Python revolver for her before he stashed it, so it was locked and ready to use.

Judge returned inside, just as Avery brought her hands back on top of the desk, undetected.

He shuffled straight to Ford's desk, where he discarded his Desert

Eagle from the waistband of his khakis and set it down. With an exhausted plop, he collapsed in the chair afterward.

Avery carefully studied his every move. She learned that his eyes drew heavy the longer he lounged. He was tired and not as overbearing as usual. Judge was the rock of Ray's crew, staying awake longer hours than the rest, to stay ahead of his friend's plans. He led surveillance at night on the runners' houses and even tracked any law activity in the area. Any failures on his part would reflect poorly on Ray to Oscar, which he wanted to avoid.

"Tired?" Avery asked him, in her attempt to break his sullenness.

Judge's head was slow to acknowledge her, and he just stared without saying a word. Nervous, she broke eye contact and returned to focus on her daily paperwork. It was still deer season in these parts, so it was important to maintain accurate numbers of hunters and their deer intake for her reports. She was also conducting continuing reports on which state lands and routes to patrol to ensure hunting licenses were current in their county. There were always those who hunted illegally during the season, especially around Christmas.

"Got any coffee 'round here?" Judge mumbled.

Before she could rise, he stood and put his hand to her to remain seated. "Just point me in the direction."

She pointed to the small kitchen near the back of the office space.

"Stay put," he said.

Within a half-hour, the police scanner crackled, which brought life to Avery and Judge's ears. It was followed by a text from Ford, which beeped from her phone on the desk.

Avery put her headphones back on and plugged them into the scanner, while Judge stood behind her to monitor the communication between the two with a hot coffee in his hand. When he reached across her body, she froze with fear. He unplugged her headphones, then gestured her to respond to Ford's text. She obliged in an instant and leaned forward to grab her cell and read the message.

"He just turned on Roberts Corner," she said.

Judge then gestured for her to respond to the text, and she did so with a simple thumbs-up emoji. Dawdling back to his seat at Ford's desk, he plopped himself back in the chair, which squeaked hard from his weight. He messed with his phone every now and then to see if Ray or any of the crew messaged him.

"It's going to be a while before Ford checks in again," Avery told him. "I'd like to stretch my legs outside if I could and feed my dogs."

"Bitch, shut up. You're going to stay put."

Without complaint, she returned to her work, before she asked if she could use the restroom minutes later, to which he allowed. He watched her walk to the bathroom in the corner of the room, in her steady and jittery pace.

She opened the door and looked back at him before she entered. He remained in the chair there without an expression, watching her like a hawk.

The moment she closed the door behind she burst into tears. Her hands shook and her breath shortened. Almost falling to the floor in a sudden panic attack, she composed herself long enough so she could sit on the toilet's lid with her hands clasped against her mouth. If she made a noise, it could alert Judge and she didn't want to upset him any more than he already was. She knew he didn't want to play babysitter and would rather eliminate her and Ford than deal with them. *Deep breaths help*, she remembered from past panic attacks. *Deep breaths.* She was eventually able to curb her rapidly beating heart, and her breathing returned to normal. She wiped the tears and the puff from her face with the heel of her hand, flushed the toilet, and walked back to her desk.

Judge hadn't moved a muscle. As if he were swallowed by his baggy and puffy coat, he appeared comfortable in the same place he stayed guard in, staring at her like he had when she entered the bathroom in the first place. Every so often she'd look up from her work to see him fingering his phone again.

She took this chance to covertly slide her out-of-sight right hand under the desk to reach for her gun. She felt around. Nothing. Her hand panicked, grasping, trying to feel for the cold metal. *Did it fall to the floor?* The realization hit her; it was gone.

Before she could face Judge, he was behind her without a noise and pressed her missing gun to her temple.

"What the fuck is this, huh?" Judge asked.

"I'm sorry! I— I— Ford hid it there for me! I didn't know until it was too late!"

"Bitch, don't lie to me!"

He lifted her from her seat by her neck with his free hand and restrained her to the wall, against the map, knocking the pins from it onto the desk. She gasped for air as he just squeezed her throat tighter and tighter. He then placed her gun into her mouth and cocked back the hammer.

"Ppp— Please."

Her feet kicked as she fought for air. Just before she fell unconscious, he released her. She hit the corner of the desk with her head and rolled onto the floor. In her fall, she forced a drawer to break open and its contents spewed everywhere around them.

"No more fucking games!" Judge yelled.

From the desk contents that were spread, she locked on a knife in the mix. It was Jett's buck knife he had always kept in his drawer. She quickly grabbed the knife and concealed it under her body as she tried to rise. She staggered, and coughed, and choked more as she did.

"Hide a gun but can't face me. Stand up, bitch!"

She finally lifted herself up, breathless, with her back to Judge.

Her movements were measured and guarded. He put his hand on her shoulder to force her back into her chair. Without warning, she spun around with the buck knife in her fist and slashed his throat with a quick and precise swoop. Judge stumbled backward and fell to a knee, gurgling blood, hands on his throat trying to stem the arterial spurts.

She sprang from her position and plunged the knife repeatedly in his chest three times. He dropped back, trying to grab her, but she slipped away from him and raced to the exit. He wildly fired her revolver several times but missed as she fled through the door. He still had more fight in him though, and crawled to the open door, leaving a blood trail on the floor.

Damned if he'd be bested by this woman, whom he saw as no more than a speed bump in Ray's plans. Almost empty of bullets in the cylinder, he glanced back at his Desert Eagle on the desk. *Too far to crawl.*

Meanwhile, Avery entered a department truck only to realize the keys were still inside the post. Worse yet, she could see Judge from the door, trying to will his way outside. Pain from her head wound when she fell hit her hard. She felt for blood and saw it on her fingertips.

"THINK," she yelled to herself as she scanned the front yard. "THINK!"

There it was. Her only hope for an escape was on a department snowmobile, which she knew they left the keys in, and took the chance. Snow kicked up behind her in her mad dash to one of two green Arctic Cats just as Judge propped himself against the doorway to shoot at her again. She turned the key. The engine caught and she laid on the throttle. The machine shot on its tracks like a wheelie and tore forward.

Judge leveled the revolver on her, but couldn't hold it steady, dizzy from the amount of blood loss. Unable to stop it, he tumbled backward inside.

Avery glimpsed a final time at the kennel she and Jett's dogs were still locked in. She could hear them bark and yelp at her escape. There was some remorse, but it was either them or her. That was that — her decision to leave them was made. She wasn't going to look back at the past anymore.

* * *

Ray and his crew pulled into the post from lunch. Holding two small Styrofoam boxes of food for Judge and Avery, they sensed something wasn't right. Some spotted the erratic snowmobile tracks that dug deep into the snow and twisted their way into the woods. When Ray exited from the passenger seat of the Escalade, he found small blood droplets on the front steps that led indoors. He and the crew followed them and discovered Judge lying on the floor, clinging to life. Ray's heart dropped as if the soul was sucked from his own body.

The food in his hands freed and exploded in a mess on the ground in his rush to his friend's aid.

"Judge!"

The blood oozing from his neck had lessened but still had a steady flow. He was barely conscious. Ray removed his own scarf and wrapped it tightly around his friend's gash to stop the blood. Pulling up his soaked sweater, he found three leaking puncture wounds. He then offered his free hand to his crew who stood back in awe, unsure of what to make of the plight.

"Give me your scarves! Or something!"

They hesitated to offer assistance, figuring Judge a goner. That was the way on the streets, where they came from.

"NOW! I need pressure on this. Get down here! Let's go!"

His men took control for their boss to put pressure on the wounds. Ray stood, panicked, his head on a frantic swivel. Tears streamed down his cheeks. His emotions clouded his mind as to what he should do next. Directionless, he conducted a half-ass search for Avery, but he already knew she must've done this to his friend and bailed. His crew looked to him for some sort of an answer on what they should do next — whether that was to call an ambulance or take him to the hospital themselves. Ray just aimlessly paced in a circle around them. He was a man without an answer.

The only thing he thought to do was to get advice from someone who always had them.

At that very moment, Oscar sat in the backseat of his Escalade while Diz drove him through the streets of Detroit on a light snowy day in southeast Michigan. Oscar watched the depression wipe by his window. Every week he had Diz drive him through his former poverty-stricken stomping grounds. It gave him clarity, inspiration even, to see the ashes he rose from. A homeless man pushing a shopping cart on the side of the slushy streets caught him.

"Miserable leech," he said to Diz.

His phone vibrated and Oscar answered the call from his son. Ray tried to stay composed, but when he heard his father's voice his own trembled. It was almost like he was reverted to that unsure adolescent again.

"Ppp...Pops..."

"Ray?" Oscar asked, concerned. "What's going on?"

"It's Judge, Pops. He— He—"

"Ray? Hello?"

Ray's gaze touched Judge's eyes when he faintly opened them, and he knelt by his side to rest his hand on his friend's forehead for some comfort.

His crew kept the pressure on Judge's wounds as best they could, but his color was rapidly turning blue, and he was losing blood by the minute. Fresh blood caked on Ray's hands, which made him fumble his phone into the pool next to them.

"Hello?" Oscar kept asking.

Diz, hearing the frantic confusion in his boss's voice, parked the Escalade alongside a curb. He shifted to park and stayed in place, waiting for his next instruction.

Oscar just kept repeating his son's name, without an answer.

When Ray retrieved his phone he said through sobs, "It's Judge. We— We've got a problem, Pops. The girl is gone... I told you! I told you we should've just gotten rid of them! Man, you never listen to me."

His weeping began to fade when he saw Judge's eyes gently close again.

"Son. Listen to me. Do not— are you hearing me? Do not retaliate!"

Ray's sadness transformed into rage the longer he watched his friend's demise. His vulnerability was showcased for all to see and criticize. He thought of how weak he must've appeared to his crew. He had enough. No more did he want to be reviled as a fuck-up. It was his time to rise to the occasion and handle his own problems.

"Ray?" Oscar repeated. "Are you hearing me? Tell me where you are? Son?"

"I'll make this right, Pops..." Ray coldly replied and disconnected the call.

Oscar chucked his cell at the back of the passenger seat. Diz just watched him through his rearview mirror as his boss tried to gather back his composure after a short burst of anger.

"Diz, get the plane ready."

X

Past Soo Junction, Ford slowed his dogs to a halt so he could call Avery after his latest text sent went unanswered. After a series of long rings, the call was forwarded to voicemail.

"I just cleared Soo Junction," Ford recorded on her voicemail. "No incidents."

He hung up, thought for a moment, then tried once more.

Straight to voicemail.

"Avery? Avery, give me a ca—"

His phone dropped the call. Checking it, he noticed his cell didn't have any reception bars. Fairly concerned for his partner, he knew he needed to get reception and mushed his team on to find a better spot.

He diverted from the trail and parked his sled in a section of thick woods behind a small-town diner two miles outside of Soo Junction. He patted the head of a panting North on his way by to the diner.

"Stay on my six, pal."

Before he proceeded, he checked himself to make sure his weapons weren't visible on him, then made his way toward the building. He covered his holster with his right hand when he walked, so as not to startle workers or patrons. When he entered the establishment, it was pure habit for him to scope every inch of the place. There were only a few patrons in various sections, mostly elderly with the gift of gab, seeing how the day was still young. Named after its owner, McClane's was a popular greasy spoon with a lot of country character. The place had a sizable menu with just about every regional cuisine there was — of course, with that usual small-town twist. Fried with lots and lots of butter.

A younger, wholesome waitress approached him with a flirtatious smile. The kind of smile that stayed glued on her face day in and day out to earn her more-than-the-usual twenty-percent tip.

"Good morning," she said. "Just you?"

Ford read the name *"Dana"* on her tag then asked, "Do you happen to have a phone I could use?"

She smiled politely and led him to a wall in the back kitchen, behind a saloon-style door, where a landline phone was connected. She left him there, and he dialed Avery's number. This time her cell didn't even ring, rather, it went to voicemail. Ford hung up and peeked around the corner before he tried again to dial Avery. Same result, straight to voicemail.

Now, he was more concerned, so he decided to settle in a diner booth near the window to try her again in a bit. He looked to a Snoopy clock above the front counter; it was almost nine. Dana approached him with a menu in hand.

"I'll need to use it again in a few," Ford told her.

"Go ahead," she said. "Would you like anything while you wait?"

"Coffee. Please. Maybe a handful of bacon too."

Dana didn't even have to jot down the simple order. She turned around without a word and went to put it in and get him some coffee. While he waited, Ford peered through the large window next to him and saw four men in black and silver ride in on black Ski-Doo snowmobiles. He thought it was odd how they strutted toward the diner with purpose. There wasn't a moment of conversation between any of them, just a look of grim determination. When they entered, they removed their helmets and took a gander around the joint. Their faces were covered with neck gaiters, so Ford couldn't recognize them off the bat. He did catch a glance at the white skull and crossbones painted on the helmets though, which he remembered was Ray's crew's insignia. Each of the riders eventually set their sights on him and ambled toward his section. *That was peculiar.* His suspicion grew. He knew they weren't just passing through the area. It was rather early for Ray's men to make their way towards Drummond Island to meet him there. A day too early.

And it wasn't plausible that these men were the thrill-seeking snowmobilers or wannabe hunters from downstate that Ford came across each winter. Those were the sort of riders who imagined they were bigger and badder than anyone around. They were charlatans, spewing their lies to unsuspecting small-town folk, the types Ford loved kicking out of town. The bad bunch coming at him, though, had contrasting intentions.

Two of the men from the group slid in a seat at a small round top table across from Ford to his left. The other two, one reminiscent of some lost ZZ Top member, and the other that looked exactly like a black Mr. Clean, took their seats in the booth behind Ford. A flanking position. They might be junkies, or they could've anticipated robbing the place, only to discover he was just there by a crazy coincidence. He doubted it, though.

When Dana, with her flirty smile loaded, locked in on her next customers and asked a rider across from Ford who had a stretched 313 tattoo on the side of his face if they wanted menus, they ignored her. Instead, they just gawked at Ford — their lone target. The tattoo-faced rider then shifted in his chair at that moment and Ford caught the shape of a pistol grip latched to the inside of his partially unzipped snowmobile suit. There it was, the confirmation he needed. These men were killers, no doubt about it.

Ford carefully inched his left hand toward a steak knife on his table. The eager ZZ Top guy behind him stood at that exact moment, approached, and wrapped Ford in a headlock. Ford sunk the steak knife into the goon's peeking kneecap, and he dropped back and hollered a piercing howl.

Ford reached into his holster, jerked his Sig Sauer, and put a bullet into each of the two tattooed mercenaries across from him, who were awfully slow digging their pieces out of their snowsuits. Everyone in the diner, employees, and patrons alike, scattered and fled the sudden chaos. Dana dropped Ford's plate of bacon and cup of coffee with a clatter, shattering them in her escape to the outdoors.

McClane's had become a war zone.

Ford ducked behind his booth firing behind him at the black Mr. Clean guy, but the man was quicker than he looked, and the shot missed. Mr. Clean made it to cover behind another booth.

The mercenary on the floor with a bullet wound in his chest glanced around for his lost weapon. In his frantic search, he found his tattoo-faced buddy lying next to him, his eyes fixed to the side, dead. On his stomach, he tried to crawl to Ford. Along the way, he grabbed his riding helmet that had been knocked to the floor during the skirmish.

Across the diner, Ford and Mr. Clean traded shots at each other from their respective covers.

The ZZ Top mercenary, the steak knife still lodged in his knee, joined in on the shootout from his own cover behind a side booth. Just as Ford came back around to fire again, the crawling gunman with the chest wound sprang to his knees as if he were Bruce Lee and bashed the helmet across Ford's face, knocking him a couple of feet back.

The crossfire ceased.

The gunman mauled him, and the two wrestled for Ford's gun. He grabbed Ford's gun hand and got his finger on the trigger.

Mr. Clean abandoned his cover to take advantage of Ford's misfortune. Rushing at them, he had his Glock 22 ready to execute his target. Ford noticed him from his peripheral, kneed the gunman he wrestled with in the crotch, trained his gun — with his adversary's finger still warm on the trigger — and unloaded most of the clip into Mr. Clean. As he fell, he popped off several wild shots, clipping ZZ Top's ear. The guy cursed obscenities as he clasped his hand over his ear on his way to the floor.

Ford used his free arm to elbow the mercenary he was wrestling with in the face again and again, until he loosened his frozen grip on the gun — finally winning the battle — then planted his foot on the man's chest and pushed himself into a slide across the floor away from him to attain a clear shot straight at him. The killer threw his hands forward in a panic.

"No!" he yelled.

Ford fired through the man's hand into his skull, ending him where he lay.

The ZZ Top mercenary struggled to a stand after he realized everything had gone bizarrely quiet all of a sudden. He kept his gun locked and ready while he clutched his bleeding ear.

"Hello?" he shouted in hopes his own would respond.

Not a word.

"We get that son of a bitch?" he asked, as he limped through the destroyed diner.

Body after body of his crew he discovered, much to his dismay. There was a split second of revelation where he thought maybe he was the only survivor of the battle. When he tried to slip into the kitchen, he felt the hot barrel of Ford's Sig pressed into the back of his brain stem. His short-lived revelation crumbled. Instantly, the mercenary released his weapon to the floor.

"Please, bro! Don't do this! I was just following orders."

"How'd you find me?" Ford asked and pressed his piece further into his stem.

"Ray!" ZZ Top blurted.

His answer left Ford confused.

"Easter? Why?"

"Your chick reneged on the deal. She sliced up Judge pretty good."

Ford's face dropped in anguish and confusion.

"What? Avery killed Judge?"

"Yes!"

"What happened to her?"

"She bolted, man!"

Ford grabbed what little hair the man had on top and yanked it back toward him.

"Don't fuck with me!" he shouted.

"I'm not! Ray made the call, man! Ray made the fuckin' call!"

"What call?"

"To clean house. You, the chick, the cook..."

"The cook?"

"That's all I know! Please, don't do this! Please!"

At that moment, Ford came to the sobering realization that his whole world was screwed. He had become a moving target. Before the pleading mercenary could beg for his life anymore, Ford swiftly executed him in the back of his skull with the last bullet he had left in his clip.

He then retrieved the bacon from the floor nearby and exited the diner, reloading his piece with another clip from his utility belt. Without stopping, he fired two shots into each of the four mercenaries' Ski-Doos to disable them in his march behind the diner.

Still rocked from the fight, he staggered some when he was closer to his dogs. He fed them the bacon and returned to his sled. When he stepped on the footboards, he reflected on what the mercenary said to him about Avery. He fingered his cell in his hand, chewing thoughts of his next plan. While he wasn't sure what he was going to do next, he was damn sure that he couldn't stay in one place for a long period of time. Keeping on the move was his best play. From the back of his throat, he hawked some bloody spit in the snow, grabbed the sled's handle bar, and clicked his tongue twice. Off the team ran. Their destiny — their fate — unknown.

XI

Footsteps creaked on the wooden stairs. Tom Two Feathers ascended from his dungeon of a basement. It was an eerie spectacle. Various tools lined the walls in no particular order. Some for cooking. Some for general home maintenance. And others for cleaning whatever animals caught in a hunt or a trap. Numbers of barrels of methylamine flown in from Niko's pilots on his payroll were positioned around the walls, encasing the unfinished basement like its own fortress of solitude, or fortress of poison for that matter. Two vats of his latest batch brewed. Fumes were filtered outside through a duct overhead that ran the lengths of the space. Here, Tom was his own version of Bob Dylan. A one-man band. There are some who could write symphonies or those who could make rockets fly or get paid millions to play a sport, but Tom Two Feathers was an artist of the drug trade.

Give him a lab and a few essentials and he'd concoct a narcotic that felt like Disneyland in his customers' veins. A single hit of his magic and they fell under his spell.

"Hey there, I need some more wood for the vat fires," Tom said as he searched upstairs for Drifter. "Hello?"

He folded back the top part of his Hazmat suit and tied it around his waist. His red undershirt was drenched in sweat, and beads of it streamed his flushed face. He went straight to his ancient, decrepit 1950s fridge, once called an icebox in its heyday, and stuck his head inside to cool off. Leftover venison burgers from last night seized his attention, and he grabbed the tinfoil-covered plate to settle his appetite while he waited for Drifter, who he assumed must've gone hunting.

Motor revs from a distance were heard as he prepared the tastiest of burgers around groups of cats that licked their whiskers, vying for a taste of the tender deer meat.

"Down, girls," he told his cats as he shooed them to the floor so he could go and check on the noise.

Pulling back his twisted blinds next to his front door, he spotted four black Ski-Doo snowmobiles approaching his property. Most outsiders who entered his area — and there weren't many — either ended their machines stuck in narrow, dead-end trails or fell in thick snow that dropped into the ditches. It's just the way Tom devised his secret home. These outsiders were unlike others.

They knew exactly which twisted trails and turns to take that plunged into the spot where his house was located below the ridge. Not a single stall between any of the four. This was calculated and decisive. Clearly, they were coming to wreak havoc.

Tom snagged his shotgun from above the bear traps that hung on the wall, kicked the basement door shut, and padlocked it to secure his livelihood. He rushed to the window again and then squatted to stay hidden. Long, controlled breaths kept him patient as he pressed his trusty shotgun against his chest.

From the corner of his window, his eye touched light. He observed the men approaching his homestead in a staggered V-formation and assumed they were either military or the law.

They had white skull and crossbones on their helmets, and each had a semi-automatic rifle slung over their shoulder by a strap. When they were within several yards of Tom's front door, they stopped and patrolled the area.

"Fuck..." Tom whispered to himself.

Crunching footsteps neared his house. His knuckles white against his weapon, he knew going into defensive mode was imminent. He gently pulled the hammer of his shotgun back.

* * *

A fork in the trail brought Ford's sled to a gradual pause right in between the two directions. He checked his cell to see if he had any reception here, not even a single bar. He knew the reception in these parts was sparse at best. Any possibility of more bars were five miles up the trail on the right. It was more field than trail, and the only trees in that region were naked. He considered the trail to the right to continue to keep his plan of staying on the move.

Especially now, since he was marked for a hit. But the nagging thought of Tom also being a mark troubled him. Tom had always done right by Ford. The least he could do was drop in to warn him, so Tom could go into hiding, away from there. It was better than being a sitting duck.

"Haw!" he yelled to North.

His team veered to the left trail to travel to the cook.

It took him a half-hour to arrive at the full sprint of his team. When he approached, he immediately detected the area was riddled with bullets, in the surrounding trees, the shack where he kept his dogs overnight, and mostly, of course, Tom's house, which had the windows completely blown out. He was too late. Everything had been destroyed. Plumes of smoke filtered from the back of the house. Devastation everywhere.

Ford took his Sig from his holster and steered his sled with his left hand behind a cluster of trees, dipping into the gully where the main house was.

Four sets of snowmobile tracks caught his attention. They came in the property from where Ford had started, then three sets of tracks exited the other way, continuing along a trail he knew led to a dead-end, some six or seven miles northeast. Only one snowmobile remained on site. Most of Tom's cats lay on it, under it, and around it. Some scampered.

Ford walked through the war zone and around many more cats. As he inched closer to the house, he saw the body of a man with a shotgun blast to his chest, helmet still on, sprawled feet from the door, which was kicked in and hanging by a rusted hinge. A little smoke puffed from inside. Ford pressed himself against the left side of the doorway with his gun extended in front of him. He crept along the way, ready to fight whatever threat awaited him in the house. When he reached what was left of the door's frame, he took a breath, stepped into the open, and entered the house. His gun hand gripped the Sig, feathering the trigger, and his left hand cupped under its grip.

He heard a metallic *click* from inside, by the window side. There, in the haze of smoke leveling his Winchester on him was Drifter, who shielded Tom Two Feathers' bloody body that lay beneath him. When Drifter recognized the supposed intruder was actually Ford, he dropped his aim, as did Ford, who quickly leaned in closer to discover Tom was alive, but barely.

Much like the killer outside, Tom also had several bullet holes in him, clear as day. Regardless of the pressure Drifter put on them, it didn't look good. Ford knew the breaths his buddy still drew were probably his last.

"Aye," Tom said. "They're looking for you, friend. I made sure to send them a different way."

"Along Merle's Swamp?" Ford asked.

Tom nodded as he began to lose consciousness.

"There isn't much time. Got one of them fuckers, but there's still three of 'em."

"Did they mention Avery at all?" Ford asked. "Anything about her?"

Tom shook his head with a wet cough that was followed by trickles of blood that colored his lips.

"Carry the fuck on, friend," he said. "Leave me to go with the place. Take your pups and run. Run like hell."

Ford nodded to Tom, keeping a brave face on for him.

"Where you gonna go?" Drifter asked Ford with his teeth clenched, urgency in his voice, but still soft and quiet.

"Don't know. I just need to keep moving."

"They took Tom's latest batch."

Ford sighed as the smoke became thick from the dark misery of the basement where the fire raged.

As he scanned the room, he noticed the two rusted bear traps that hung on the wall below the rack, where Tom always kept his shotgun. He stood and unhooked them from their spot.

The vengeful expression on Ford's face resonated with Drifter. Whatever trouble Ford was about to catapult himself into, he knew he wanted in.

"I'm coming with you," Drifter told him.

Ford eyeballed the Drifter, trying to gauge how he would fit his on-the-fly plans, "Bring your rifle."

* * *

A blur of black whisked along a trail that split into Merle's Swamp. When the three gunmen rode in, they were quick to realize the trail was not sufficient for regular snowmobile rides. Visibility was minimal at best, and they knew these trails were barely trekked, because they didn't find any signs of activity. Only hunters and trappers liked such trails, as they could catch treasure troves of smaller game. During the winter, the swamps were a city of small game such as snowshoe hares, ruffed grouse, and bobcats that inhabited the swamp because the dense underbrush blocked the frigid winds.

Jungles of skeleton trees twisted and grew into each other like mangled snakes over the thin pathways. Not a prayer a rider could make more than a few miles per hour through here, with their head ducked below their windshields for fear of being clotheslined. Tree limbs smacked and scraped against their helmets throughout. Each saw an opening ahead and they rode to it, bowing down under a large hollow tree that had fallen across the path, only being suspended by other near-dead trees. Successfully passing under it, the trail ended at a ten-foot bank that neither snowmobile nor dog sled could ride across without struggle. Beyond it was a clearing. There wasn't a single dog track or sled track seen across the bank. Even worse, snow began to fall from the steely skies, which limited their visibility even further. It pelted their helmets from the wind's whip that increasingly bared its fury.

The lead rider wiped the wet snow from his helmet's visor then flipped it up, revealing the top half of the ugly, scarred portion of his face that wasn't covered by a neck gaiter. A mug that had every bone broken from his days of amateur boxing in Motown. His large nose lay flat, almost touching his top lip. Standing, while cradling his purring ride between his legs, he now understood they had been duped. Tom Two Feathers had the last laugh.

"Dumb hick motherfucker," the lead mercenary said to himself.

As hard as it was riding into the swamp, it was even harder trying to escape its dreadful maze. Each rider had to reverse in a single file the same way they entered. Tree limbs, again, smacked and scraped their helmets, and they stalled their machines a few times. They left the trail circling their exit until all three riders were in the clear of the trees. When they were, the lead mercenary laid on his throttle, leaned his body forward, scrunching his brow line to an angry V, and darted away. The other two mercenaries followed, each kicking up a wave of snow that completely covered their tracks that led into Merle's Swamp.

Trying to make up for lost time, they backtracked towards the correct trail to their destination, which they reached in less than an hour. This was confirmed when they identified dog paw prints, followed by sled tracks heading in a southeast direction. Through the falling snow, something ahead caught the leader's attention and he squinted to distinguish it. The object was brown and long. Closer, he and his gunmen rode in at a steady pace as they approached. Nearing the object, they saw it was Ford's sled, abandoned. Each dog was still secured to it, and they just sat patiently. Snow accumulated on their coats, which meant they must've been there a while.

Before he could stop, the leader's sled rode over something that made a *clunking* noise, causing his machine to stall abruptly and throw him off past his windshield, and into a mound of fresh snow face first. His associates braked when they witnessed this and hopped from their own rides. They swung their semi-automatic rifles around from their shoulder blades, and then pulled and let go of their bolts to lock them ready to fire.

After a moment, the leader scrambled to his feet, bewildered, the wind stolen from his lungs. His visor had broken in the tumble and parts of his face, seen through the opened helmet slot, were whitewashed to a fine raw red. He wobbled back to his machine to investigate what the hell had happened. Doing so, he discarded his helmet to the ground, his sandy and curly hair a puffy mess. To his surprise, he found a bear trap in his machine's track. His crew filtered in behind him, gazing at the trail they didn't quite trust now.

"Yo, what the fuck is that?" one of them yelled as he inspected the contraption.

"A bear trap," a female voice answered with a thick Kentuckian accent.

"A what?"

She said, "Had an uncle who used to hunt 'em."

These gunmen in silver and black became keen to their surroundings. Was this bad luck or set for them?

They saw two sets of boot tracks near the trap. A set went right off the trail, into the many pine trees that seemed to grow on a small hill. The other set headed left, straight past the abandoned dog sled, and into another section of pines that curved downhill into a sloping pattern.

"Hard to outrun snowmobiles," the woman said. "Think he heard us comin' and fled on foot?"

"Possibly," the leader said, still reeling in pain from the accident. "A while ago, though…"

Each surveyed the spot, practically back-to-back, checking every tree, mound, or bush that surrounded the trail. The lead and the woman worked their way backward simultaneously to investigate the abandoned dog sled further, while the third mercenary stayed on the foot tracks to see where they led.

Maisey squirmed in her spot when the strangers inched closer.

North held strong, still sitting in place. His lip snarled in a growl; a deep-seated growl that started low and began to intensify. Vicious jagged teeth revealed from his muzzle made the gunmen proceed to the sled in caution.

"Look at that!" the lead mercenary marveled at the fierce North. "He's like a goddamn wolf!"

"Careful," the female warned her comrade.

The leader stared into North's intimidating golden eyes that were dilated. Raising his rifle, he aimed it straight at the dog's face.

"What are ya doing?" the female asked.

"Do you wanna check the sled with this fucking monster attached?"

Even with the barrel pointed at him, North continued to make his presence known to the crew. Right before the lead mercenary could pull his trigger the snow behind them jumped, and another bear trap hidden beneath chomped down on the third man's leg, ripping through flesh and bone with its rusted, alligator-tooth spikes. The mercenary clutched his bent leg and cried out with a hair-raising shriek. His weapon fell free to his side and he tucked himself in the fetal position to paw at it. Amid his torture, he flung his helmet in terror, revealing him as a ginger-bearded man in his forties.

Both the leader and the female whipped around toward him. At that instant, a shot rang out from the left side of the trail, beyond the dog sled. The leader mercenary dropped in front of the woman. Panicked, she fired sporadically past the dog sled, where the shot rang from. Her bullets flew into oblivion, unknown to her if she hit any meat.

A second shot crackled with a more thunderous echo from the right side of the trail, hitting her in the neck. She collapsed like a dropped bag of sand, next to the leader, spewing blood. Face to face, the female saw the leader take his final breath.

Pools of blood painted the snow and ice around them a dark red. She clung to life, pulling off her helmet, then placing both hands over her wound, but doing little to stop its drain.

Drifter appeared from the thick of the pines from the right side of the trail with his backcountry snowshoes on his feet and his Winchester cradled in his arms. Ford, also in snowshoes, met him from the left side of the trail, with his handgun drawn. Both locked on the third mercenary still wailing while he pawed at the clamped bear trap that had shattered the majority of his leg. As they approached him, Drifter didn't waste a second, finishing the job with a single shot to his forehead.

Ford approached the female, a butch and bald woman, who spluttered blood in her struggle to get control of her rifle close to her side. Ford easily kicked it from her reach and pointed his own burner at her face. Rather than give in, she didn't cower. She gradually rose to her knees, removed her hand from her neck, and gave him the bird. She then belted a hell of a gang war cry, "Long live the 313!"

Ford ended her right then and there. Observing his latest kill, he sort of admired the woman's fight. When he turned around, he saw Drifter looting the dead bodies for anything valuable he could scavenge and possibly pawn.

Ford left him to it and retrieved the batch of meth that was stolen from Tom's place. It was shared in packaged bags between each of the three mercenary snowmobiles, hidden in large compartments under their seats.

Amid collecting, Drifter spotted droplets of blood that weren't anywhere near the bodies. He followed them with his sights, and they stopped on Ford's arm — the source of the droplets. Smoke was still visible from the bullet wound. The wound occurred when the female mercenary was freely firing at the trees. Perhaps a ricochet.

"Get you?" Drifter asked.

Ford, not having realized this prior due to his crazed adrenaline rush, undid his utility belt and sat on the lead mercenary's snowmobile. He wrapped the belt around his arm to apply pressure.

"Want me to go into town to get something for it?" Drifter asked.

Ford didn't think much of the offer, rather, he went to his sled to retrieve a map that he produced from his backpack.

"Could use your help planning a different way to Drummond

Island," he said. "Easter's gunmen know our routes. They'll be scattered everywhere on these trails. I figure someone like yourself would know the ins and outs of the land."

Drifter studied the map.

"Best routes are through the thick," he said as he ran his finger along parts of the map, averting the original marked plans. "The shit nobody wants to truck through."

"Sounds like my kind of running," Ford said, marking the routes with a pencil that followed Drifter's finger.

He folded his map, tucked it in his backpack, and shook Drifter's hand to thank him.

"Sure you don't need any help?" Drifter asked. "Want me to clear the bodies at least?"

"Leave them for the law."

He then stood on his footboards, ready for the next part of his adventure. His team of dogs stood ready with him. And with another double-click of the tongue, the sled's nose jerked to the sparse clouds, and they were gone. He glanced over his shoulder at Drifter a final time, who remained in the middle of the trail, watching him leave. Falling snow whitened him completely out of sight in seconds.

XII

Camera flashes brightened the cold corpses in McClane's diner. A Sheriff's Department photographer snapped the grisly aftermath photos of the gunfight. Mercenary bodies were strewn throughout among the debris, congealed blood, and hollow shells. What was considered a charming Ma and Pop greasy spoon, was launched into hell on earth.

Behind the photographer, a budding deputy with thinning, chestnut hair, and the last name of Jarvi stood observing his work. His care for the photographer's job was a front for his actual motive, which was to approach Sheriff Anson, who had always intimidated him. He watched Anson. He thought of him as having a 'man's man' stature to him — something the deputy always admired. There, the sheriff stood with a cigarette clenched between his thin lips, looking over the slain. All Jarvi could wonder was what Anson was thinking.

Did he already have a good feel for the case when he stepped foot on the scene? What does he already know that I don't?

"Sir?" Deputy Jarvi said, unsure, trying to catch his superior's attention.

Anson turned around, his cigarette smoke carried with him and exhaled into his deputy's face. Jarvi just took it in, even though he wanted to cough. He eventually released his cough in a masked, throat-clearing sort of manner, to avoid any embarrassment.

"Witnesses in the parking lot said our man did this and disabled their snowmobiles," Deputy Jarvi said. "A 9mm was used. We found his tracks leading to his dog sled."

Both men scanned the shot-up snowmobiles from the windows. Past them, they saw patrons, now terrified witnesses, who stood in the parking lot among a clutter of the sheriff's department deputies, a couple of Michigan State Police cars, and jungles of police tape. Two of the deputies interviewed each witness for their account of what had happened earlier.

"They only see Ford?" Sheriff Anson asked. "Not Kinnomen?"

"The waitress said he came in alone to use the phone when the deceased entered," Deputy Jarvi replied. "Shortly after, the shooting started."

Anson removed his trapper hat and rested it against his barrel chest as he took in the room again.

"Got yourself into a little trouble," Anson muttered to himself.

"Oh, and we ran those prints on them," Jarvi added. "Each are from Detroit. They've been identified as part of the 313 Disciples gang down there. Why they came here is anyone's guess?"

The sheriff shed his knowing smirk, grasping the shit that had come to his sleepy town. Putting his hat back on, he said, "I think I've got an idea why."

"When's the rest of the State Police arriving?" Jarvi asked. "Aren't they going to take control here?"

"With the holiday and the storm on its way, we won't see any outside help til probably after the New Year. Besides, we don't need 'em."

"We don't?"

"Buckle up, deputy. We have work to do."

With that, he left the diner for his truck, flinging his finished cigarette into some slush puddles.

* * *

Ford discreetly shuffled his way past empty and former post-mining boom storefronts, on foot, along the town of Rudyard's main street. His destination was the local Rite Aid drug store that was tucked between a dive bar and an antique store. When the mines in the Upper Peninsula of Michigan began to close in the 1980s, Rudyard suffered the biggest economic hit.

What before had been a thriving town that included a bowling alley, multiple grocery stores, fast food chains, growing local businesses, and a fairly large high school, succumbed to a one-trick pony street. It was the only busy street the decline had left in its wake.

Ford pulled the belt around his arm tighter, grinding his teeth in pain. Right before he could slip through the drug store's automatic doors, a Michigan State Police cruiser drove by. Ford kept his back toward the cruiser and slipped into the store. His arm throbbed with pain so bad that it felt like it had a heartbeat. Reading the small signs above the aisles, he spotted the first-aid section and made his move.

Nearby, a female cashier stocked canned goods. When Ford hastily scuffled past her aisle, she caught a slight blur of him. Curious, she walked to the edge of the aisle, and at her feet, discovered a spot of blood. Her curiosity heightened, and she followed where she thought the direction of the blur passed.

In the middle of the first-aid aisle, Ford searched for what he needed. Coming across his find, he stuffed his jacket pockets with tweezers, gauze, rubbing alcohol, and a brown bottle of peroxide. Through the convex mirrors in the corners of the store, he could see the cashier nearing his area with each curious stride. When he swiped what he needed from the shelves, he departed the aisle for the store's exit.

"Sir?" the cashier said, can I help you?"

She followed him to the front of the empty store, just before he made his way to the exit.

"Sir? Wait! Hey!"

As she switched her walk into a light jog, Ford did also and dashed through the doors. She pursued him outside to find he had vanished. The officer patrolling the streets was on his way back when the cashier saw him and flagged him down.

* * *

A blizzard swept through the entire Upper Peninsula that night. Wind chills plummeted to minus thirty degrees, and it was absolutely punishing at twenty miles per hour. Shielded from the blistering wind, Ford and his dogs were tucked in the thick of the woods, mostly around pine trees, where they made their camp. Earlier, Ford dug a small trench in some thick snow, which took him hours to accomplish with his one healthy arm. Using the tarp that covered the meth cargo on his sled, he draped it five feet above the trench at an angle, so the snow wouldn't accumulate on its top. Then, he tied it down and around a couple of trees to secure it firmly in place and plunged the spikes from the bottom of his snowshoes he used as stakes into the ground to provide extra hold.

The tarp and trench were long enough to cover him and the dogs, albeit a tight fit, for their campsite for the rest of the night. This was also necessary, as they could use each other for body heat.

Next to the fire he'd built with his hatchet and some dry wood he'd been able to find, Ford squatted to a sitting position, absent his jacket, his bibs unbuckled and pushed to his waist. Underneath, his gray long johns were damp with sweat. He discarded his blood-soaked neck gaiter he had wrapped around his arm, revealing the nasty wound. It was deep and the blood around it pale and crusty. He began to prepare to treat the wound with the stolen essentials from Rite Aid. His tweezers in hand, he applied the rubbing alcohol on them for sterilization, then dipped the tool into his wound to feel for the bullet. Within a handful of seconds, he clinked a hard object, inches in, and yanked the bullet free. Blood spilled from the hole, and he twisted it at a downward bend so he could empty most of the heavy flow onto some wood between his legs that he eventually threw into the fire. He brought the tweezers to his face and went after the bullet that was lodged in his arm before he disposed of it to the fire as well. He then poured the peroxide onto the open wound. A milky white foam materialized from the hole, which he wiped away. Next came the most painful part of his backwoods surgery. Of course, until now, the pain was killer, but nothing came close to what he was about to do.

To prepare, he grabbed his trusty utility belt and inserted it into his mouth and bit down. From the fire, he produced a metal rod, which had been resting in the flames. Its tip was a bright cherry red. His teeth dug deeper into the leather of the belt, and he held the cherry to his now bullet-less wound and pressed on it to cauterize. It sizzled like a fish fillet, and he could smell the foul odor of his burning flesh. A muffled scream buried deep into the belt, but not loud enough to alarm most of his dogs, who lay around him. The spot where their camp was created was near perfect, as the winds masked any sounds he or his team made while in hiding. It was not like anyone would be outside searching in this shit storm. Not even Easter's men, regardless of how relentless they were. Most parties — law or outlaw — were likely inside on this Christmas Eve.

North arose from his lying position, concerned for his owner when he heard his distressed groan. He repeatedly licked the frost from his human's stubble beard.

"Shhh," Ford whispered to him. "I'm all right, buddy. I'm all right."

Whatever energy Ford could muster, he used to wrap the gauze around his arm to a firm hold. In a weakened grunt, he tipped himself to the side, near collapse, to retrieve his cell from his backpack. Before he could even check, he already knew there was still zero reception.

Bushed, he let the fire's flames mesmerize him. Any second he could drift to sleep. He thought of her.

The girl who made him feel things he'd forgotten along the way. Avery Kinnomen. An innocent he influenced into a criminal life. He hadn't a clue where she was, or if she was even alive for that matter. There was no way of knowing. A thought crossed his mind to forgo the mission at hand, futile as it may seem at first. Say he could avoid the law and return to his house for the money. Would Easter and his crew be waiting for him? It was possible they were holding Avery captive. If so, not following through with the mission would mean her death. He didn't want that stink on him.

A certain joyful thought of her possibly meeting him at the ice bridge teased him a little. Maybe she was able to escape and work her way to Ford. She knew the end leg of his journey. She knew he would eventually arrive at the ice bridge, so that would be the perfect meeting place, if she could hide herself decent enough, of course. If Avery wasn't there, Ford knew for sure Easter's men were. No doubt, he knew they were waiting for him. What better way to find him than in the barren tundra of the ice bridge? Nowhere to run. Nowhere to hide. Him versus them.

Niko was a problem, though. Missing another delivery, on top of having one lost on his hands to begin with, wasn't a good idea to settle on. The kid had the resources to find him if he decided to abandon the peninsula entirely. Ford hated the feeling. The feeling of constantly looking over his shoulder. Between the law, Niko, and the Easters, he was stuck in the middle and he understood its consequences.

North licked his face, which snapped him from his reasoning, comatose state.

"Someone important once told me that sometimes the best way around a problem is straight through it," Ford said to North.

North just pawed at Ford's forearm, wanting more affection from his human. Ford cracked a slight smile as he put his arm around the pooch and scooted him closer for warmth. North nuzzled his wet snout into Ford's jacket.

"Straight through it is for us..."

North licked the side of his face again.

"Merry Christmas, buddy."

He and North continued to watch the flames and the pelting snow outside in the heart of the mighty blizzard.

Every so often Ford would run his hand through North's coat and burn the loose hair in the fire that floated from his fingers. Huddled around them, the other dogs slept, practically on top of one another as if they were puppies again. Some snored, others twitched and yipped, gone in the world of canine dreams, whatever they might be.

XIII

Elsewhere, another homicide scene was in the process of containment by the Sheriff's Department. Bundled head to toe in department puffy coats and thick trapper hats with the ears down, Sheriff Anson and his eager Deputy Jarvi fought the howling wind through the charred structure of Tom Two Feathers' house. It continued to smoke and smolder, but the ongoing blizzard helped calm the fire to its weak embers. Inside the black, crumbling remains of the house's frame, they found the body of Tom Two Feathers covered with a blanket. Some snowflakes had since collected on him.

When Anson squatted next to it, his knees cracked and creaked. He gently lifted the blanket from the body's top portion to take a gander for himself. He gazed on the face, then the condition of the body. Inexplicably, it hadn't been burnt bad, given that the kitchen floor they stood on was mostly intact.

"Know him?" Jarvi asked.

"Know of him, yes," Anson replied. "Tom Two Feathers. A real knucklehead dealer. I busted him back in '98 for slinging. Doesn't surprise me he was cooking again. How about the other bodies reported?"

"We got 'em. A few more Detroiters, like the guy we found about ten miles from the Rudyard trails."

"The marks on their helmets—"

"Yes," Jarvi said with anticipation and dug for another part of the file. "Got...that info here. The insignia, the skull and crossbones, are that of the 313 Disciples. Which we know. I have a bunch of information on them. Um, their main drug of choice to traffic is meth. Big time. Yup. After the head of their chapter, Otto Farmer, was murdered, they were then hired under a security contract by Detroit businessman Oscar

Easter."

"Oscar Easter?" Anson asked, his ears perked.

"That's right. Who's that?"

Anson nodded, "Most downstate know about Oscar. Son of Ellis Easter. Might be before your time, deputy."

"Oh, yeah, I know of Ellis Easter! 'Nobody to Love Me.' I love his songs! He ended up dying in that plane crash in Wisconsin, right?"

"That'd be him. Oscar tried to claim some of Ellis' estate way back in the 1980s. He claimed he was Ellis Easter's illegitimate son from another woman he'd met on tour long, long before."

"Oh, wow."

"The Easter family fought the assertion, and they went to court. They won. Big story back then... Anyway, Oscar has his hand in just about every goddamn cookie jar downstate. Politics, travel, hotels, business developments, you name it, he's got a connection."

"So, is he not actually Ellis Easter's son?"

"He lost in court," the sheriff answered before he gave a deep, heavy sigh in his rise from the body. "Damnit..."

"What?"

"This here reeks of gang-territory shit, Deputy Jarney."

"It's— it's Jarvi...sir."

Anson looked back at him confused.

"Gangs?" Jarvi continued on, changing the subject from the awkwardness of Anson not remembering his name. "Up here?"

"Afraid so."

Both let the distressing thought of gang activity in their parts sink in for a minute. Jarvi was genuinely scared at the thought of such an anomaly. Anson, on the other hand, was somewhat intrigued by the thrill it brought. Finally, something interesting happened that he could dive fully into, that wasn't the usual highway or backwoods drama.

"No updates from Rudyard yet," Jarvi reported, breaking their thoughts. "Deputies are searching the area as we speak."

"Medical supplies," Anson mumbled to himself of the reports of what Ford stole, then faced Jarvi again. "I'd bet this last gunfight damaged him pretty good."

"Think he killed Two Feathers here?"

The sheriff took a second, then shook his head. He proceeded to point at the two bodies, the walls, and outside of the house.

"Took the time to cover the body," Anson pointed. "Multiple wounds and bullet holes here and there from different weapons. Did you see those mess of tracks on the way in? I wouldn't doubt this was from the dead men you found on the trails. To tell you the truth, I think...Well, I think our boy's being chased."

Jarvi sat on the sheriff's theory before he remembered the copies of files he had brought with him, which he held tight in his mitts. He presented them to the sheriff, proud of the research he'd done. But Anson didn't attempt to grab them.

"I got those background files you wanted," Jarvi said with a certain joy, reaching for justification from his superior.

"Read them to me, would you?"

Jarvi nervously split the file apart to do so.

"Um... Avery Kinnomen is clean. Seven-year veteran. No priors. Much like Prevo, pretty much a lifer of the area. Cyrus Ford, same, other than transferring from Hebbronville, Texas. No priors. A traffic violation from years back, but nothing else.

I also spoke with Prevo's mother and father, and they really couldn't give us any insight on the three. It's possible they're holding back. Maybe they are — I don't know. Any family Avery had around passed away or relocated to another state. Same with Ford. No siblings. Parents gone. Pretty much on his own."

"When did he begin working for the DNR?"

"Uh..." Jarvi dug further into the file, almost spilling the papers in the process. "Three...years ago. July third was his start date."

"July third?"

Anson sat on the specific date. It rang a bell.

"Hebbronville is close to Mexico," Jarvi said. "You think he has cartel ties, maybe?"

Anson puffed his chest and strolled by what was left of the cook's house. As if this moment were some *Law and Order* episode or a detective show, he took in everything, emulating the likes of a Rust Cohle or a Fox Mulder, trying to build to that cheesy gotcha moment with a witty one-liner that would amaze Jarvi, who was easily influenced.

"What do you think?" Jarvi asked.

Before Anson could say another word, a colossal wind gust from the white hurricane knocked around a section of framing from the house and tipped it completely over.

Holding onto the frames from the window for support, Anson shifted Jarvi to the side of him with his arm and the frame collapsed behind, just missing them.

"We're going to have to get this scene contained," Jarvi expressed to Anson as he waved in some additional support from outside.

"Get on home, deputy," Anson told him.

"Now? We're in the middle of this thing, Sheriff."

"Nothing is going to happen in this weather tonight. Besides, it's important you're there for your kids when they awake in the morning to see those gifts from Santa. Trust me. Never miss those moments."

Jarvi gave in to his superior's order. He waved in other deputies to preserve the crime scene so the storm wouldn't ruin it any further. Anson didn't spend much more of his time there before he ventured back to his office at the Sheriff's Department, where he buried himself in work. Last thing he wanted to do was go home and spend Christmas in an empty house. Working was the sole thing he consumed himself in since the divorce. His ex spent the holidays with their adult children, and he spent it working the job he chose over her and even them. Always the same, even after all these years have passed.

Aside from Christmas lights draped throughout desks, windows, cabinets, and doorways, darkness pretty much claimed the downtown Newberry building. Anson's desk lamp was the only light on.

Most of the department was home for the holiday. Bags under

Anson's eyes told the tale of a fight to understand what was happening under his watch. To him, these bags were trophies of pride. Of his labors. Of future justice.

A file labeled *JULY 3RD* was positioned in front of him next to Jett's burner cell and iPod marked as *EVIDENCE*. His computer's bright screen was the only thing keeping him awake during these late hours. Newspaper archives rolled down his screen. He kept skimming past stories on the week of July third from three years prior.

FIERY CRASH CLAIMS UNIDENTIFIED VICTIM IN LUCE COUNTY

The headline forced him to stop his scroll of the mouse. *July 1st was* the date. Reading the article, he shot from his chair like a match lit under his behind. He went straight to his office's file cabinet in the corner and maniacally dug through it, knowing exactly what he was searching for.

XIV

Oscar and Diz strutted the halls of the Luce County Hospital with purpose. Their deadpan expressions cut straight through the festive atmosphere. Nurses and doctors, many with reindeer antler head dressings and Rudolph noses on their faces, turned their attentions to the swaggy duo. Not a usual sight around here to see two fancy-dressed black men in fur coats, especially on Christmas Eve.

In between various vital sign monitors that beeped and hummed, a barely alive and unconscious Judge lay motionless on a hospital bed. His neck and chest were extensively dressed. Aside from the damage to his jugular, he suffered a collapsed lung, various broken ribs, and his sternum was busted. But the amount of blood he had lost severely affected his condition the most. At this juncture, it was touch-and-go on whether he'd survive. Ray was in a chair next to the bed. Since Judge was brought there, he never left his side.

He clasped his friend's limp hand tightly with his own and he silently prayed to himself for most of the day.

Oscar and Diz passed by what was left of Ray's crew standing in the hall, outside Judge's room. When each of them spotted Oscar, they straightened their posture and gave him a slight nod, which wasn't reciprocated. Diz stayed behind as his boss proceeded into the patient's room. The door closed behind him.

Seeing the intimidating manner in which his father entered, Ray was quick to release Judge's hand and straightened his posture in his padded chair. He knew his father was traveling his way but wasn't sure when. By now, though, Oscar had seen and heard enough.

"The woman did this?" Oscar asked as he took off his fedora.

Ray nodded, ashamed to make eye contact.

"Find her?" Oscar asked, taking a step forward toward his son.

Ray shook his head, his eyes prisoner to the floor.

"What about the other one?" Oscar asked, inching even closer.

"Still out there. I got a couple of men stationed by the ice bridge and they said he hasn't appeared yet. He's not riding the trails we planned, so I don't expect him 'til morning, with the way the weather is."

"Tell those men to stand down."

Ray finally looked up to his father for the first time since he arrived.

"What?" he asked, dazed.

"You failed," Oscar told him. "Stupid me for thinking you were ready for your own territory. This place isn't right for you. It's beyond what you can handle."

"Seriously? I got this, Pop. I've been waiting my whole damn life for an opportunity like this. Don't take that from me."

Oscar pointed to Judge as the crux of the issue. "What is this, Ray? Huh? I thought we were past this nonsense. When you returned home you said you had changed. This man here ain't nothing but the same street trash I warned you about. And I should know better than most."

"Nah. Judge and me have known each other since we were kids. He ain't like all that."

"They're all like that, son. They're leeches. Any way to get a hand in your pocket, they'll surely try. Why do you think I never give back to the streets I come from, huh? Because they ain't grateful. They didn't earn it like I did. No handouts. This man here, your friend, represents everything I motherfuckn' hated about my past. He ain't no better than them. He's just a hired thug."

Ray's demeanor began to crack, unable to contain his emotion.

"Are you fucking crying?" Oscar asked and hovered over his son, mad as ever. "Are we in our feelings again?"

Ray choked back tears. The giant was a child in his father's mind. He had always been considered a child to him.

"I— I don't know what's wrong with me," Ray said.

"You don't fuck the help."

Ray bowed his head again in shame at the chided tone of his father's ridicule. Yet another embarrassment in a long line of embarrassments he was all too familiar with, going back to his adolescent days. He could feel Oscar's stare beaming straight through him. That disappointed stare of judgment, rejection. It cut through him like a knife.

"Look at yourself," Oscar said. "Every opportunity you were blessed with just pissed away."

Ray's fingers rubbed the palms of each hand, and he twiddled his thumb ring. He began to feel that he couldn't take the abuse anymore. More and more his tears surrendered to building anger.

"It's my fault, really," Oscar said with resignation. "I raised an entitled boy. A weak faggot."

Ray rocketed from his seat in a frenzied rage, towering over his father's dominance. He snatched him by the lapels of his fur coat in a swoop and pinned him hard against a far wall in the room.

"Don't take away what's mine!" Ray yelled, his voice strained with a subtle boyish and volatile plea. "It's all I have."

Oscar's eyes popped wide. Fear washed across him. This was a side of his son he had never witnessed. Ray was pushing back for the first time ever.

Ray released his father and the Michigan kingpin hit the floor with a thud. Swinging the door in his exit, Ray gave a last glance at Judge, knowing he had to fix the mess he made. His crew had seen the family spat through the window and were at odds whether to follow Ray or stay with the man who paid them their wages. However, when they witnessed the bold measure in which Ray took the reins, his men chose to leave with him to finish what they'd started together.

Lying on the floor in a sad pile of his mink fur, somewhat embarrassed by his son's physical power against his meekness, Oscar stood and straightened himself just as a nurse entered the room. She had heard the commotion clear across the hallway. As did most of the hospital.

"Sir, please leave, now," she told Oscar.

Oscar strutted past her, putting his fedora back on and paying her no mind. Diz coiled directly in behind him when he reached the hallway and walked with him. When the nurse saw they were indeed leaving, she checked Judge's monitors and then left the room shortly thereafter. By the time she had closed the door, Judge's eyes partially blinked open.

   Everything that had transpired, he'd heard.

XV

Through the unruly aftermath of the historic Christmas Eve blizzard, Ford rode the higher grounds of the Chippewa County hillside in the bitter, windless morning. The higher grounds provided him an advantage of being able to obtain sights on anyone following him from below. What he hadn't realized, though, was that the blizzard had changed the landscape dramatically in his favor. His tracks were nearly covered throughout. The accumulation would prevent any law enforcement, including the DNR, to dispatch search parties for him, until township plows had cleared the roads. Areas that were accessible by snowmobile trails alone were currently blended with the terrain, making the law wonder where the trails were located to begin with. Even worse, the thick snow made it near impossible to ride through. The sun was out, but in order for the trails to return to rideable shape, they needed a warm day or so to harden. Dog mushers were the lone snow travelers today, aside from the plows. For Ford, it wasn't necessarily a cakewalk either.

The remaining bits of his journey would prove the most physically trying. When the snow became too thick in numerous areas, he would dismount his footboards and run, pushing his sled over tall embankments and unreasonable new-fallen snow terrains. At a certain point, in a heavily wooded section on the hills, he slowed his sled and searched the ridges below after he heard what sounded like motor engines. Near the bottom of the hill, he spotted two ambitious Sheriff Department deputy cars that followed behind an orange county snowplow. Come hell or high water, their search for Ford refused to quit on the account of some snow. A meandering and useless process that wouldn't score any results as far as Ford was concerned.

Further away from them, he located a group of three DNR officer snowmobiles, combing the area behind another set of snowplows. He figured it wouldn't take long before his own department joined in on the hunt for him. Their efforts would also go wasted. They weren't even headed in the right direction he was traveling. Unfortunate they had to ruin their Christmas Day tracking him, he thought, but fuck them. At least their lives weren't in danger.

It wasn't until closer to noon when Ford reached Drummond Island. When he did, any life the normally busy streets had was gone. Winter had become victorious, forcing everyone inside, which left the inland a ghost town on another level. Nothing was open to the public.

Even though he could ride freely without detection, he was still on high alert. He knew he was close to whatever Ray had in store for him.

Away from the main stretch, Ford finally embarked on the ice bridge between Michigan and Canada.

"Slow, North!" he said.

His sled slowed to a complete stop, each dog's tug-line from the gang-line trickling to a slack. He took his cell and texted Calvin Witter where he was at, then mushed on. Passing between the two pine trees and the *LEAVING MICHIGAN, USA* sign he rode the ice bridge, possibly for the final time, he feared. An afternoon sun had already begun to thaw the snow to firm ice for riding on the giant lake, which further assisted his dogs to run at any speed.

A mile into their journey, here they came. Three black Ski-Doos and one red Ski-Doo rode in fast behind, bullets on skis— that's what they were. When they were within a hundred yards, Ford noticed his dogs' ears flickered backward. He peeked behind his shoulder to see the hell riders were coming in hot. His jaw tightened and he gripped the sled's handlebar hard in his lacerated fists and his dogs' brisk run transformed into a full-on sprint across the empty ice bridge.

"Speed!" he yelled. "Go, North! Speed!"

From the only different colored Ski-Doo, which was red splashed with white, a machine meant for more racing than leisure, Ray led his death hunters at their target with untamed ferocity. Everything that had hindered him in his past had reached its boiling point, and it fueled his crazed actions in his pursuit of the man who caused his troubles. Now in his possession, he raised Judge's Desert Eagle past his windshield and fired a shot that missed Ford's head.

Ford swung around in retaliation, raising his Sig Sauer in the same motion, and returned fire. He careened his sled back and forth, dodging the enemy barrage that commenced after Ray's initial call to war with the first pull of his trigger. It was on.

One of the gang, a skeleton of a man with the baggiest of snowsuits, burned ahead of the musher and met his sled side-by-side. He aimed his drawn Glock 22 he kept in front of him and fired. Ford ducked, and from his squatting position, shot a round that hit the mercenary under his chin like a boxer's uppercut, throwing him off his machine.

A bullet from behind hit Ford's left shoulder, shattering it. He ejected his empty clip, then slapped another in place from his utility belt. Standing back up, ready for whatever else came his way, he fired repeatedly at the remaining trio, hitting and disabling a helmetless rider's snowmobile with pinpoint accuracy. Ray braked and let the rider hop on the back of his whip.

Meanwhile, a third mercenary reached Ford and winged him in his left leg. His next target was the dogs. If he could shoot any of them, the sled would certainly stop its momentum.

"Slow!" Ford yelled. "Slow!"

Ford's sled dropped its speed so he could float closer to a side-by-side position with the shooter, and the two engaged in hand-to-hand combat on their respected rides that wouldn't quit. Blows were traded, each gathering the upper hand from every melee. Amid the brawl, Ford's Sig was knocked free from a hard jab to his ribs, and it was lost to the ice. The killer took advantage and pistol-whipped him, making Ford vulnerable. Just before he could blast his face, Ford drew his hatchet from his belt and brought it downward in a precise hack, lopping off the man's two fingers, one being his trigger finger. He then dove from his sled like a missile and knocked the man from his ride, sending his own sled and the snowmobile onward, driverless. On the ice, the two rolled around. Each fought for the killer's gun, visible just paces away. Ford knew it was his only chance as his hatchet was also lost in the scuffle. He used the mercenary's momentum to force them toward the piece that they ended up rolling on top of. Their scuffle for the gun ended when it suddenly sounded off. The lake's wind carried away the cannon-like echo of the shot.

Ray and the helmetless rider rode in to find his own man lying still on top of Ford, who also appeared motionless.

By the same time, North had realized he lost his rider way behind and turned the sled around himself and returned for his human. North led the trot back to where the havoc was. The moment he saw the blood and bodies littered throughout the area, he hovered his nose above the ground and sniffed for Ford. A ferocious growl deep inside him ignited and the hair on his back stood at the sight of Ray Easter and the seemingly last living mercenary.

Ray ordered his man to check the entangled bodies, presuming both were dead by the rivers of blood around them. He turned back to Ray to give his assessment when Ford moved, aiming the Glock from under the dead killer and fired. The bullet went straight through the man's leg, and he fell back, bellowing in agony.

Ray and his man traded shots with Ford, who, using his free arm while the other held the gun, dragged himself behind the dead killer. Each emptied their clips into their dead friend's corpse that Ford now used as a shield, hoping some went through. Ford's shots hit their target, however, and killed the last mercenary, effectively ending the dogfight.

One of the shots fired ricocheted off Ray's piece, knocking it from his grasp.

As he tried to retrieve it, Ford, completely empty of ammo, threw aside his bullet-riddled human shield, rushed at Ray, and tackled him with surprising speed. They tumbled through the snow and ice. Ray easily overcame Ford and tossed him aside like a rag doll, each time punching him repeatedly in the face and gut before throwing him onto the frozen lake further and further away.

Ford's dogs barked violently and hopped in place to try to break free from their restraints. North frantically thrashed his head back to bite at his harness, trying to assist Ford, but he was trapped.

Ray searched for his gun again, while Ford tried to recover from the blows, but it was lost in the great sheet of white. Even worse, the sun's blinding glint reflected a glare that limited visibility on the ice bridge.

"Fuck this," he yelled. "I'll end you with my bare fucking hands, possum cop!"

He stomped his way to Ford again intending to snuff him out for good. Ford continued to try to recover and stand from his latest beating, but to no avail. Every ounce of his energy was nearly gone. Ray lifted him again. Face to face they were, but Ray had the edge. Ford's arms and feet dangled, too heavy and injured for him to use as if he had cinder blocks attached to them. His unbreakable will was stubborn, however, not ready to quit, a will that wouldn't let him give up.

If it was his day to die, he'd die fighting until his last God-given breath. The only thing left for him he could use was his head, and he used it to head-butt Ray, busting his enemy's nose wide open. Ray wrapped his massive hand around Ford's neck and delivered punches to his face with the other hand. After several blows, he heaved Ford to the ice again, sending him into a skid in front of North. Due to streaks of blood and the amount of swelling on his face, he was practically unrecognizable and nearly blind. North sniffed the familiarity on him, then started to lick the blood from his face. Ford reached his hand behind North's neck and detached the restraints of his harness.

Ray felt his nose to assess the damage. For sure, it was broken. Using the sleeve of his puffy coat, he wiped the blood from his face. Exhausted, too, he was sluggish as he stumbled toward Ford again, now woozy and coughing. Ray wrapped both hands around Ford's throat and raised him as high as he could, while he squeezed. Every ounce of strength he had left poured into his hands to end this monumental pain in the ass forever.

Ford fought to breathe. He could feel the bones in his neck were on the verge of breaking, along with his windpipe. His bloodshot eyes bulged, and he started to lose focus.

From the blinding glare of the ice, North lunged at Ray and sunk his froth-covered teeth deep into his leg.

He refused to let go and shook his head, his dagger teeth digging further into his skin. Ray's wail caught the wind and echoed across the ice, and then he released Ford. He desperately tried to shake the large-pawed beast. Using his other foot, he kicked him in the snout, forcing the mighty dog to fall back onto the ice himself. North yelped to a halt near the sled.

Ford fought the stars clouding his vision as he hacked and dry-heaved. He observed Ray, who was also fighting to rise. The brute was leaned forward in a sitting position, breathless. The ice beneath him was cracked in an outline of his body. Ford knew it was now or never — he had to strike now. He snagged North's loose neck-line near the other dogs, bolted to Ray, who was hunched, wobbly on his feet, and wrapped the line around Ray's neck. He swung around so he and the giant man's backs were touching. And then he yanked downward with all that was left in him. Ray's head snapped back and now he was the one struggling for air. He pawed at the tightly wrapped leather line and his body flailed wildly. Veins in Ford's head and neck popped, and his fists turned a ghostly white as he pulled with all the pressure he could muster. Everything he possessed went into his grip and he hollered with a rage that was prisoner deep in him. Ray's fight eventually weakened, and his limbs went limp. When he didn't feel any more fight, Ford released the line and the Goliath gangster died with a powerful face-first thump onto the ice.

Ford lay back exhausted, practically unconscious himself. His frozen breaths puffed like a locomotive smokestack, and he bled from every wound. North trotted to him and began to lick his face again and whine.

"Uh...I'm...okay," Ford muttered to his leader, coming back to full consciousness. "Okay...I'm okay, North. Shhh..."

He rolled to the palms of his hands and knees and staggered back to his feet and studied Ray's body gaping from the ice in front of him. To assure himself the fight was truly done he kicked him. North then led him back to the sled, where the other dogs waited. Ford tied the alpha back with the rest of the team. To the back of the sled he shuffled and stepped on the footboards, then felt around for the handlebar. His vision was better but still blurred. From the depths of his soul, he knew there wasn't a moment for him to rest, but his body said otherwise.

North glanced back at him. His human was barely able to hold onto the sled's handlebar, let alone gather enough air in his lungs to click the command to mush. So North pounced in place and clawed the snow wildly. His antics riled his team, who followed his actions and barked and wagged their tails when they did. He ran first, northbound again to Canada, followed by the rest. Now the dogs were in control of the sled and in full motion. Behind, the slain bodies of what remained of Ray and the 313 Disciples were left to their icy justice.

Calvin and his eight border patrol officers waited onshore. Through his binoculars, he spotted Ford's sled approaching, slowly but surely. Ford appeared keeled over the handlebar.

When the sled finally reached the Canadian side, he fell from his sled; a bloody and beaten shell of the fighter he once was. Calvin and the others pulled the sled onto the shore fully and helped Ford to his feet. They grew confused at the sight of him and North covered in blood. The dog was drenched from his left eye across his body and to his paws; almost as if it were his war paint.

"Well, you look like shit, champ," Calvin commented to Ford. "What happened?"

Ford's half glare at him gave him his answer.

"Doesn't matter," Calvin said. "Good work."

Calvin's men thoroughly frisked Ford, removing any weapons that he didn't already lose. They unbuckled the lines from the dogs and each man took a side of the sled and carried it to the van and slid the entire thing inside.

"This everything then?" Calvin asked after he saw the meth loaded. Ford gave a half nod, "Niko... Take me to Niko."

"As you wish," Calvin said and signaled his men with a flick of his wrist.

The patrol officers unexpectedly drew their weapons and fired upon Ford's sled dogs.

"NOOO!" Ford screamed, trying to grab for Calvin.

But he was quickly restrained and knocked out cold by the butt of Calvin's rifle.

"Leave the carcasses for the coyotes," he heard Calvin tell his men.

With the little vision he had left, he could discern the shapes of his murdered dogs lying on top of each other in a heap of red and fur. And there lay his sidekick ahead of the pile. North's lifeless large white paws were the last thing he ever saw of his friend again. Everything went black.

XVI

Ford came to in the back of the same van next to his sled. From his slow return to consciousness, he witnessed Calvin busting his burner cell in half. Another border patrol officer next to him rifled through his backpack. He had big teeth and freckles. Every piece of content he came across he threw onto the floor.

"Welcome back," Calvin said to Ford, cocking his head to the side. "Thought I killed you with that last blow there, champ."

Ford noticed the meth he lay next to and put his hand on it for balance in his attempt to sit up straight. He felt the van idling amid his rise. Poking his head around the sled, he saw the van was pulling next to a series of large factory buildings. At the very moment it rolled to a stop, Ford was forcibly removed by Calvin and the two patrol officers that rode with them. He was then held at bay.

Since it was Christmas Day, there wasn't a factory worker in sight.

Most semi-trucks and forklifts were stowed away the night before to keep free of the blizzard. Squinting through the sun that became hotter as the day changed, Ford could barely read the *KROWCHUCK SYRUP* sign above the largest building there.

Calvin went ahead of the van's front bumper to speak with a Latino security guard on duty, next to the main building. Ford watched the conversation rapidly go south. With animated arms from Calvin in the face of the guard, he seemed to berate the man before he returned in a huff.

"Get him back in the fucking van," Calvin yelled to the patrol officers.

"What happened?" the freckled officer asked in a gravelly voice.

"Our other ride hasn't returned from the base. They aren't answering any communication either. Fucking amateurs."

"What do you wanna do then?"

"Niko wants to see him."

Ford was reloaded back into the van by the patrol officers, again, rough and forced. His awareness was clouded — groggy even. He was still reeling from the loss of his dogs. The misery in him ran deep as if a family member had been taken from him.

This time, Calvin sat in the front passenger seat of the van. Motioning to the driver he said, "Take us into town."

The driver, an obese man with a buzzcut and a noticeable surgery scar on the back of his head, did a double-take, confused. But he asked zero questions, put the van in gear, and did as he was told.

From winding roads that seemed to snake downhill, away from the factory, Ford saw the landscape they rode through turn from a rural setting to a quaint but endearing small town.

Within minutes, they were in the holiday-decorated and empty streets of what must've been the downtown area. The van halted when it reached a certain point. It remained in the middle, not parked on the side like other vehicles were around them. Ford wondered where they were. From his obscure vantage point, through the side window of the van, he could only see a few nicely dressed people on clean shoveled sidewalks. They were watching something beyond the van's blind spot. It wasn't what Ford could see, though, it was what he could hear that triggered him. Almost angelic, seeping into the atmosphere, he could hear harmonizing voices singing "O Holy Night."

"Stay here," Calvin told the two patrol officers in the back, and he and the driver exited the van together.

Now that he had a clear line of sight from the windshield, Ford could determine where the alluring voices hailed from.

A choir of about sixteen in burgundy-and-gold robes sang from the steps of a massive white brick church, amongst two-hundred bystanders. They stood everywhere, in each direction, some together and others by themselves. Each seemed mesmerized by the harmony. Smack dab in the middle of the choir, Ford spotted Niko singing in the crowd of the angelic people.

Calvin and the driver leaned against the grill of the van and indulged cigarettes in sight of Niko. In their uniforms they seemed unsuitable, given the crowd wearing their Sunday best and the festive atmosphere. They watched the choir finish. Niko picked them from the mass and advanced straight to them. On his way, he took on many handshakes from residents and eager business owners. Many thanked him, others creating small talk. Ford knew Niko was an important figure but didn't understand how important he was to this tiny, seemingly thriving, town.

When Niko finally reached Calvin and the driver, his previous charming smile disappeared, and his amiable disposition vanished. It was time for business. Calvin opened the passenger door for him, then entered the back himself to scoot near Ford again. Niko paid no mind to Ford and what was in the back, rather, he just waved to the friendly citizens of his community. When they reached a portion of the town, where there wasn't a soul in sight, the youthful Canadian gangster stripped his robe and bunched it in the corner of the dashboard.

He snagged his shades from the inside of his suit jacket and slid them on.

"Why the fuck is my batch in the back?" Niko coldly asked Calvin, his head glued to the front.

"My guys bringing the plow were supposed to retrieve it, but they're unreachable," Calvin replied, obviously not pleased. "I don't know why. Sorry, Niko. I'll be sure to take care of that situation."

"My mom?"

"She was picked up after the service."

Calvin pointed ahead to another, much larger, white van by an empty portion of the town that was under construction. Frames of unfinished structures stood near and far around them. Frames for storefronts, offices, and apartments. From the van, a middle-aged man with a skullet, wearing a nice sweater and khakis, was lowering Joëlle Krowchuck in her wheelchair on a chair lift. Niko left to go to his mother, kissed her on the cheek, and wished her a Merry Christmas.

Snagging a blanket from her van, he covered his mother with it to keep her warm. In the other van with the batch inside, Ford was again removed by the patrol officers and brought before Calvin and his mother.

"Take the batch back to the factory and unload it there," Niko told the man with the skullet. "No one is working there today, besides my security. It'll be okay."

The man nodded, and Calvin pointed at one of his men, next to Ford, to accompany him. Both left in the van with the latest batch shortly thereafter.

"Avery didn't join you?" Niko asked Ford for the first time since he joined them.

Ford's dead glare at the kid pierced through his eyebrows. Niko had to know of Ford's struggles this past week. He couldn't care less, though.

"Just the one batch then, eh?" Niko asked. "Not the other owed to me?"

"One batch," Ford coolly replied.

Niko's own brow line straightened. He placed his hands on his hips and took a minute for himself to think.

Disappointment was obvious, but he tried to keep his frustration in check. Mostly for his mother.

Clapping his hands together, he pointed to the section of town under construction, "I've always wanted to show you where I come from, not just how we make our money. Call it my passion or what have you. This town was named after my father, Carson. He was born here. His father was born here, and me; the Krowchuck name started in this great place. Everything we make with our family's businesses — the syrup, meth — goes right back into Carson. Ford, don't you understand?"

Ford observed the surroundings he spoke proudly of.

"Unlike Oscar Easter's greed that maintains Detroit's shithole, and the people there stuck in poverty, my family's money is Carson's money. The Krowchuck brand bolsters that.

For us, that's the reason we do what we do. Our community is our heart."

"Suppose the people here knew the ground they walk on was built from dirty money," Ford said.

"Suppose they did. You know, my mom used to tell me I should never be concerned about the way we help people, as long as they're being helped."

He rested his hand on his mother's shoulder.

"Rise and fall, that's the name of the game in the drug business, ain't it? With that comes loss. More loss than gain. My approach is different. Unique. I intend on raising my own children here in Carson."

He pointed across the street to a group of buildings in the middle of the remodel.

"Right there is a coffee shop. Down Henson Avenue, a new bank. This area we're in will become the new town square. A record store... A mall... I can see it. Homegrown. See, I'm a man of simple tastes. There was some bloodshed along the way, yes, but that was mostly how my father ran things. Not me. I only carried on the legacy. We conquered Canada. From Newfoundland to British Columbia, everyone knows that there is no drug better than Krowchuck meth. It's so good that it's seeped into the States, and that just gives validity to how popular the brand has become.

Me, I could give a shit— oops, sorry for the language, Mom... I couldn't care less about that kind of growth. But I never get in the way of giving the people what they want. We'll get to that in a minute. My stateside contacts told me about Tom Two Feathers. His lab was destroyed. Sheriff's got everything on lockdown currently. Won't be much longer before Canadian feds come sniffing around here."

He stepped forward so his mother wouldn't hear him and whispered to Ford, "Man, the Easters sure made a fuckery of things, didn't they?"

Ford just stared and spit a stream of blood at Niko's feet. The kid chuckled some at his employee's expense, amused by the act of defiance.

"Seems you've had your trouble with them as well. Did they get

Avery?"

"She's just...gone."

Niko nodded, assuming she met her demise at the hands of the Easter posse.

"So, what now?" Ford asked. "Are you going to put me down like you did my dogs, right here? If so, I suggest you quit runnin' that momma's boy mouth of yours and give me my bullet already."

Niko glimpsed back at his mother, a contented grin wrinkling under his pathetic blonde mustache.

"Let's take a ride."

XVII

Sheriff Oren Anson walked the lengths of the empty department building. Usually, his secretary was seated at her desk, but today, he had to play multiple roles. Her fax machine behind her desk hummed and spit a piece of paper out that landed on a pile of others below. When he went to grab the stack, a phone rang on the desk. He answered.

"Hot off the press from *Texas Parks and Wildlife* as you requested, Oren," the lady on the other end of the phone said.

"Perfect," Anson said, carefully reading the documents. "Thanks, darling. Merry Christmas."

He further studied the copies sent to him before someone in his own office caught his attention. Anson peered through his partially opened door to see an elderly Native American woman wearing a black-and-red flannel parka seated in a chair in front of his desk.

Anson put the phone back on the receiver and entered his office with the stack of papers faxed to him in his hands.

"Merry Christmas, Ms. Cadotte," Anson greeted the Native American lady. "Give me a second, please."

He dug in his file cabinet and pulled out two file folders and fanned them on his desk before Ms. Cadotte. They showed an automobile accident from years back, mostly of a burnt F-150 truck.

"Thank you for coming in today, it being the holiday and all," Anson said.

"Ain't got nobody to spend the holidays with anymore," Ms. Cadotte replied in a deadpan voice. "Just another day to me."

"Right... By chance, do you remember that US-2 pickup accident a few years back?"

"Of course. Horrible what happened to that driver. Dear Lord. Burned to death like he did."

"These are graphic, just so you know."

"I've seen my share of graphic before. No need to prep me, Sheriff. Lay it on me."

Anson couldn't help his amusement at the tough old dame's apathetic attitude. The next photos he laid in front of her were the accident photos of a charred body — completely unrecognizable.

"That day, remember when the State Police interviewed you?"

"Yes."

"That man you saw flee the scene. Had a bag or duffel, you said. This him?"

And he placed a photo of the driver that was faxed in on top of the charred body photo. She studied it for a minute before she shook her head.

"What about this man?"

Another picture he slid on top of the faxed copy, a DNR photo ID of Cy Ford. Observing, she recognized the specific photo without skipping a beat.

"That's him," Ms. Cadotte said. "Yeah. I remember those eyes. He had a beard, though, before."

Anson's face lit up. He always knew something wasn't right about Ford. It wasn't out in the open, but there was an inkling he had about him. There was just an impression he carried with him. A past he kept close to the chest. Others probably couldn't detect it, but Anson was well-versed in bullshit. If his theory was correct, then the fake Ford was the biggest bullshitter he had ever come across in his tenure.

Escaping through the woods as he did that fateful day, Anson knew Ford had made a compelling choice. Until that point, Anson assumed Ford's metaphorical well had run dry. Maybe it was the feverish heat to blame that afternoon. Maybe even the thrill of identity theft. Anson wondered, *Was this his first time in a while? Or was it an addiction he couldn't shake?*

Maybe up until that day he had forgotten what the ruse felt like. Often, Anson wondered if the wanderer thought he could pull off this latest identity without a hitch. His motive didn't appear malicious. It appeared more out of necessity. Survival. Anson knew he solved the mystery that was Ford, at least for this identity.

XVIII

Endless acreage of Ontario's northern wilderness seemed under Krowchuck's control. Ford stared out the side of the van's window in the backseat. Their journey eventually ended by a small bluff, which overlooked a pond that wasn't quite frozen; likely because of the small, active waterfall it possessed that flowed from the St. Joseph Channel. It was a channel that ran over the waterfall and exited an inlet of the pond into Lake Huron.

Ford knew the drill. He led himself out of the van before Calvin and his patrol officer could force him to do so again. Niko exited his side, too, but not before he made sure to crank the heat in the van so his mother wouldn't freeze.

Confusion was drawn on Calvin's face, bringing Ford to this particular spot; a place he was familiar with. He looked to Ford, then to Niko, unsure of the situation.

As the freckled patrol officer and the obese driver stood next to Ford on each hip and Calvin ahead of him, they peered at the land that the secluded inlet pond was carved in. Next to it was a wide — rather than long — hayfield. At the tree line of the field was a house still under construction, much like Carson's downtown area.

"Regardless of what you may think," Niko said to Ford. "I don't have some big plan of a takeover. The only thing I want is the Upper Peninsula territory. We found it the best gateway into the States without your law giving us a hassle.

It's crucial we have control. If Oscar wants to battle for turf, then I won't cower from it. Sure, I'll hit him head-on. I'm not scared. As much as we've tried to avoid the bloodshed my folks went through decades ago, we might be forced to fight for what's ours again. This time stateside. That's where you come in."

Ford's ears perked up with uneasy anticipation.

"In my short nineteen-and-a-half years, never have I come across someone like you. Pitch after pitch, I've tried to angle it in a way to salvage your services. Without hesitation you declined every offer most would jump at.

Now, here we are, Ford, I've brought you here to offer you a Christmas present. My last pitch."

Even Calvin became perplexed about where the conversation was headed.

Niko pointed all around him, "That house on the hill. This pond. The land it sits on, all of it, I'm offering to you."

Calvin was taken aback by his boss's words.

"I get it. A runner's life is a bitch. It wears. How about I bring you on the payroll? Call it a promotion. With it comes a larger piece of the pie — a percentage of the Upper Peninsula's take. You get to set up the entire operation. Pick the runners, cooks, the whole lot."

"Whoa, hey, wait a minute now," Calvin said, facing Niko.

"Calvin—" Niko said to him.

"This is my home, my property. Property you already gave me. What the hell is going on, I thought we had something different in mind?" He leaned towards his boss and then whispered, "I shot the man's dogs for chrissakes. Served him to you just like you wanted."

"I only ordered you to deliver him to me, nothing more."

"We were done with him, you said. Suddenly you wanna make him a partner? What the fuck, Niko?"

"I changed my mind. It's the better business move."

"Changed your mind?" Calvin scoffed, turning around in a huff, then back to Niko. "You know, it'd be real nice if you'd let me in on these changes. Maybe show a little respect, eh?"

"You mean like how you've been skimming off the top from me for a while and didn't tell me?"

Calvin's expression instantly changed. Ford could only watch the heated argument turn awkward.

"Exactly," Niko shot back unapologetically. "So please, Calvin, tell me more about respect."

Calvin ate his words, his body frozen by the revelation. Standing there before his boss, he mulled over a list of excuses in his mind, but he knew whatever poured from his mouth didn't matter; his subversion was apparent.

The freckled patrol officer slithered in behind Calvin and swiftly slit his throat to Calvin's, and even Ford's, shock. Ford teetered back, as did a queasy Niko, who just watched the blood gush from his right-hand man's neck before he fell to the side in horror of his life being snatched from him.

"A goddamn knife?" Niko scolded the freckled officer. "Look at this mess."

Niko squirmed at the gory sight and motioned to the officer who did the deed to dispose of the body. But not before he nabbed Calvin's Glock 19 and kept it for himself. The way he held it between his thumb and index finger was awkward, which revealed his inexperience in weaponry. He then moved aside so the officer could drag Calvin by the arms towards the edge of the bluff.

As he did, the body left a blood-skid mark behind. Calvin was ultimately rolled over the cliff and his body fell like a dummy into the pond below. The current caught him, and he flowed through the inlet and was whisked into Lake Huron, where his body would likely never be recovered.

Niko readjusted himself, trying not to let his fear of blood affect him. He took the gun and slid it into his jacket pocket.

"Mom and I would be honored if you would accept our invitation."

A speechless Ford tried to get past the shock of what had just occurred. He'd be lying to himself, though, if he at least didn't feel a faint satisfaction of that final stupefied expression on Calvin's face. In the same notion, though, it gave him warning of what could happen to him. He stayed alarmed but calm in his response to the kid.

"Your entire offer to me is based on the fact that you win against

Oscar's retaliation."

"Of course. We can get you hired into border patrol immediately, or if you'd rather work from an outsider's perspective, that's entirely your call. Essentially, you would become my advisor of strategy. My lieutenant."

"Your soldier — like good ole Calvin was."

"However you want to label it — sure."

"There was a time in my life when I'd jump at that offer, believe me, but that's not who I am anymore. As I've said from the very beginning, I want to make money and move on."

"Money doesn't entice? Everything I've offered?"

A bold Ford shook his head, "I've earned enough. Now I'd like to go enjoy it."

"Then you need more time."

"No, Niko. I don't. I've made my choice."

Niko sighed, dejected, "Listen, you're clever. You know I can't just let you walk away after everything you know. Everything you've seen."

Undaunted, Ford nodded his understanding, "And you know I could just bullshit you by accepting your offer, then just bail later. But I want our business to end like men. I'd rather not have to look over my shoulder."

"Me too... Me too."

Ford watched the optimistic expression on Niko's face turn into a grimace and his sights floated beyond to the obese driver behind him. He could practically hear the officer draw his side piece from his holster to use on him. Ford countered. He threw himself backward, with an elbow out, into the driver's gut. Like a bomb, the gun fired over Ford's shoulder. All he could hear now was a piercing ringing in his ears. He wasn't to be stopped, though.

Ford reached into his boot for his concealed Kershaw knife and plunged it upward into the driver's throat. Removing it at ease, he then chucked it like a baseball at the freckled officer near the bluff, who was on the verge of a charge.

Straight into the chest the knife sunk, and the officer backpedaled with momentum. Ford kept coming. He pulled the knife from him, then jammed it into the man's temple in the same action and threw him aside as if he were a used condom. The savage in him returned and wouldn't stop until the mission he struggled to fulfill was complete. *Kill the kid.* He swung around to deal with him next.

POW.

A bullet entered his already smashed shoulder. As if he were in a daze, where everything appeared in slow motion, he casually observed the newest of bullet holes.

POW. POW.

Two more struck his chest. Standing with the smoking barrel of Calvin's gun aimed true at him was Niko. The kid had the fear of God on his face and his hands shook madly.

Ford fell to a knee. The cold swiped his breath in an instant. He struggled to exhale.

Unsure if he had stopped him or not, Niko was cautious in his approach. Ford slowly looked to him with what remaining energy he had. The kid squatted to his level, still a few feet from any possible reach. He studied this dying man before him.

"Hate this sorta shit sometimes," Niko said to him. "It'd be nice to live a life like others my age get to live. I never got to just be a kid, you know? Since I can remember, my father tested me and prepared me. Still... I never could stomach the violent parts.

Here I am holding this thing, though. Can't be too bad, eh? Guess it's why I'm still alive and you're...not... You were a hell of a runner. Business is business, though."

He stood tall, lifted his leg to Ford's chest, and kicked him clean off the bluff and into the icy waters below. He stretched his neck past the rocks to see where he landed, then tossed Calvin's gun in the drink with him. There the kid kingpin was, left alone among the dead in the snow.

Taking his time, he walked around the slain, grabbed the keys from the driver's jacket as he tried not to get any blood on his hands, and returned to the van.

"I got it under control, mom," he said out loud.

Joëlle's eyes were drooped and fixed. To him, they appeared as if they were glass. Her mouth hung as usual, but there was blood on the corners.

"Mom?"

When he reached for her hand, he noticed she was cold to the touch.

"M— M— Mom?"

He then yanked the blanket he covered her with to discover she was hit by a prior bullet in the heart. It was a stray from the obese driver, who Ford had killed. She had expired amid the fight.

"Oh...Mom...no... God..."

His head collapsed into her lap, and he cried uncontrollably. His plea for help went unanswered.

XIX

Anson ducked under weaves of police tape that covered the entire crime scene, including the kennels, and went inside the post. Judge's blood was stained to the wooden floor. The crime scene was still intact. Not a single thing was moved or cleaned as if everyone who had inhabited the space had simply disappeared. Anson's reason for being there was desperation. It was already Christmas midday, and he had his case just about wrapped. He knew who the players were. He knew their motives. Every battle aftermath was thoroughly investigated right to the Canadian border — where his jurisdiction ended. What was missing were the suspects. Any clue to guide him to their whereabouts, he wanted badly.

Whatever was relevant was already intricately combed through, so he knew he needed to search for something that on the outside might not appear as anything special.

Searching behind pictures, dipping his hand into dark crevasses, digging through garbage, knocking on walls and parts of the floor for hollow points, he was obsessive.

Avery's desk didn't reveal much. Neither did Ford's. Clean as ever. Paperwork was stacked on the corner. His trash was emptied as well. Jett's desk was the heart of the struggle between Avery and Judge. It had a lot going on, but nothing that caught his interest.

Dog barks lured him to the backyard and into the kennels. Sadly, Avery and Jett's sled dogs were left behind amidst the bedlam. Christmas was a big reason why. The incompetence of Anson's deputies mostly, though. Paul and Ringo were hopping in the air and yipped their pleas at the sight of a human. It was probably over twenty-four hours since they were last let out of their cages, or even fed, for that matter.

A dog lover himself, Anson felt for them. He took each dog from their cage to let them do their business, then loaded them in the back of his truck to transport them to the Humane Society. There, he fed them with the Alpo left in the tool shed. Lastly, he entered the kennel to prepare Lucy for removal. Her pants were shallow, and she whined. In and around her doghouse she circled, lying, sitting, and then pacing. Being comfortable was impossible. Her backside began to bulge. She was at the beginning stages of labor. Anson figured it wasn't a good idea to move her, despite the need to find her a new home.

To make her cozier, he grabbed blankets from the other dogs' cages and arranged them around her to nestle her for delivery.

When he returned from taking Sadie, John, Paul, Ringo, and George to the Humane Society, he swiped himself a desk chair from inside and set it in front of her cage, so he could relax her as best as he could through the labor. He felt it best to keep her company, rather than go at it alone.

"Just me and you, old girl," Anson said to her. "Not such a bad Christmas, I guess."

He checked the kennel as if someone was listening, then leaned back in his chair.

"Heck, wanna hear something nuts? My own kids won't even give me a call today, can you believe that? They never have before, doubt they will change anytime soon. Can't blame 'em I guess. I don't make it easy. Never did. I was never a dad to stay home much, even on days I didn't have to work. There were constantly other things to do. I don't know why. Well, I do know why. Between you and me, parent to soon-to-be parent, it's menial work raising kids. There, I said it. My mind didn't work like other parents'. I couldn't sit there and watch 'em grow. Everyone told me having children was the greatest joy ever. Watching them become adults is a privilege.

"Yeah, the feeling was there for me, sure, but it wasn't much fun. Didn't take nearly as much joy in it as I thought I would. I love my kids, I really do, but I wasn't a good father.

"My ex-wife used to get on me about barely being around. I gave her every excuse in the book why I had to be somewhere else. She was smart, though. She knew I didn't have the mindset or the knack for patience. Probably best she divorced me when she did. I probably would've kept on ignoring her if she hadn't. I would have used the job to keep busy, just to stay away from home. I wound up a lonely old man, that's the truth of it. Ain't much a good feeling either. I don't know if what I did is worth that feeling... Do me a favor, Lucy. Be a good parent for as long as you can. Shit, I'm sure you will. Dogs got the instincts for it, am I right? Maybe they'll keep you young.

"That's the saying. True, the Humane Society will ultimately separate you, but for the short time you get them, treat them right. Watch them grow. Maybe you'll become fulfilled... Go ahead, girl. Let your babies into the world."

Most of the day he remained there in front of her cage in that desk chair, smoking cigarette after cigarette, almost emptying his pack. Every now and then he'd stroked Lucy's coat. At three o'clock in the afternoon, she finally gave birth to her first pup, a male with a color similar to hers. Anson watched Lucy clean him with her tongue in amazement. Of every beautiful thing in this world, new life still takes the cake.

Lucy's tail swept a portion of hay in the middle of her giving her new pup a saliva bath, revealing a crack in the wooden floor below her.

Intrigued, Anson flicked his cigarette aside and swept away the hay and blankets from it. He found the crack bent into a sharp right angle, most likely forming a square, or more specifically, a door. It was a hidden door, with Lucy on top of it.

Anson safely transferred her and her pups into her cage's doghouse and made a bed in there, so he could investigate the secret door. Lifting it, to his pleasant surprise, he discovered a packaged batch of crystal meth.

Unknown to him, he had just discovered Jett's lost batch that the 313 Disciples stole from him that tragic night on the trails.

Ray wasn't sure where to hide the batch, and he had better sense than to carry it with him. So, he decided to plant it in the space under Lucy's cage, where he would leave it until he could figure out what to do next.

XX

Oscar stood behind a large plexiglass window next to Diz, who remained expressionless and silent — his usual soulless disposition. On the window, the reflection of Ray's body was shown on a cold metal table. Oscar just gazed at his only child. Oddly, he didn't cry, nor did he fume, almost as if the reality hadn't set in yet. Showing any vulnerability was never of much interest to him. The only person he'd been able to reveal that to was his late wife — the true love of his life. To him, she was an angel, and there wasn't a woman who could ever fill those shoes. Marriage was a one-time deal for him.

"Too much attention is on us now," Oscar said. "Let's push reset on the whole damn thing."

Without a word or even a hint of a reaction, Diz left his boss's side to carry on the assumed order. Oscar continued standing behind that glass, his dark gamut of emotions lost on Ray.

He had already identified the body to the coroner, and when an employee wanted to cover Ray or roll him into his future cold chambers, Oscar shooed them away. He wanted extra time with his son. The sort of time he'd taken for granted when he was alive.

* * *

Across town in the county hospital, Judge was wide awake. He was still weak, but able to walk from his bed to the bathroom without assistance, even though he shouldn't. The short-handed staff on this shift were preoccupied with a small holiday party they'd arranged for the younger sick patients of the ward. Judge was left to find his bearings by his lonesome. Not that he was bothered a lot. Nurses avoided his room because they feared him. He wasn't the most personable guy, and the eye contact he gave them was intimidating, to say the least.

As he moved around the room, holding his Holter monitor hooked to him, he glimpsed through his window to the parking lot below. Among the sparse number of vehicles in the frosted lot, he spotted Diz marching toward the hospital's entrance. Diz arriving alone wasn't a good sign.

It might as well have been the grim reaper himself. There wasn't any question in Judge's mind that Diz was coming to snuff him out. He didn't need to see the gun he had in his coat to realize that. To the room's closet Judge shuffled and grabbed as much of his belongings he could hold.

Every move he made hurt like the worst pain he'd ever felt, but he toughed through it.

When Diz entered the room a short while later, he discovered Judge was gone. The nurse who had previously booted Oscar from the room entered behind him with caution. Judge was gone, but the Holter monitor wires and IV were left behind.

"Where did he go?" the bewildered nurse asked Diz as if he knew of Judge's disappearance.

Diz ignored her, turned in a single stride, and left the room to find his target. He walked the halls, peering into every patient room and nurse station. Trailing behind him every step of the way was hospital security, unsure of what to do.

By the time Diz stepped into the cafeteria, Judge was on the other end of the hospital, exiting the facility. He knew he had to get to somewhere warm or his already serious condition would only worsen. He ventured to the parking space where the doctors parked and watched a white Lexus pull in. Judge walked to the ride to hijack it.

Only when the doctor barged into the hospital, fearing for his life, and rambling on about a black man who carjacked his vehicle did Diz understand that Judge had escaped. He promptly returned to Oscar at the coroner's office and relayed what had occurred and prepared himself to hunt the loose end.

"Fuck it for now," Oscar commented to Diz. "There are other fires of Ray's foolishness that we have to extinguish that take precedence."

XXI
FIVE WEEKS BEFORE

Basketball dribbles echoed in a church gymnasium of a school that was closed for over a decade, now the property of Oscar Easter. Ray worked a sweat playing by himself. He rocked a Detroit Pistons practice jersey and shorts, and his kicks were vintage Allen Iverson. Both knees were braced. Shot after shot, dunk after dunk, he looked solid, a throwback to his former glory days.

Regardless of the flashes, he still favored his bum knees. And it exasperated him. Bent over, sweat dripping at half-court of the old wood floor, he palmed the ball and dashed at the basket with purpose and came around with a thunderous jam that rattled the backboard. It practically brought the whole rig to the floor.

He heard a clap behind him in the rickety metal stands that ascended to the giant windows above.

Near the bottom row was his father, holding another basketball with both hands.

"What's going on?" Ray asked.

"Came to take you somewhere," Oscar said.

"Where? I've got a half-hour left of my workout."

"That can wait. Get your stuff, All-Star. Let's ride."

Ray retrieved his bag, threw on his thick North Face coat, and walked with his father. Oscar still held the ball, rotating it in his mitts. A piece of him wanted to try a three-pointer, but he didn't want to embarrass himself.

"Go ahead," Ray said. "Shoot."

Oscar was hesitant at first, but his son egged him on. He set himself behind the faded three-point line and chucked an attempt. Airball.

"Sports were never my thing," Oscar said, watching the ball bounce into the shadows of the dark gymnasium.

Ray tried not to break the laughter he held and said, "Neither was watching your boy play them either.

* * *

Diz drove Oscar and Ray far outside the city to a massive landfill near Auburn Hills. He backed the black Lexus they were in to the edge of a ridge that overlooked a mile-long by mile-wide ocean of trash. Oscar and Diz, followed by a baffled Ray, exited the vehicle.

"Jesus," Ray muttered, covering his nose with half of his North Face.

The rancid smell of the dump didn't faze Oscar and Diz. They just stood in place with their leather-gloved hands in the pockets of their peacoats.

"So, you wanna be me?" Oscar asked his son.

Ray understood the significance of his father's question. Only when he was serious did he ask him these sorts of questions. He didn't break face to show his passion and confidently nodded to his father.

"Think you can do what I do?"

"Yes."

"You want the throne?"

"Absolutely."

"Great. Go open that trunk and grab me the carpet inside."

Ray thought it was a peculiar request but did as he was told. When he popped the trunk, he saw a rolled-up carpet stuffed inside. At the end, closest to him, a pair of bare, black and pale feet protruded. Ray flinched, stepping away from the trunk at the gruesome sight.

Oscar chuckled to a stone-faced Diz, "He's his mother's son."

"The fuck, Pops! Doesn't Diz handle this stuff?"

"We all have had to get our hands dirty. Is this too much for you?"

Ray pondered the question. He didn't want to punk out in front of him. Here was a chance to show his father he had some brass. His fingers rubbed their palms. He hesitated. Following a few deep breaths, he pulled and removed the carpet from the trunk. Heavy, it rolled from his arms to the dust of snow on the ground.

"Go on," Oscar told him. "Toss it in the pit."

Ray knew his father's business. Hits, drugs, shady negotiations, the corrupt politics, whatever someone could go to hell for, his old man had a ticket waiting for him. Ray never witnessed it first-hand, though. His late mother shielded him from the wicked life. A life of lawlessness, masked to outsiders by lavishness. Ray knew. He always knew. But still, he yearned for justification from his father.

Instead of carrying the whole carpet in his arms, he dragged it from the end that didn't have feet sticking from it and pushed it into the pit. Peeking his head past the edge, he saw it fall in and blend into the garbage below.

Within a day or two, it'd sink beneath the top layer.

"The north territory," Oscar said. "Do you think you can handle it?"

Ray faced his father, "Hundred percent."

"Good. Yours for the taking then."

"Wait, but... Pops, that's Krowchuck territory."

"For now, but I still want it. You're gonna get it for me."

"How?"

"Welcome to the pros, son. This isn't learning some dumb jump shot. Think you can handle what I do? Prove it. Take the north and I'll leave it to you to control, if you can."

"Bull. I wanna hear a cut."

Oscar was impressed, which Diz could see by his expression. His son's unlikely business mind finally came to life.

"Eighty you, twenty me," Oscar said.

"Get the fuck outta here."

"I'm serious."

Ray acutely focused on his father, gauging his actual seriousness. Could be a sick joke, but Oscar wasn't the joking type. If his mother was alive, she wouldn't approve, but Ray felt it was his calling after basketball. He believed he failed at everything else, so in his next chapter he vowed he wouldn't repeat the same mistakes.

"Thank you," he said to his father. "I don't know what else to say. This is huge. You probably aren't expecting much... I'll prove you wrong. I will."

"Your show, son. Do what you gotta do to get me the north."

Ray accepted his father's challenge by shaking his hand. "I'm gonna piss, then let's get outta this place. Freaks the hell outta me."

Oscar entered the back of the car, and Diz, his usual driver's seat. The heat remained on full blast. Waiting for Ray to return, Oscar situated himself behind the passenger seat. His eyes met Diz's in the rearview.

"If I can't have the north right now, then nobody can," Oscar said to Diz. "If Ray succeeds, then maybe he does have what it takes. If I'm being honest, I expect him to fail miserably. When he does, the law's presence alone will devastate Krowchuck's operations, which will force him to back away for a while until the heat subsides. During which, I'll intercede and take control of what he leaves behind."

Ray returned to the car a minute later. His father's snide smile from the thought of his secret, devious ploy was now wiped clean.

XXII

Tiny knives were stabbing his entire body. That's how it felt, anyway. Lake Huron's frigid waters were unreal. Ford had drifted into the Great Lake from the channel he was kicked into. If there was a silver lining to his dire predicament, the water and air's freezing temperatures of the environment had helped stop the blood flow from his wounds. Floating above the ice that saved him from sinking into the depths, the partially cloudy sky was all he could see. An object floating next to him caught his attention and he saw it was his Alaska postcard. It must've fallen from his coat after his plunge. He pinched its corner and brought it to his view. An aching chuckle slipped out. Everything he wanted or even cared about was snatched from him. There wasn't a thing he could do other than laugh at himself. The thought of the hypothermia getting him before dying of blood loss made him chuckle.

Although this was his end, he took solace in knowing his death would be peaceful, to say the least. So, there was that.

Currents had pushed him closer to the shore, near the rocks of the bluff that skirted along what was known Krowchuck country. Ford embraced his fate. Hell, he knew he deserved what was coming eventually. In what he assumed were his final moments, he thought of his dogs, Avery, Jett's wiseass jokes that he secretly enjoyed, and other past moments in his former lives that brought him joy. Even closer he inched to shore, but the stacks of ice that had formed like glaciers in the shallows hindered him from ever touching land. He had become a human bobber and was too numb and too weak to prevent his drift.

Waves crashed against the ice and their brutal force pushed him further and further into the water. Fuck hypothermia and the loss of blood. He was going to drown. He took his last breath before his head was completely submerged.

When he came to after an unknown amount of time, he realized he was on the shore, somehow, someway. As if he were having an out-of-body experience, he could feel himself moving. Floating even. He could even breathe, but barely.

Further from the water, he watched the stacks of ice become smaller. *Am I dead?* It was Drifter carrying him over his shoulder, trudging through the slush on a beach to a massive snowplow. At first, it didn't hit the disoriented Ford, but Drifter had rescued him from the waters.

He leaned Ford against the plow's wheel so he could remove the dead bodies of Calvin's two patrol officers from the cab. They were the men that were supposed to arrive at the factory for the meth load earlier. Drifter was the reason they were missing in action.

Every inch, every layer of clothing Drifter stripped from Ford and covered him with three blankets across the backseat of the plow. Ford's ice beard made him appear as if he were a winter Neptune. Drifter cranked the heat in the plow's cab and drove the rig as far and fast from Krowchuck country as possible.

* * *

Ford found himself in a Hobo camp off the beaten path. Heated tents were everywhere in the space, with holed barrels of fire throughout. The camp itself had maybe twenty-five that occupied the space, and it was mitered with sleds of scavenged possessions of mostly junk, but still of value to the people living there. Ford lay on a cot made just for him, while Drifter rigorously worked on his injuries. He plucked bullets and shrapnel, reset Ford's shoulder, sewed wounds, and applied ice to swelling areas of his body. A hung propane lantern was his main source of light.

Often, he'd glance at Ford and see him go in and out. Whether he felt the pain, he wasn't sure. Drifter figured he was going to sleep for the next several hours.

When he was able to fully regain consciousness, he was buried in a sleeping bag with layers of thermals on, including thermal socks that toasted his feet. His face had swollen from the beatings he suffered, which still affected his vision. The ice Drifter used on him helped lessen the swelling a bit. His entire body was bruised, and it ached to no end. He noticed the many rags of blood scattered in the tent. Remembering he had been shot multiple times, he felt around his body with his lacerated hands. His chest holes were stitched. His shoulder had been reset, but it continued to hurt like hell, and was mostly unusable. His leg on the same side he barely felt any pain from was also treated. He rose from his lying position and groaned when he sat upright on the cot. He then dropped his legs over the side.

Hearing Ford from outside the tent, Drifter left a burn barrel he shared with others to check on him.

"Am I dead?" Ford asked.

"No," Drifter replied with a slight chuckle.

Still muddled and groggy, Ford scratched his scalp and tried to fathom what had happened.

"I snatched you out of Huron," Drifter said. "Damn near dead when I found you."

"H— Ho— How? How did you find me?"

"You left a kill trail that led right to you."

"Why, though? Why'd you follow me?"

Drifter shrugged, "I guess you seemed like you needed a guardian angel."

Ford was at a loss for words. There hadn't been many instances in his life where someone had shown him this kind of gratitude. What could he say to him? A piece of him sort of wanted to die, because he'd wrapped his mind around the idea in the Huron.

To cut through the awkwardness, Drifter went to check his patchwork.

"Heck of a job," Ford said.

"I was a Navy Corpsman with the Third Battalion Seventh Regiment Marines. Did a few tours in Iraq. I did this sort of shit regularly. Gotta say, you're a lucky bastard. Bullets went straight through, just missed some real bleeders."

Ford glanced around the tent, already scheming his next move.

"In case you're wondering where you are," Drifter said, "We're not far from Carson. There are good people here in this camp. Trustworthy."

"Close bunch?"

"We are."

Ford nodded his acceptance.

"When you were out, I did a little tracking. Niko's back in Carson. He doesn't know you're alive. Figure when you're able to, we can go back after him."

"No," Ford said after a bit of hesitation. "I'd rather just get back stateside."

Drifter didn't expect this answer from Ford. "You don't want to finish the job?"

"There isn't a point to it anymore. The kid thinks I'm dead, I'm dead then."

He rejected Drifter's help in his fight to stand. When he finally rose, he walked a bit around the tent. His curiosity continued to pique, and he picked through random bloody dressings and tools strewn throughout. Almost as if he was avoiding what he actually wanted to say.

Then finally, "It just makes sense to me. I get it. I get why Niko does what he does for his town. I'm just...done with him... Now... Now, I'd rather just find Avery, get my money, and start somewhere fresh again."

Drifter nodded and said, "Dangerous."

Ford grunted his agreement. He rested a hand on a small antique school desk, so he didn't tip over. Reaching his hand into his jacket on a string that was hung across the tent where his clothes dried above a portable propane heater, he recovered the damp Alaska postcard he carried with him on his journey. He handed it to Drifter.

Finally, Drifter understood Ford's motives. His want.

Though he was a complicated man, he had simple desires.

Like a time-traveler from another decade, he just wanted what he earned and nothing more. It was as if he was a prisoner, who yearned for what others took for granted. An actual life.

"I could use your help getting back," Ford said. "I can pay you. Figure you'd know the best routes around the law."

"It's probably best if we make the trip once you're healthier—"

"Can't. We don't have enough time. The longer we wait, the more Avery could be in trouble."

Drifter wasn't behind the idea. For the number of bullets and beatings Ford endured, his even standing was a feat.

"Don't worry about me," Ford said. "Just help me get back to Michigan."

Drifter was still uneasy, but when he considered the postcard again, then saw the longing in Ford, he accepted his proposal and handed him back the postcard.

* * *

Early the following morning, Drifter traded the plow in for a stolen 2006 Yamaha snowmobile with a Snowcraft trailer, a ride he jacked in Carson. Enclosed in the trailer portion was Ford, bundled with a haul of warm blankets. They rode the ice bridge under the warm sun that had finally shown itself in full. Ford took it in through the trailer's mesh windows.

The routes they used to ride back into the states were predominately railroad tracks and abandoned logging roads. Many were straight shots. They had to break most of the wooded trails they rode through, which prolonged their journey. Fortunately, when they crested Chippewa County, most of the tracks were in the high country, so Drifter was able to Eagle eye across the countryside. Law or DNR in the areas stuck to lowlands. Any willing to venture higher could be met with unforgiving mounds of snow the blizzard had left in its wake that made it impossible to scale.

By day's end, the two arrived at the post to see the law had made their mark on it already. They kind of figured as such. With his trusty Winchester rifle shouldered, Drifter helped Ford from the trailer and proceeded to let him use his arm for leverage as they walked into the post together.

Immediately, they saw the bloodstains on the floor. Something bad had happened here. Desk to desk, room to room, they searched for clues that would show any sign of hope for Avery's whereabouts. Her office was mostly clean, except for the ridiculous amounts of scratch-off instant lottery tickets that occupied a good portion of her trash can.

Ford sifted through the opened mail on her desk. To his shock, he discovered countless past due bills and a crumpled eviction notice on her house. If the mail told her story, then Avery Kinnomen was broke.

"Found something in the back," Drifter said, poking his head in the office doorway.

Ford put his hand back on the man's shoulder and followed him to the kennel to find Lucy lying on her side and a litter of five puppies feeding on her. Five beautiful newborns. His face lit up at the sight of them. They were the most hopeful sight he'd seen in the past few days.

Drifter led him to the cage and Ford opened it to greet Lucy and her pups. Even though his face was battered, Lucy recognized him by his smell and wagged her tail.

"The Humane Society is coming later to pick them up," Sheriff Anson's voice sounded from behind.

Drifter swung his rifle around to see the sheriff aiming his Ruger GP100 revolver true at him. A weaponless Ford returned the puppy inside the cage to its momma.

"Knew someone would come back for the meth," Anson said.

A blank expression spread on Ford. He didn't have the slightest idea what he was talking about.

"I've been waiting here for someone to show. Can't say I'm surprised it's you, Connor Lafleur..."

That name made Ford freeze. Anson tossed a case photo of a

partially burned Illinois State driver's license at the drug runner's feet. Ford barely gave a squint at it.

"Or is it Kit Keith or Michael Price?" Anson added and tossed the other case photos of two unearthed ids on top of the first. Kit Keith was a Canadian identification and Michael Price was a Montana identification.

"Sure as hell not Cyrus Ford. He died in that wreck you both were in. Ring a bell?"

Ford gazed at Anson, refusing to break face.

"Figured the real Ford was running from something when they discovered the LaFleur ID in that scorched pickup three years ago. Some road worker found those IDs hours south on the same highway weeks after. All along that guy was you. Playing with someone else's life... Tracked a Connor LaFleur to Chicago. He was a firefighter. Perished on the job. Now, I'm assuming Kit Keith or Michael Price was your next stolen identity. Maybe either of them was a backup, huh? Maybe they're identities you've already squeezed dry? Spill it, just tell me. Who the fuck are you?"

Ford remained silent. Stiff.

Anson grinned. "I'll find out in good time, don't you worry."

Drifter kept his aim steady on the lawman. If Anson made the smallest of jerks, he'd be met with hot lead.

"Crystal methamphetamine. That's what you, Avery, and Jett were transporting, right?"

Ford said nothing.

That was the answer he needed to justify his whole investigation. But really, he didn't even need that.

He knew he'd been right the second he put the final pieces together. Just felt good to hear it aloud. A sort of pride in himself he held close, having solved the biggest case in his life.

"What happens now, Sheriff?" Ford asked.

Anson, still leveling his gun on Drifter, carefully released his left hand to his belt to finger for his cuffs and threw them on top of the case photos of the fake ids.

"Not sure who your friend is here, but I have another set in my cruiser if he wants to join you."

"He's not a part of this. Just helped me get here — that's all."

"Fair enough."

Pain slashed through Ford as he bent over to reach for the cuffs. At that moment, they heard footsteps crunch in the snow and saw Oscar Easter and Diz entering the kennel with their guns on them.

"Someone forgot to send me an invite to this rendezvous," Oscar said.

Anson backpedaled to the side to turn his aim on Oscar and Diz. Drifter turned his aim on them as soon as he heard their approach. The standoff was set.

"Drop 'em!" Anson yelled at Oscar and Diz. "Now!"

"You first," Oscar said.

"What do you want?" Anson asked.

"Just came by to grab something that belongs to me," Oscar said.

"The batch ain't here," Ford said. "Your boy took it."

"We heard it was here. I don't suppose you'd mind if we took a little look for ourselves, would you?"

Time stood still. The question lingering was who'd shoot first. Ford was the only person weaponless. He could feel the tension rising and quietly fell back, so as not to trigger anyone's actions.

"Drop your weapons and back away," Anson repeated.

Locked in on Diz, the sheriff saw his pupils dilate with anticipation.

"Fuck," Anson said.

Diz fired first, hitting Anson in the stomach. Oscar followed an instant later, hitting Drifter. Anson and Drifter each got off a single shot, but both were wide of their marks.

Ford raised his hands, "Enough!"

The victors turned their weapons toward him now, letting Drifter and Anson lie in their own blood.

"The territory is yours now," Ford said to Oscar.

"You and I didn't make a deal. That was with my son. His death is your doing."

"He died because of you. Just like the rest."

"Well, no. Not quite. That was Ray's show, unfortunately. He never had the smarts. He wasn't built for this sort of life. The weight of the Easter name...too much..."

Movement behind Oscar and Diz caught Ford's peripheral and he kept the conversation flowing, so they wouldn't see for themselves.

"Your last name," Ford said. "Is it true what they say? Are you actually Ellis Easter's son?"

Oscar chuckled at the question, "Sometimes you gotta play the part to earn the respect, you see."

Oscar kept his gun aimed at Ford. "A shame you had to get caught in the middle of this."

Before he could fire, a headshot dropped Oscar and his body slinked to the snow. The bullet hole was large and brain matter splattered on Diz's dress pants. Diz whipped around to spot Judge holding Anson's 30-06 rifle he snagged from the Sheriff's truck, marching toward him. Both began to shoot at each other at close range.

Ford hit the ground, trying not to catch any strays. When the dogfight ended, Diz slumped dead against the fencing of the kennel, a single shot from the powerful rifle hitting him square in his chest. Judge fell back against Astro's empty cage and slid to his ass, his dreads like spider legs, everywhere.

Ford got to his feet and saw that Judge was still sucking air but struggling mightily. Every passing second his breath became frailer and shallower.

Before he died, Ford grabbed him by his opened North Face and pulled him forward.

"Where is she? Where is Avery?"

He said nothing. Ford shook him hard against the fence.

"Don't fuckin' know," Judge said. "Bitch knifed me and bolted."

"What do you mean?"

"She...fucking bailed before ya even made it to Rudyard..."

He chuckled as blood spilled from his mouth.

"She played yo ass... L— left...left ya holding a live grenade."

Ford released Judge after hearing his revelation. The thug gurgled and the struggle to his end wasn't a pleasant one. When Ford reached for his rifle to give him his peace, Judge jerked it away and spat a heap of blood at him and wheezed. Ford backed away.

"I loved Ray..." Judge revealed.

Words he never was able to tell Ray when he was alive.

He then closed his eyes and never opened them again.

Ford checked both Anson and Drifter and saw that both were still breathing.

Drifter held his gut, which leaked like a sieve — the most serious of his wounds. He also had a wound to his collar bone and another to his arm. Ford knew he was too far gone. Checking the damage, he came across a Marine emblem tattoo across his chest with the words *SEMPER FI.*

"After the war, I lost myself," Drifter said, coughing, barely able to speak. "There were things I did there...I needed to escape...me."

He extended his hand for Ford to shake. "I'm Sam. Sam Bass."

"Thank you, Sam," Ford said, forcing a half-smile as he shook his hand and then held it tight to his own chest.

More uncontrollable coughs followed and blood painted Sam's lips. The muscles in his face started to relax.

"Cut the shit," Sam said. "Tell me... Tell me who you are? Your real name."

Before Ford could speak, Sam's eyes glazed like glass and his chest stopped. Anything Sam had ever known, loved, felt, and desired bled from him onto the ground. Sam was a forgotten soul. Ford knew him as a nice guy. A real give-the-shirt-off-his-back nice guy. Now Sam lay before maybe his only friend, cut down far too young. Ford would never forget Sam Bass.

Ford took Sam's hands and folded them on each other and placed them on his chest.

After, he grabbed Sam's Winchester and got ready to leave on the snowmobile they rode in on. His conscience eventually overcame him, and he checked the sheriff to see how he was. Anson moaned in pain when he did. Ford took a scarf from Diz's neck and applied pressure to his gut wound. Anson shivered. Ford then removed his own jacket and covered him with it to keep him warm.

"Before, you mentioned you knew someone would return for the meth," Ford said. "That's what Oscar was after. Only, I don't know what meth you mean."

"Damn you, Ford... Don't act dumb. Your little payday under the dog's cage. I found it. That's why you returned."

Ford stood. "I'll call for some help..."

"D— Don't get too excited. I'll— I'll find you again."

Ford just watched his adversary try to hold the control he thought he still had.

"Caught you once," Anson added. "I'll catch you again."

"Good luck, Sheriff..."

Ford made a move again to leave the kennel but forgot something— the dogs. Limping across to Lucy's cage, he took the five newborns and nestled them in his bibs, and lastly led Lucy from her cage. Furious, Sheriff Anson tried to crawl to Ford, his silver cross necklace spooling on the ground underneath him. The ache from his gut wound was too much for the old man to continue and he gave it up.

Ford left the kennel.

Together with Lucy, he placed the pups in the trailer buggy, then went to Anson's truck. He lifted the back gate and found Jett's stolen batch; a prize he considered a hidden delight. Next, he went to the front of the cruiser and grabbed the CB mic.

"Shots fired at Newberry DNR post. Shots fired. Officer down."

He tossed the mic in the seat and limped back to his snowmobile.

XXIII
THREE YEARS BEFORE

Tangled in a mess of shrubbery was a BlackBerry cell phone. Feet from it in the mud a set of keys on a keychain. A navy-blue Chicago Fire Department hat with an English font *CFD* stitched on the front fell not far from the keychain.

Seconds later, a ball of clothes. A long shadow from the day's end stretched on asphalt, and from a backpack, discarded items hit the earth.

A haggard Ford walked an uneven highway lost in some North American wilderness that stretched forever before him. As if he were the keeper of the land or a wandering spirit of the forgotten highway that split through, he trekked for hours along its lonely shoulder. His only possessions were secured inside a nylon and mesh hiking backpack that clung to his back after he disposed of the original items. On his right side, he balanced himself on a stout walking stick he'd whittled during his travels.

Intense summer sun beat down on him, creating streams of sweat from his mangled long, brown hair and unkempt beard. His clothes and shoes were mostly freebies he scored from Goodwill stores and stolen from donation bins around homeless shelters and churches. A typical traveler who had lost himself somewhere along the line in the battle of life. At this turn, he was as enigmatic as the universe was uncharted, and he kept mainly to himself as if it was his religion.

His steps eventually ceased. In his hand, he fingered an Illinois state driver's license with the name "*Connor Lafleur*" on it. This was the last piece he was about to discard, but instead, he just stared at it as if he didn't have the heart to dispose of it. As if it had a special meaning. The longer he stared, the more tired he became. Today's travel was harder than other days. Finding shelter to take the rest of the day off from his aimless journey was his intention, before an apple-red Ford F-150 drove into the formidable area. It was the first sign of life he had seen in hours. He never longed for much company, but the thought of getting off his feet in a vehicle, especially with air-conditioning, sounded better than trying to last in the heat, where he would surely boil on the highway like an egg. Ford decided to stick out his thumb. The truck zoomed by, but its brake lights glowed, and it promptly rolled to a stop.

Ford stuffed the ID in his bag without much thought, then mustered what energy he had left in the tank to advance toward the diesel lifesaver.

* * *

He was slow to awaken from the passenger seat of the truck, his head leaning against the window. Had it been hours or minutes he'd been sleeping? He wasn't sure. He scooted his backpack closer to his leg, away from a good-sized military duffel bag that was squished in the footwell.

"Traveling for some time, I take it?" the driver asked with a thick southern accent.

Ford nodded, hesitantly.

"Me too," the driver added. "Going on seventeen hours, coming up this way here to bum-fuck-nowhere on a transfer."

"How much further?" Ford quietly asked, his rough voice barely audible.

"Not much. If ya don't mind, I'll drop ya off when we get into the town ahead. Rudyard, I think I was told. Not far now."

Ford politely nodded.

"I'll buy ya a beer," the driver added. "Get some dinner in ya before ya move on to wherever next."

"Thank you."

"Where is next anyway? Shit, where ya from?"

"All over, I guess."

"Like a real rolling stone, huh?" He chuckled some. "Kind of a go where the wind blows sorta man."

"Something like that..."

Just before the driver could speak another word, a deer sprang from the surrounding trees into the middle of the road to cross. The driver swerved the wheel hard to the left to avoid striking the animal, and the pickup veered from the pavement. Ford braced himself for the crash he knew was coming.

***

The once slick-looking red pickup lay on its roof, totaled, in the deep ditch. Debris was everywhere, and black smoke was billowing out from under the smashed hood. After a few minutes of hell inside the cab, Ford was able to break his window and roll with the smoke out of the cab to safety. He grabbed the brown grass and pulled himself to all fours to puke. Dazed, he sat upright to catch his breath. Everything was a blur. He tried to find an easier way to the driver with no such luck. Before he knew it, the fire that originated from the engine block claimed the front end of the truck and exploded enough to damn near incinerate the windshield. The hungry fire had no quit. It continued to engulf the mangled metal with increasing ferocity.

Ford knew the only way to the driver now was to go back the way he came, so he scrambled back under the pickup to try to save him. He threw out the contents of the cab in a panic, including the driver's military duffel, but his own backpack was not in sight. When he finally made it across to the driver, he was still hanging upside down, the dashboard pinning him in.

His hands draped past his head and were flattened inside the cab's roof. There wasn't any immediate indication he had survived the explosion of fire and smoke, but Ford knew he had to at least try to free the man. He tried every option possible to undo him in the small space he had to work with, but the growing flames became unbearable. It seemed the harder he tried to free the helpless driver, the more stuck he became. The dash wasn't budging, and who knows if anything was squishing his legs from the floor.

Intense heat and the constant flow of smoke forced Ford back from the cab and back onto the ground next to the burning truck. As he started to move further away, he found the driver's duffel was entangled around his leg. He untangled it and crab-walked away from the inferno.

A passing car stopped. Just as it pulled onto the shoulder of the road, the pickup exploded in a massive blaze, forming a growing cloud that would be visible for miles.

A highway patrol siren sounded in the distance.

Hearing the oncoming siren, Ford chose to leave the scene and fled into the thick pine trees of the dark forest that was masked by the smoke. He was spotted by the onlookers who helplessly watched the body in the truck succumb to the flames. They were left with the stomach-churning smell of death and burning diesel fuel in the summer air.

* * *

When night fell, Ford emerged from the woods. Hours earlier, he had located a small motel near the edge of Rudyard. He surveyed the area to get the lay of the land to decide if it was safe for him to stay for a day, maybe two.

He wasn't sure if anyone was searching for him now on what he assumed would be described as *"the man who fled the accident."* His backpack somewhere in the F-150 would raise heavy suspicions for the local law and that worried him. He could only hope the fire destroyed everything.

Regardless, he knew it was probably best to buy a room for himself when it grew dark, rather than chance being seen in the daylight. New faces in small towns could raise suspicions, and towns like Rudyard normally closed at day's end, so he figured it would be better to move after dark.

There wasn't much business at the Cass motel. Not surprising. Now it was referred to as *'ass'* since the sign's light on the letter *'C'* was burnt out. The shittier the motel, the fewer the people.

Perfect.

The parking lot contained two cars parked on opposite sides of the motel. One a rust bucket full of holes as if someone took a shotgun to it, and the other a 1995 Chevy Cavalier. From the woods, he'd seen the Cavalier had gone for most of the day, only to return at dusk. Ford figured the person had business in town. A normal traveler. Someone cheap, nonetheless. But the rust bucket hadn't moved an inch from its spot the entire day. Just before mid-afternoon, he did catch a glimpse of a heavyset, middle-aged woman, who most likely was the owner. He didn't think she was a threat.

She had only made two trips to her heap that afternoon. Her first was for her pack of smokes, and the other for a pair of sandals she kept in the trunk.

Ford hobbled across the street with the duffel slung on his back and he slipped into the motel office, where a neon sign flashed *VACANCY* above the door. His ankle was sprained earlier when he fled from the wreck. He was able to soak it in a stream along the way, but it provided only temporary relief. The pain made him wince the more he stood on it.

There wasn't a single person he could find working the front desk. He checked his surroundings constantly and scanned the lobby for any cameras. There was none. The office itself was in desperate need of a remodel. It held onto a 1980s vibe and the musty smell reeked of it too. When he approached the chipped wood counter, he saw a dusty service bell tucked behind a vintage Macintosh computer monitor, away from public view. An odd place to keep it. He tapped the bell and waited. Rustling was heard behind the office door in the back room. An old woman in a fuzzy bathrobe waddled on the cold floor behind the counter with bare feet. Ford noticed her toenails were long and yellow and crusty and her skin looked as tough as leather. Her droopy eyes scanned him through her thick lens glasses that sat on the tip of her nose. She keyed in on the wounds and his overall grim appearance. The scowl on her face didn't change at the sight of him, and she just continued her wobble to the computer.

"How many?" she asked Ford.

"Just me."

She pecked at her keyboard.

"Queen okay?"

"Yes."

"How long?"

"I'll need it a day. Might be two, but for right now a day is fine."

"Two then."

Ford gave her an odd look.

"You'll pay for two. If you end up needing the room just the one day, I'll reimburse you."

Ford nodded his acceptance.

"That gonna be a problem?" the old woman asked.

"No, ma'am."

"Good."

She stiffly pecked at the keyboard again, while Ford patiently watched. He couldn't help but hone in on her struggled breaths in between key clicks. By the smokey smell of her and the labored sounds of her breathing, he figured she was a heavy smoker with emphysema. Now at the back end of her life, he assumed she didn't care that she had the disease.

"I'm not gonna get any trouble out of you, am I?" she asked.

"No, ma'am."

She fixed her stare on him for an uncomfortable amount of time, making her point, as she tried to inflict as much intimidation as she could.

Ford wouldn't be surprised if she had a gun under the counter. She probably wanted an excuse to use it. She backed away from the computer and snagged a room key from one of the gold hooks next to her head on the wall and handed it to Ford.

"One twenty-two is your total," she told him.

Earlier the same day, Ford found a wallet inside the side pocket of the Texan's duffel he carried with him from the pickup. To his luck, there were two crisp one-hundred-dollar bills. He pinched the bills from the wallet and handed them over to the old woman. She returned his change.

"I'm going to need an ID," she said.

"Right."

He dug back inside the wallet and carefully handed her the Texan's driver's license. He held his breath as the old woman held the card with her forefinger and thumb, a good two feet in front of her, and squinted to read its wording. His poker face was hard to maintain, given the circumstances. Of everything he thought he had planned, he neglected to think about this part of the transaction. There wasn't much time to do so. All he knew presently was if she made a move under the counter or for the landline on the wall, that he'd run straight out of that office faster than he had at the accident.

Mere seconds later, which felt like minutes to Ford, the old woman finally said to him, "Cyrus Ford. Well... To be honest, you'd look better with a haircut and a shave, if you ask me."

"You're probably right," Ford replied with an uneasy chuckle. "I'll consider it."

The old woman then pecked the name into the computer, slid the service bell back behind the computer, and left the office without saying another word.

"Okay then," Ford said to himself with a raised eyebrow.

* * *

Exhaustion tried to win his body, but he refused to sleep. He paced around his musty room for hours, which, like the front office, could have used an update to its decor.

Every ten minutes he'd pull back the thick plastic shades to gander at the parking lot and the road at a distance. The longer he stayed awake the more paranoia took over his thoughts. He'd eventually drift to sleep but first had to calm his racing mind.

Dumped on the bed were the real Cy Ford's belongings from his duffel. Aside from a few articles of clothing that were most likely rejects from the man's suitcases, there was an Acer laptop, his transfer papers to a Department of Natural Resources post in Newberry, Michigan, a wad of money worth eight-thousand-dollars that he carried with him after emptying and closing his bank account before his trip north, a pair of size ten Timberland boots, a pair of Puma shoes, a cheap watch, extra pairs of socks and underwear, and a no-frills pocket knife. Ford tried to analyze the Texan's life from the items he carried. This wasn't his first rodeo. He'd stolen identities before that were far harder to assume. The only problem with this identity was that he hadn't had nearly enough time with the real Mr. Cy Ford to get into character as he had in the past with other marks. Normally, it'd take weeks to become someone else. Much like an athlete studies game tapes, or an actor rehearses for a role, he'd have to remember even the most minute details. Birthdate, hometown, name of parents, and any siblings. There wasn't any room for half-assing. In the risky game he played, if he didn't go all in, the ruse was a bust.

What he compiled from his observations of the Texan was that he was, or appeared to be, excluded from any outside conflicts that could blow his cover. He was basically a loner at this crossroad in his life. Hard to believe, because the man seemed as extroverted as they come. Maybe, he thought, the man had a lot of friends but kept them at arm's length. Trust issues possibly. He wasn't sure and would never know.

If there was anything bad from assuming this identity he would discover in good time, he was sure of that. Mr. Ford was divorced. No kids. No social media accounts to speak of. He was an only child to parents who both passed away years ago, and there weren't any burdens to keep him close to Texas. From the emails he gathered on his laptop from his personal and work accounts, the reason for his transfer to Michigan appeared to simply be that he wanted to start a new life for himself. There was nothing left in Texas for him. For a thief to land such a beautiful mark was comparable to winning the lottery. In this unknown crook's line of work, there were always loose ends. Always. He prided himself in religiously side-stepping these to perfection in every identity he claimed. It was truly an art form.

Much the same as his other stolen lives, the dead ones were the easiest to maintain. It was the live ones that created tedious obstacles. The only time he had ever used living identities was when he needed to travel to a place fast, much like a car thief does when they hop vehicle to vehicle. Living identities weren't meant for long-term use, mere days at best. Ford's rule of thumb was that the dead identities could last for years.

Of course, he could just use any original name and create his own life; a fresh beginning. He'd done it in the past. Those types of identities never lasted as long, though.

Without social security numbers and any history behind the fake person, he would end up using driver's licenses like toilet paper to cover his tracks repeatedly. It was possible to legitimize a fake person, but that took a lot of money, something he never seemed to have. This type of theft took longer to establish and was harder to maintain. Assuming the identity of someone who'd died was much easier. The mold already existed and all he had to do was just step into it. Staying the course with little obstacles was the new Ford's preferred method.

Two in the morning was when he rested his eyes for the first time in days. A knock on his room's door jolted him awake soon after. He was instantly in fight or flight mode; it didn't matter which. Inch by inch he crept to the window and carefully slid aside the plastic blinds to check who it was that could possibly want him at this hour. Nobody was there. He pulled the shades back further to reveal more of the outside world and couldn't find a soul.

The lot remained empty, aside from the same two cars. Ford then slid to the door and cracked it open. His view drifted to the doormat where a small leather bag had been left, with a handwritten note on top. He grabbed the bag and the note and immediately shut the door.

"This was my late husband's. Keep it and do something with your bird's nest. —Cass Motel"

Ford placed the note aside and unzipped the bag to find clippers, scissors, shaving cream, disposable razors, aftershave, Brute cologne, and deodorant. Every fixing he would need for his personal vanity and hygiene. The old woman's odd gesture amused him. He considered the gift for a time. It was only when he saw his reflection in the mirror above the dresser that he gave in. His general appearance resembled a crazy type most would want to avoid, and he knew he should try to look better. Through his haggard appearance though, he had always maintained something almost melancholy in his unwavering gaze. A change in the physical sense he figured was good for him, regardless. Playing the desperate wanderer had run its course.

Hot water from the motel's shower felt like he was covered in a warm blanket. He didn't want to leave its embrace. It had been weeks and a couple of states since he was able to satiate in such a simple luxury. Illinois, actually. Up until now, if he chose to wash himself, he would have had to settle for lakes and streams. And there were days he couldn't stand the smell of his own odor. Normally, he'd tough it out and reside in his stink. It was kind of a human repellent. Not many people want to go near a crazy bastard that reeks.

When he really observed his naked self in the motel bathroom, he was in awe of how thin he'd become, probably the thinnest in his life.

He was frail and his skin was tanned and burnt; a jarring turn from the virile man he was used to staring back at him. Most of his travel after his last stolen identity of Connor LaFleur was on foot. He was a foot nomad. If he wasn't hitchhiking or catching freight trains, he walked. Those hundreds of miles he hoofed in the middle of a sweltering Midwestern summer had taken its toll on his body, and his sanity. In the old days, he'd just opt for jacking a vehicle to get him as far away as he could from one life to the next. He'd hop around that way, always keeping ahead of the law after a car theft. This time, with no car, the law wasn't after him. It was plausible he was just paranoid, or maybe it was something within telling him to change his ways. He wasn't sure. A fool would chance stealing a car or pass through more populated areas to distance himself from LaFleur's life in Chicago. Ford might've been losing his shit, but he wasn't reckless. He didn't have the confidence to chance it this time around. He wasn't even sure if there *was* any heat on him, but it was a nagging gut feeling he had. He always went with his gut over his heart — always. It never led him astray. Freeing himself from Connor LaFleur left him with a perilous sense of caution. Before, he was always looking for signs that were compromised. Looks from Chicago pedestrians that lasted longer than they should. A random man who followed him on the L-train on his way home, those sorts of things. It was just too much.

LaFleur had extended family in the same state that were close by. He had a wife and a few kids that were still around elsewhere in Florida. This was amateur hour. It was damn sloppy, and Ford knew as such. The LaFleur identity began as just a steppingstone mark to carry him to the next identity he was searching for. But unpredictable circumstances made him keep the mark longer than he felt comfortable with.

Coming to Michigan was by chance, not necessity. Fleeing Illinois was inevitable. There wasn't any other maneuver he planned for, aside from taking on his next identity, which he hadn't even started to prepare for until after that deer jumped in front of that F-150. Ford wasn't a God-fearing man, nor did he believe in karma. Lady Luck, though? A different story. In a weird, crazy way, she was on his side.

As is the case with any new identity, in comparison to the art of money laundering, it must be cleaned before use. So, Ford decided to stay another night at the Cass Motel. On his last night, he snuck into the woods behind the building and dug a small pit to burn Cy Ford's credit cards as well as his laptop. Earlier, he had jotted down everything he needed from the laptop to complete his transformation. With the accident that incinerated contents the real Ford owned in his life, including turning his own body to ash, what remained of the Texan drifted to the skies as smoke.

By way of helpful locals, Ford was able to acquire an address for the Newberry DNR post. He was already well locked into the guise. There was no turning back now.

He had to play the part. There wasn't room for error. The idea of hitchhiking wasn't going to happen, either. He needed a real ride. Following his first walk around Rudyard, it didn't take him long to find it. Just off the main drag, sitting in between a Speedway gas station and a McDonald's, Ford spotted a blue and silver 1998 Dodge Ram for sale. When he checked on it, he discovered it had 192,500 miles, which was high, but the just under two-thousand-dollar price tag he couldn't pass up. The small lettering on the front windshield sign directed him to the McDonald's, where he went. He walked inside to the counter where a gangly male teenager with shaggy hair was waiting to take his order. He noticed the teen's hat barely fit on his head due to the amount of hair he had. His bangs mostly covered his eyes, to which he had to brush them to the side every so often.

"What can I get you, sir?" the teen asked.

"Can I speak with the owner about that Dodge outside for sale?"

The teen turned without hesitation and shouted towards the back grillers, "Joel!"

The teen left the front counter and was replaced with a bald and chubby fellow with a manager's name tag hanging from his McDonald's polo. Instead of a casual half-wave or generous greeting, the manager just raised his chin to Ford. He probably thought he was about to handle the usual customer complaint or job applicant.

"I'm interested in the truck for sale," Ford told him.

"Oh, all right," Joel said. "Sticker price stands. I ain't going any lower than I already have."

"$1,900 is okay with me."

"Do you have any questions about it?"

He then moved on from behind the counter when a family of four walked in the doors to order.

"Can I get someone up here?" he called to his staff for one of them to man the register.

With a hand he showed Ford to an empty booth nearby they stood in front of but didn't sit.

"It's got some miles on it, huh?" Ford commented to Joel.

"I've had it many years. No big problems to think of recently that haven't been taken care of. Radiator blew last year. Got that replaced. Has a new suspension as well. No main engine problems. No leaks or nothing. She's gotten me through some bad winters, and up here that says a lot. She doesn't owe me a thing."

"Great. Just what I'm looking for then."

"Wanna test her out? See how she rides?"

"No, that's okay. I trust you. Besides, I know where you work."

Joel's face dropped, not quite understanding Ford's joke. Only when he chuckled did Joel's stiff disposition loosen.

"Right," Joel half-heartedly chuckled. "I'll grab you the key."

Joel shuffled to the back office, while Ford removed his wad of cash from a denim jacket he bought from a nearby clothing store. He counted the right amount needed for the vehicle and put the rest of the wad back into his jacket pocket when Joel returned. Joel handed him the key that was connected to a miniature chain and Ford proceeded to pay him. Joel then squeezed in the booth and counted the money in his lap, far from anyone's sight. Ford couldn't think of why he did that, but he was under the assumption small town folks were cheap and nosey, so his inconspicuous behavior fit.

"Right on," Joel said of the right amount he counted. "She has a full tank as well. Title is in the glovebox, already signed over."

Ford shook his hand, ending the deal, and left the restaurant. He glanced behind his shoulder on his way to his new ride to find Joel watching him from the window. To Ford, it was an interesting display of typical male behavior to let go of something that held memories. For this Joel guy, he knew he bought a piece of memory from him. Could be that this was his first vehicle ever, or possibly he kissed his first girl in this thing. Ford never had those sentimental feelings about anything that wasn't breathing. To him, there wasn't a need for it — making yourself sad like that. In the end, people are bound to lose everything they love.

Ford climbed into the Ram and dropped into the sunken seat. He felt for the lever to adjust it and cranked himself forward, so he wouldn't sit as far back.

He then positioned himself in and slammed the door shut. He gave the truck a once over and could tell Joel took good care of it. There wasn't a smoky smell. The interior roof didn't have rips or cigarette holes and it must've been vacuumed on the regular. He turned the key and the truck caught and started with a rattle. He glanced back at the McDonald's to still see Joel overseeing his baby's departure from the window. That fake customer service smile stuck on him. Ford couldn't resist and pressed hard on the accelerator, spinning the wheels in place, which kicked up gravel, and then he slapped the truck in gear and tore out of the lot onto the street. He couldn't see from his line of sight but took joy in the thought of that plastered smile melting off Joel's face.

* * *

His moment to shine came the very next morning. To sell himself, he'd have to manage this rush job of an identity to perfection. Miles from the main road, he found the post was seemingly in a low-key spot, far from likely detection and generally separated from the public eye. *Oh, this was almost too ideal* he thought and grinned.

High-pitched whines perked his ears, which persuaded him to walk toward the sounds, rather than to the front door of the rustic building. He found the kennel on the right side of this post.

To his surprise he saw there were over a dozen sled dogs inside it, eating and playing in the dirt without a care on this bright midday that provided a nice breeze, which dried hints of the nervous sweat he perspired. Ford walked to the kennel's gate and most of the dogs caught notice. A few barked. Some yelped and whined and rushed to the gate's entrance to greet the unknown visitor. He squatted to their level and ran his hand along the chain-link. He felt the array of saliva-drenched tongues that popped through for a lick. From under the legs of the dog who he would later learn was Astro, a dusty gray dog with hints of black squeezed into sight and slithered himself in front of the pack to get a closer look at Ford. It was a baby North. His happy face was practically squished to the gate from the dogs behind that excitedly pushed their way to the front. Ford kept his gaze on the pooch, and he stuck his fingers through the fence to pet him, but he dodged his head to the side, unsure of the stranger.

"He's from the new litter," Avery said behind Ford.

Ford only half acknowledged her, still trying to find his footing for his new identity. What was just a quick glance, turned into a longer gaze as he was struck by her appearance.

North hesitated at first, then took advantage of Ford's distraction to lick his fingers that he left through a chain-link loop. Ford looked at the pup and tried to pet him once more. This time he let him.

"You must be the fresh blood," Avery said. "Cyrus Ford, right?"

Ford smirked, "That's me."

XXIV

A seemingly wide-eyed, healthy Ford watched the spring countryside of the Upper Peninsula of Michigan that passed by his passenger window. He was in the confines of a DNR cruiser that traveled on a highway. Nearly ten months of experience was under his belt at this point in his brand-new life.

"You don't talk much, eh?" Jett said, from behind the wheel.

Ford looked at him. Jett had a dark, thin mustache and wore a Michigan DNR baseball cap. His left hand gripped the steering wheel and the other hovered above a spitter in his lap.

"No worries, greenhorn," Jett said. "I ain't judging. It makes you a good listener. Personally, I happen to like good listeners."

"What's the location we're headed to called?" Ford asked.

"Drummond Island. That's where this small boat wreck that was called in is. We'll assess the damage and take care of whatever washed onshore. Good times."

"Why aren't the Coast Guard or State Police handling it?"

"Whoever called this in said it appears to be an abandoned fishing boat, no casualties or anything. Guard and State boys don't wanna bother with something this lame, so it falls on us, I guess. You'll learn that as the job goes. Not sure what you were used to in Texas, but sometimes we get to do some pretty dope things wearing this badge. Other times we're nothing but the piss boys."

"Good to know."

"Damn straight."

Jett gave him a wink as he drove across a bridge that connected De Tour Village to Drummond Island. Minutes after, they pulled into a beachfront, where Tom Two Feathers stood in the parking lot, awaiting them. His long hair was tied back into a ponytail and his hands were stuffed in his torn jean pockets and he was barefoot.

Avery drove into the lot close behind their vehicle and parked beside them in her own department truck. She exited with her thumbs in her utility belt like she was a cop and locked in on the lone twig-thin man.

"Were you the person that called the wreck in?" Avery asked Tom Two Feathers with authority, who stood and sized up the trio.

"I did," Tom said as he pulled a hand from his pocket to greet them. "Name's Tom."

Avery, then Jett, and lastly, and most skeptically, Ford shook his hand. Ford couldn't help but notice Tom's teeth were brown and his breath smelled like hot mustard when he came in close.

"Got a last name, Tom?" Avery asked.

"Just Tom."

The officers found it an odd response but went with it.

"Can you show us the wreck, 'just Tom'?" Jett asked.

"You betcha, friend. Follow me."

He turned around, his dry, skeleton hands back in his pockets, and walked onto the sand of the beach. The three thought it weird of his easy-going, matter-of-fact disposition, but nonetheless proceeded to follow him with mild suspicion. When they moved into the beach's wide view, where they could see side-to-side and miles onto the blue of Lake Huron, they searched for any sign of wreck debris.

Neither could locate anything but sand and water. Tom continued to lead them to a muscular man in his thirties, standing near an unmarked Bowrider. He wore dark shades and a small Coast Guard polo shirt that was so tight, it appeared painted on his weightlifter body. The man was erect with his hands on his hips and a booted foot on the bow of the boat as if he were striking a hero's pose.

"Thought the Coast Guard wasn't gonna bother?" Ford said.

"Yeah, what the hell?" Jett said. "Just Tom, what's up? What's this?"

Tom's feet touched the water in front of the boat's bow, and he stepped aside to let the muscular Coast Guard man speak to the trio.

"Thanks for coming," the Coast Guard man greeted them with a deeper voice that sounded more forced than natural. "We were able to clean what we could. In fact, we found the owner of the boat. Doubt her license is current and her boat probably isn't registered. Might be in your best interest to speak with her."

Ford's sights pivoted to Jett and Avery, who were as confused as he was about the strange encounter. Avery's patience wore thin, and Jett replied just before she could ask what the hell was going on.

"Sure, we'll talk to her," Jett said, sounding interested. The Coast Guard man helped him into the boat.

Ford and Avery gave each other a glance before they, too, decided to seek the mystery further and take the man's hand.

Onboard, Ford felt for his gun holster on his belt, and pure instinct placed himself in front of his co-workers to separate them from the Coast Guard in the event of any danger. Tom climbed into the boat without any help.

"Is it necessary for him to join us?" Ford asked, referring to Tom.

The Coast Guard man shrugged, "I don't give a shit."

"I ain't gonna bite," Tom said with a breathy laugh.

The Coast Guard man started the boat. It revved with a monstrous rumble and kept a soothing hum when cutting through the water. It sped far from land until the DNR trio onboard couldn't see the beach anymore. Soon they spotted a white thirty-foot charter boat. The Bowrider floated to its side, where Calvin Witter awaited on deck. The Coast Guard man threw a rope and Witter hauled it in closer to the charter. He then followed this by sliding a ladder to them to climb aboard.

"Up you go," the Coast Guard man said to them.

The trio was hesitant but decided to do so. Ford noticed the Coast Guard himself remained behind. He did not attempt to join them or leave without them.

"Follow me," Calvin said after the four boarded.

"No," Ford said, which made Jett and Avery halt with him.

"Excuse me?" Calvin said back around.

"We've followed enough orders. Now you tell us what the hell's going on? What are doing way out here and why are we speaking to the Canadian Border Patrol? Until we get some actual answers, we're not following anyone anywhere."

Calvin's annoyance grew and he placed himself in front of Ford. As he leered up at the five-foot-ten DNR officer, he seemed to enjoy his resistance. Both stared at each other with an unspoken understanding that whoever spoke first lost. Jett squeezed in between the two to play mediator.

"Whoa, okay. My friend here, he's not much for social interactions," Jett explained and scoped the angry man's name tag. "Listen, Witter? If you can just please tell us—"

"He's right," a female's French-accented voice projected from behind.

Everyone turned to see Niko's mother Joëlle approach from beneath the charter's deck, from what they assumed was a luxurious cabin. Rocking her Gucci shades with her hands in her white, sleeveless, wide-leg jumper, she had a certain confidence to her presence that commanded as much attention as it did respect. Her hair was short and highlighted and her tall physique was fit and toned. She appeared to be a striking French-Canadian queen of a small empire. There wasn't a hint of the stroke that would convert her to a vegetable state in a year's span.

"Calvin, dear," she said. "Please step aside. They want answers and they are entitled to them."

Calvin did as she said, but he continued to glare at Ford.

"Pleasure to finally meet you, I am Joëlle Krowchuck. However, I'm not sure if you recognize that name. Maybe you have heard of my family's company, Krowchuck Syrup? Any of you? Oui?"

"Oh yeah," Jett remarked with enthusiasm. "I love that stuff."

Joëlle followed her pleasant nod with a smile, "Good."

"Man, my favorite flavor y'all make has to be butterscotch. Hands down the best—"

"Will you shut up," Avery snapped at him.

And he did.

From below deck, Niko Krowchuck wandered in behind his mother holding a blue tote in his arms, and stood next to her, without her even knowing. He was dressed like he could fit in as a Kennedy in his white sailing sweater, wicker slip-ons, and khaki shorts. Unlike the trendy tyrant he'd become, he knew his place in this world at this stage. His mother seemed like his end-all-be-all, and he followed her every step of the way.

"Pardon the vagueness of this meeting," Joëlle told the officers with a pleasant smile. "I was always big on extravagant surprises; the child in me. I specifically wanted each of you here on my boat today. You're probably wondering where we are. Well, my *chéris*, we are smack dab in the middle of the border that separates your United States from my Canada."

"I take it there wasn't a boat wreck then?" Avery said.

"Correct," Joëlle said before the sight of her son made her acknowledge him. She placed both her hands on his shoulders to present him. "Oh. Please meet my only child, Niko. Since his father's passing, he's become an invaluable asset in continuing the growth of our family's businesses. Krowchuck Syrup," she shed a flirty smile at Jett when she said this. "And narcotics..."

That word she knew would trigger the three DNR officers. She stopped her speech just so she could observe how they would react.

"Narcotics?" Avery said. "You're fucking with us."

"*Ma chérie*, I'm afraid not. Methamphetamine, in fact."

"Why, how?"

"Dogs."

"Dogs?"

"Your department has service dogs. You own sleds. You have means to travel as you please without suspicion from the police."

"You need smugglers," Ford said.

Joëlle pointed at him, "Precisely, Mr. Ford. Winter exclusively. The water this boat floats on right here will freeze over. A nice, big, thick, beautiful sheet of ice that leads straight to St. Joseph, Canada. You've met Tom Two Feathers here, oui? He has agreed to join our operations as our cook in the northern territory of your state. His product is far, far superior to any of what our current cooks can produce in Canada. We want a partnership with him to bring his product to our country and then, of course, beyond. We've researched every method of transport across our borders.

"Air, water, road, in terms of law enforcement, each comes with critical, devastating roadblocks that carry heavy risks. The only weak part we found was winter travel on the lakes. We need trustworthy mushers. We need the three of you officers."

"Lady, I don't know how you found us, or how you even know about us for that matter, but you're way out of line," Avery said, her aggravation apparent. "You're lucky we're not on land right now."

She had already turned to climb down the ladder to the Bowrider when she heard a clatter behind her.

Turning around, she saw Niko dumping a mound of money stacks from the tote he held. Ford and Jett had already paused their actions and stood in awe.

"I'm not someone who trades threats," Joëlle told the officers. "There aren't any guns allowed on my boat. The only guns I see are yours. The three of you can leave my boat whenever you want; I promise you.

"I know you'll probably then contact the proper authorities when you reach the US, and how do you say, a *shit storm* will come my way. Then of course, as I'm sure you're wondering, yes, my wealth and my reach will beat any hearsay. So why don't we stop with the *la bêtise* and get to the proposition, oui?

"At your feet is an opportunity. No strings. Just a job and earnings. Right here is how much each of you, as a team, make in a single run. Just one run. Know that if you do business with us, you are a part of the

Krowchuck family. Our success means your success. You take care of us; we take care of you. *Toujours et àjamais.*"

Ford, Avery, and Jett didn't know what to say. They were completely out of their depth, and they knew it. While Avery was surefire against Joëlle's proposition, Ford and Jett's silence betrayed their interest.

Joëlle turned toward the stairs that led below deck, "If you want to talk further, Niko, Tom Two Feathers and I will await below deck with drinks. Please feel free to join us or leave as you came. My feelings will not be hurt either way."

She disappeared with Niko, Tom Two Feathers, and Calvin below, leaving the three alone with the most enticing bait imaginable glimmering on deck at them.

"Come on," Avery told Ford and Jett as she made another move to the ladder. "Let's get the fuck off this crazy boat."

Jett had to force his eyes from the money and was practically zombified when he followed Avery, out of habit, like she was his older sister or mother. Ford remained behind, and instead, just squatted to the pile of cash and grabbed a single stack to observe the bills to see for himself if they were real.

"Let's go, Ford," Avery said, her foot on the ladder.

He turned his head toward her, "There's gotta be almost a hundred grand here, and it's real."

"I don't care! Being here on this boat with that woman could get us in God knows how much trouble. Let's get going. Hurry!"

"What do we make, not even fifty a year? We need to discuss this."

"You can't be serious. Okay. Listen, I don't know how they do things back where you're from, but I've seen the small-time busts back home. They ain't pretty, Ford. They ruin lives. That meth-head Tom Two Feathers, or whatever he's called, I'm sure he's had his share of being on the wrong side of those busts. You want to partner with that? Huh?"

"Look where we are and who we're dealing with. She's not talking about a small-time trafficking operation. If I'm being honest, she kind of has a point. We do have the means."

"What are we talking about here," Jett said. "Are we actually considering this?"

"No," Avery replied. "We're leaving. Now!"

"Both of you are true locals," Ford said. "You know every piece of land and trail there is across the entire U.P. We've been using the dogs for part-time tasks as-is, so there isn't anyone who'll suspect us. If we cover each other's asses and play it smart, we could make some serious money."

"Who are you?" Avery asked him, her fist balled as if she wanted to punch him in the face, right then and there.

Ford swallowed hard and yielded his rock-solid composure a bit before he answered. "I have many regrets. Where I come from, you get what you deserve. Any opportunity that comes your way you grab it because it may never come back around. I was married before. Same time I was working three or four jobs, trying to get by like any other asshole. My main job was as a third-shift security guard for a high-value storage facility. They housed big value items for jewelers, museums, collectors, what have you. Stuff they couldn't find room for.

"There was a certain night a few hours into my shift where I came across a gang of masked individuals that had broken in. Ten or fifteen of them against me. Who was I to play vigilante for a barely minimum wage gig? They tied me up and stole artifacts, jewels, paintings, anything they could within twenty minutes that had value and wasn't nailed down. They weren't a violent bunch. Case in point, before they left, they had offered me half of this rare coin collection they snagged from some wealthy collector's unit.

"To this day I'm not sure why. Maybe as a thank you for not being difficult? I don't know. I rejected them and they left. Fast forward months later, my wife became real sick. It was a bad stretch. Just... We didn't have health insurance, not much of a savings to speak of, and what we could afford wasn't helping her much. Every single night I went to work I'd hoped those thieves would return, and maybe I could get a piece of the cut that time. Even thought about robbing the place myself. My wife eventually... I still carry some guilt with me because I feel it's my fault. I should've taken care of her. I had the opportunity. With money, I could've got her the best doctors and hospitals. I could have given her a better life. See, my opportunity passed, and not an hour goes by that I don't wish I would've taken those thieves' offer."

"From a guy who never talks much you sure know how to bring a tear to your audience," Jett said, his voice not its usual bubbly self.

"Ford, I'm really sorry about your wife," Avery said, "I mean it, but to hell with you. Come on, Jett."

Jett stood his ground, not budging. "Avery," he softly said. "He's right."

Avery couldn't believe Jett was leaning towards Ford's side.

"You always bitch about living paycheck to paycheck," Jett said. "Tell me, if you had this sort of cash in Vegas, would you have stayed?"

"If I had *talent* I would've stayed."

"Ford is right. We don't make shit as it is. We work inside a fuckin' secluded-ass-post, and maybe see our superior twice in six months. If all we gotta do is smuggle some drugs across some imaginary lines with our pups, then I don't see the harm in that. We're not killing anyone like they do in the cartels. This ain't *The Godfather*, either. We're just bringing some shit from point A to point B, collect our fee, and boom, paid. What's the risk?"

"Our jobs," Avery said. "Our lives. Boys, we get caught and we're done for. And for what? To get our hands on some dirty money?"

"We're in this together," Ford said. "I failed my wife. I won't fail you guys, because we have each other's backs."

"Avery, my folks could sure use the financial help," Jett said. "Like your folks, they also worked hard their entire lives and never got ahead. It'd mean the world to me if I was able to help them."

Avery's tough exterior and stance were hard to break, but Ford and Jett's words chipped away at her, and she crumbled little by little.

"Let's hit a dollar amount and cash out," Ford added. "Keep that goal in mind, and when we hit it, we bail."

"I could— I could possibly get behind that," Avery said. "But there's that whole conscience thing. My parents, God rest their souls, they'd disown me for getting mixed up in this sort of racket."

"Why don't we take this a step at a time then? Let's hear what Joëlle has to say about the operation and go from there."

"I'm down with that," Jett said, then eyed Avery again for her compliance. "Good?"

Avery was still at odds with the decision. The money, her co-workers' differences in opinion, even her own wants, made it hard to refuse the offer. Ford could see her struggling with her conscience. He stepped toward her and lifted her chin to him so she could look him in the face and hopefully realize she could trust him on the matter. He wanted to prove to her that he could become the rock she needed for the first time in her life.

"We're not going to do this without you," Ford said. "It's either all of us or none of us."

With tears in her eyes, she finally said in a whisper, "Okay."

"Are you sure?" Jett said.

"Yes," she said a little louder. "Promise me, though, we never get greedy. Not us. We don't let the money control our lives. I saw how it controlled my family growing up. I don't want to make the same mistakes."

"Deal," Ford said.

"Deal," Jett echoed.

The corner of Avery's mouth wrinkled upright at Ford, and he offered a comforting grin.

Jett led the way and went below deck with an obvious spring to his step now, followed by Avery. Ford took a moment before he signed off on something that would inevitably change their lives.

He gave a last glance at the calm water that the charter boat was anchored in, and it suddenly became rocky. The wind swept the blue and gently hit his face. Paying it no mind, he entered the cabin behind his co-workers.

XXV

Up until the shootout at the post, Ford had remained cautious of being made by the law or anyone. Currently, his and Avery's faces were plastered everywhere across the state. Newspapers, radio, television, the works.

Regardless of the muddy waters of the Krowchucks' and Easters' hands in the drug case, Cy Ford was notorious. As he made his way home, without detection, he remained cautious of his surroundings. While he was incredulous of Judge's last revelation, he'd be lying if he didn't think the nagging thought persisted. He broke past the police tape covering his property like spider webs and entered his ransacked house. He already knew his arsenal of weapons, much like his truck, were confiscated by the authorities. There was still a chance, though, that the hidden money hadn't been touched.

First the kitchen. His counter's framing had been ripped apart intentionally. The money was gone.

In the living room lay a mess of destroyed furniture and fireplace bricks that'd been pried apart by a crowbar that he found in the middle of the debris. How the entire chimney didn't collapse was baffling. Despite this, Ford felt around where he kept his hidden stash, and it, too, was gone. His bedroom produced the same results. Stuffing from his slashed mattress, torn pages from his Bible, and his books lay strewn on the floor without a care. His floor's register had been pulled from its slot and stuck inside the wall of his distant empty closet wall, as if it were slung by an NFL quarterback. He knew before he even dug his hand in the filthy vent that he wasn't going to find any money there.

Last was the basement. Almost immediately, he tripped over empty paint cans littered about the floor. Gutted. Absolutely gutted, he felt. He knew this wasn't the work of the law. It didn't have the same approach he was familiar with. Those final words Judge affirmed rang true to him now.

Ford knew Avery had ravaged through his house, leaving him nothing. How could someone he cared for so much betray him? This was the same woman he thought he knew everything about, more than anyone in his prior lives. He loved the way she made coffee every morning in the post, even though she never drank a cup. She just liked to have that cozy, homey smell in the air. He loved the way she never cared much about doing her hair, yet somehow it always managed to look perfect. There were days she'd leave tiny plants on his desk to give the space some happiness, instead of the mess it normally was.

Or there were other days she'd have him finish whatever lunch she ate that day, because she was too full to eat. She'd always claim she made too much, but Ford knew she was just making sure he had something in his stomach. It was that nurturing quality she possessed that he knew was pure and trustworthy. Ford wanted to think he could possibly give her a break in this murky situation. Maybe she acted out of fear. Or what if she truly thought he was dead? It didn't matter, the facts said otherwise. Plain and simple, it was greed. No different than anyone he's worked with before.

For once, since she went off-grid, he knew exactly where she was hiding. South of here, at her grandparents' cabin in Brevort was his next destination. Avery couldn't seek shelter in her own house with this much heat, nor could she hide with any friends; she didn't trust any of them. Her grandparents' cabin, for a few days at most, was the best hiding spot to lie low that Ford could think of. His mission was simple; get his fucking money back.

* * *

He stuck to routes he knew. Unused railways mostly. The ride itself had its treacherous terrain, but he worried more for Lucy and her puppies than his own recovery. Young pups as they were, they were newborns.

Best Ford could do was keep the family warm. Every so often he'd stop to check on them in the trailer buggy where he housed them.

There was a pup of Lucy's that reminded him of the pup's father, North. He had similar marks, and even though they were barely twenty-four hours old, the others huddled around him when they ate or slept.

By morning, Ford had reached his destination, on the outskirts of Brevort, along Lake Michigan's shoreline. It was exactly how Avery had described the area. He parked his ride in front of a stretched-out chain across a private dirt road. He then made sure Lucy and her litter were comfortable, as he wasn't quite sure how long he'd take. From his pocket, he produced an extra burner cell and texted the coordinates of the exact location to Sheriff Anson. The only essentials he brought with him were the Colt Delta Elite Rail sidearm he snagged from Diz, a buck knife from Sam Bass, and a sack he heaved over his good shoulder like he was some bad ass Santa Claus. With that, he made his lone journey along the deep and snow-covered dirt road of the Kinnomen cabin.

Avery was holed up by herself inside the cabin. It was a place she admired and held onto as one of the only good memories of her youth. Now it was her temporary asylum. She had a bandage on her temple from when she hit the desk during the previous skirmish with Judge. Aside from her grandpa's old .357 Magnum he buried in a drawer, the only other items that were left in the open were Ford's money that she had counted. There it was, laid on a table in stacks of five-thousand; all seven-hundred thousand of it, right to the penny. Counting it the last two days kept her from going crazy. That, and alcohol.

She always remained ready during her stay here. Any moment she thought the law, the Easters, or even a DNR counterpart would discover her and bring her to their own form of justice.

Her plan was to stay here a few days, possibly a week, until the heat in the area had eased, then she'd make her next escape away from Michigan. Away from this rural country of nothing but cold and white she had lived in for as long as she could remember. Florida, perhaps?

Mexico? She wasn't sure of her next destination. The only thing she knew was that she had the money to do whatever she wanted now, and her former life was just that, her former life.

While she stayed in hiding, she had drunk most of her grandfather's homemade moonshine he hid behind the protruding broom closet. Not so secret, seeing how everyone in the family knew where it was. Avery remembered her father sneaking nips when he wasn't around. When Avery and her three brothers were old enough to rebel, they also snuck a few nips of grandpa's moonshine, whenever they had a taste for it, which was often.

Avery had retired to the bathroom, pulled down her snow pants, and relieved herself, while she rubbed away some gunk on her grandpa's gun. Amid her peeing, something didn't feel right in the air. The wind blowing outside sounded different around the cabin. It shifted and then silence.

She didn't hear anything in particular. It was just an ominous feeling. She finished her business and returned to the main room to check the two front windows. There, she saw a silhouette figure limping along her road with a hump, which she quickly realized was a sack over their shoulder as they approached. At first, she thought this was some sort of sick joke, seeing how it was around Christmas and the silhouette was doing their best Santa impression. If it were the law, they'd surround the place with guns before she could even touch the window. Zero screwing around, just tactic.

Only when the dark figure drifted closer to the cabin could she see that it was Ford. Her eyes grew the size of golf balls. He was alive. The inconceivable shock of his survival instantly turned to dread, and she checked her gun's cylinder to make sure it was fully loaded, then stuffed the gun behind her back, inside the waistband of her pants.

She then unlocked the door for him. When it swung open, she put on her best astonished face and brought a hand to her mouth to really help sell the act.

Ford hesitated to enter, stopping at the welcome mat.

Whether she'd put a bullet in his brain upon entry, or if she had anyone else in there with her was anyone's guess. Only when she withdrew back into the main room to show that it was safe did he enter, but made sure she stayed in front of him.

Behind her, he saw his money stacked neatly on the table.

He closed the front door himself and dropped the sack in front of it, almost in a blocking manner.

"I can't believe what I'm seeing!" Avery said, her breath seemingly taken from her.

Ford said nothing, walked past her, and sat in the chair next to the table of cash. Avery swallowed hard and worked her way to the other side of the room for a new mason jar of her grandpa's moonshine from his hiding spot.

"Ford. This calls for a celebration! Goddamnit, we made it!"

She grabbed two small mason jars, filled them to the brim, and slid one over to Ford.

He didn't say a word, knowing he was intimidating her. He could see that she was becoming increasingly finicky.

"How'd you find me?" she asked.

"I'm a good listener," he told her, then placed the glass of moonshine on a money stack.

"Of course. You remember everything, don't you?"

Ford kept quiet.

"So, you did it then? Niko? You did, didn't you? Of course. Look at you. You're here."

Ford still didn't answer.

"What about Ray and—"

"They're all gone," he answered before she finished her sentence.

"They left the territory?"

"They're dead."

Avery blinked rapidly as she tried to pry as much info as she could from him, "But Oscar—"

"Dead too."

"Well then...that's— that's— that's great news. We're finally free."

Ford, from his chair, looked around the room.

"What's in the bag?" she asked, motioning toward it with her head. "Christmas gift for me?"

She formed a crooked smile, hinting a giggle, but that was fast to disappear when the stone-faced Ford didn't react.

"Where do we go from here?" Avery asked. "We can't go back to our normal lives — that's for sure."

"This everything?" he said, pointing to his money.

"Sure is."

"Got it laid out like this, huh?"

"Well, yes, I counted it. Not much else to do, being stuck inside here."

Ford gave a long, cold nod, "Lost you pretty early on in my run."

"Yeah, I— Things got pretty crazy at the post."

"Hmm."

"Ray left me alone with Judge, and he took that opportunity to take advantage of me. I— I feared for my life. I did what I had to do to get away, just like you."

Tears welled her eyelids.

"Yeah," Ford said. "Bad for you, though, that Judge didn't die that day. Truth be told, he held on just long enough to tell me what really happened."

Avery held her breath, the color leaving her face. She backed away, her focus nowhere and everywhere but on him. Her fingers nervously tapped the table.

"Was that your plan from the start?"

Avery shook her head; offended Ford would even think of such a thing. "You're gonna believe him over me?"

"There are many things I'm bad at, but I've always been pretty good at smelling bullshit. Lady, it reeks on you."

Avery gestured wildly with her hands in her plea for him to believe her. "Ford, it's me. I wouldn't just— just bail."

"But you did."

He kept closing in on her — slow step after slow step.

She kept her distance. "I— I didn't know."

Ford continued to inch towards her.

"Okay! Okay, I'll tell you what happened. Ray and the others left me alone with Judge to go get lunch. Judge found the gun you hid for me and went nuts. I did, I feared for my— my life. This mark on my head, s— see? That from him. I got ahold of Jett's knife and stabbed him and fled. You gotta believe, Ford. That's the God's honest truth. I was just scared, that's all! I thought you were dead!"

"You took all of it, though. All my money. I seem to remember telling you to only look in the paint cans..."

"I did what I had to do to survive!"

Ford kept slowly approaching.

Right before he could enter her personal space, Avery drew her gun from her back at him. He just grabbed her wrist in her momentum and twisted it to thwart her from shooting, then picked her up and slammed her against the wall behind them. Her head just missed being punctured by the fourteen-point deer antler trophy mounted above. The gun freed from her grip.

Avery knew certain he wanted to hurt her. Her betrayal struck the most crucial of chords. He felt like a fool. She broke right then and there in front of him, pinned against the wall with no hope in sight.

"Thought you were as good as dead... What do you want me to say? I'm weak... I'm not like you!"

She cried and cried. Tears flowed. Ford knew *these* were real tears.

"I needed that money. Ford, believe me, I never even thought about your earnings until you told me where it was. I figured there was more. I don't know, something in me just clicked. Like, there was this answer to my debt. Everything I made I gambled away. Same as my father and grandpa. Call it an addiction or whatever. But never in my life did I ever have that sort of wealth. Guess it was never enough. I always wanted more. Thought I could win and now I— I've got nothing...

Broke... Worst part is, I betrayed our friendship. It kills me!"

Ford was far from believing her, but he listened to what she had to say.

Regardless of the many lies she told, he knew she was spilling the truth this time. It made sense. Still, he knew business was and always will be business. The money was more important to her.

"Don't hurt me! Please... Please..."

She heard a *click* sound. She recoiled back thinking it was the gun being cocked. Nothing had been fired, though. *What was that sound?*

Then she realized Ford, like a magician, had her in his DNR cuffs, attached to the deer mount's antlers.

"What's this?" Avery asked, wiggling in place. "Ford?"

Ignoring her, Ford grabbed the heavy sack near the front door he brought in and emptied the meth batch he had taken from Anson's truck onto the second table. Avery's mouth dropped open, mystified. He then limped to the other table full of his money and swept the stacks into his empty sack.

"Ford!" Avery yelled. "What are you doing?"

When he finished recollecting his money, Ford dug through the fridge and found some chicken leftovers Avery made that he could feed to Lucy and stuffed them inside his sack as well, then heaved it over his good shoulder once more.

From his pocket, he produced his burner cell and placed it on the empty table that once held his money. Avery cocked her head. She still wasn't sure what his intentions were, as he worked his way out of the cabin.

"Listen to me," Avery pleaded. "Everything we've been through, please don't leave me like this."

Ford stopped at the door.

"Ford— Cy, please. My feelings for you were always real. Please, take me with you. I'm not strong enough to go through this alone."

"You're stronger than you think," Ford said.

"What about having each other's back, huh? Before, you said we were in this together and you didn't want to fail us like you did your wife. Remember that? Have my back, please."

"Avery, I never had a wife..."

He left the cabin. Further and further, he made tracks. Avery was left to wrap her head around his lie. He could hear her cries until he was almost to his snowmobile.

He checked on Lucy and the pups, who were resting. He resecured the bag of money on the back of his sled. Not long after he was out of sight, he heard sirens in the distance closing in on the cabin.

Sure, Ford knew Avery would put the DEA and FBI on his tracks, and Anson had a case he'd present to them, but he would vanish long before that reckoning. It was his specialty.

XXVI

Scads of footsteps clucked and clicked and shuffled past a hospital room's semi-open door from the hallway. A set of feet neared and entered the room. There, Deputy Jarvi stood tall, his beanie swiftly pulled from his head. Just the sight of the injured Sheriff Oren Anson seemingly asleep in his hospital bed worried him. He didn't like to see a man he admired laid up like this. The young deputy tried to scoot to a chair in the corner of the room to wait until Anson awoke.

"Wipe that look off your face, deputy," Anson muttered, his lids cracked.

"What look?" Jarvi asked and he was quick to sit in the chair.

"You know what I mean. That 'your granddaddy is on his way out' sort of look. Wipe it."

"Yes, sir."

Anson winced and groaned in his push to an upward sitting position against his headboard. When he did, Jarvi's face scrunched like he was feeling the struggle with him.

"You get her?" Anson asked.

"We got her," Jarvi replied with somewhat of a victorious and accomplished tone. "Thanks to Ford's text he sent you. She was hiding in a cabin in Brevort. Handcuffed and in possession of quite a bit of meth. A nice Christmas present from her partner, I suppose. Wish we could've gotten him and her together. Having her is better than nothing, I guess. It's a win for us, anyway. The good guys."

Anson didn't show the same optimism Jarvi did. There was an incomplete feeling that lingered and torturously rumbled in his stomach, worse than his gut wound. Ford was the real prize. Like a mosquito to blood, he was already obsessed with finding him. The lone thought that ran through his mind since his suspicions about the DNR officers was catching Ford himself, or whoever the hell he was.

"Where is Avery right now?" Anson asked.

"Well, we brought her into county and the DEA took control from there."

"Of course."

"They grilled her for hours. We were mostly left in the dark. Only real leak that came through to us was Ford's involvement in the whole operation. I'll tell you, a lot of feathers have been ruffled. Sir, you should see it. Never have I seen our office so busy with the sort of types we've got working around there. DEA, FBI, State Police, it's quite a show."

"Did she give a location on him? A hint of where he could've fled?"

Jarvi shook his head. Anson sighed in disgust. He wanted more information than his deputy could give. If he could squeeze this lemon dry, he would, but this lemon was already spent, and he knew as such.

"Don't you worry," Jarvi said. "We're putting every resource we have into finding him. Every lawman across the state is looking. The DNR is too, and the State Police. Anything they come up with goes straight to the DEA."

"Fucking DEA. I don't want the goddamn DEA on this, or anybody for that matter!"

Jarvi grew confused by Anson's anger, "Sir, I— Why not?"

"Don't you realize?" Anson yelled, jerking forward, and cradling his stomach with a grunt. "Ford, Avery, Jett, they made us look bad. This entire time they were doing what they did, and we didn't have a fucking clue."

Jarvi tried to calm his superior as he stood, his hands forward, "Maybe you should take it easy, sir."

"The hell with that! This happened on our watch, don't you see?"

"Right, but how were we—"

"We got too complacent. They might've made a joke of us early, but I was on to them. Especially Ford. I always knew something wasn't right about that man."

He rose from his bed and Jarvi rushed to his side to help him.

"Let me go. I'm fine. I just need a minute to think."

"Sheriff, I don't think it's a very good idea to leave your bed in your condition. I didn't mean to rile you. It's probably best you get back in bed and I leave."

"Don't be ridiculous, I'm fine. Nothing is going to beat an old, stubborn son of a bitch like me down. If a divorce couldn't, bullets won't either."

He released a hearty chuckle that turned into a cough.

"Okay, sir," Jarvi said with half a laugh, even though he wasn't on the same page as the sheriff.

Winded, Anson sat on the bed, helped by Jarvi, who sat next to him. Anson gathered himself to think of what he could do to keep his involvement in the case. While he thought, his teeth gnawed at the facial hair below his bottom lip.

"Listen to me, deputy. I want you to do me a favor and run to my house, and in my office in my desk, I have the case files. Grab 'em and bring 'em back to me. I figure I'll be here longer than I thought, so I might as well be useful."

"But, sir, the DEA took the case files. Top to bottom."

"No, no, I made copies of everything and kept them at my place. When I heard of the casualties discovered on the ice bridge border, I assumed the higher-ups would get involved sooner than later. Didn't think it would happen this soon after Christmas. I made copies, though, so we're good anyway."

"Sir, forgive me if I sound dismissive, that's not my intent, but our job here seems done. The case shouldn't be our problem."

"Oh, don't act so defeated! My God, when I was your age I had my nose in everything I could in the department. Nothing got past me. Show some initiative, deputy. This is still our jurisdiction"

"Uh, it's not that. I just don't wanna put my job in jeopardy."

"Ah, yes, there it is."

"Sir, I've got a family to support. This job is— You see, I— I just can't be involved in this sort of thing."

"Yeah, sure, I guess you're right."

"I'm really sorry, sir."

"No, no. It's quite all right."

He patted Jarvi on the shoulder and slid back into his bed.

"Actually, you know," Anson said. "I am pretty tired. I think the adrenaline from the gunfight is still running through my veins. It's probably best if I rest a while..."

"Sure," Jarvi said. "That's okay. I'll leave and check in on you tomorrow."

"You don't have to. I'll be fine. Just take care of the department and help steer the ship in my absence."

Jarvi smiled and rose from the bed. "I spoke with a nurse on my way in. She said you didn't want her to call any of your kids. Did you want me to? I can tell them or your ex-wife, so they're aware of what happened."

"Oh, Jesus no. I don't want them worrying about me."

"Are you sure? I feel bad leaving you here alone."

"Deputy, stop. I'm good. Get that dumb look off your face and get the hell out of here. Do your job. That's the best I can ask of you. Just do your job. That will help me more than anything else."

"Will do, sir."

Not knowing what else he could say, even though he still felt guilty for leaving his superior in that hospital room by himself during the holidays, Jarvi put his beanie back on his head and left. He was pleased that the sheriff had enough confidence in him to run things while he was out.

As soon as Jarvi was gone, Anson paid a hospital orderly to retrieve the case file copies. He then got to work studying them and thinking of what outside contacts he knew who might help in tracking down Ford.

* * *

A couple more weeks and Anson was finally discharged from the county hospital. He arrived home in his Sheriff's Department truck the same way he always had, alone. His old blue farmhouse was located on twenty acres and was a good nine minutes from downtown Newberry. It was also the remaining asset that wasn't taken by his ex in the divorce. Not like she wanted it anyway; it had been in the Anson clan for nearly a hundred years.

When Anson parked, he saw a white Jeep Cherokee Sport sitting adjacent to his house, facing the opposite direction of the access road into the property. He spotted a clean-cut man on his porch, who looked as if he had just come from Sunday Mass with how nice he was dressed in his suit coat, covered by his peacoat and dress slacks. The man stood from the stairs as soon as Anson pulled in. He must've been waiting there for a while. Anson knew the man as County Commissioner David Saari. Funny that he made the effort to come this way to see him, he thought. In all his years with the department, Anson only saw Commissioner Saari at the office, town hall functions, and around Newberry. Saari was never much for home visits, let alone one-on-ones.

He usually was accompanied by someone from his staff or his talkative wife, who complimented his dull personality.

Anson scooted from his truck with his box of files he hid under a couple of Carhartt coats. He went to the mailbox and grabbed a hefty stack of mail that was left there while he was gone and tucked them under the coats. When he reached the stairs, he put on the best fake greeting expression his face could muster as soon as he saw Commissioner Saari step down to help him with what he was carrying.

"Let me help you there," Saari said, his hands extended to relieve Anson.

Anson pulled back out of the commissioner's reach. "Oh, that's quite okay, David. I have it. I'm much stronger than I look."

"Alrighty then."

He backed away to let Anson climb the stairs. When Anson reached his front door, he placed down the box and held in a painful grunt he wanted to release from the soreness of his healing stomach wound. He was careful to reach for his key and put it in the deadlock before it hit him that he'd have to invite the commissioner in, and that was the last thing he wanted. For a while the only activity Anson looked forward to doing was kicking his feet up on his own recliner and not having a soul around to bother him.

There, he could watch whatever he wanted to on the television, without the interruption of medical staff or the casual visitor from the department dropping by to check in on how he was recovering.

"To what do I owe the pleasure, David?" Anson asked when he turned to him, neglecting to unlock the door.

"First, I wanted to apologize to you for not coming by to visit when you were in the hospital. As I'm sure you can imagine, we're pretty busy with the recent happenings around here. Never in a million years would I expect our county involved in this sort of scandal. Part of why I enjoyed my job the most was knowing the county kind of ran itself."

He chuckled to himself.

"Listen, I don't intend to be rude here," Anson explained. "Or short, but I'd rather just be by myself today and settle back into my routine. It was sure nice of you to stop by. Really, I'm doing just fine, though. I'll see you next week when I return."

"Of course, Oren," the commissioner said. "However, there is another reason I came by."

"Okay..."

"Since this whole drug thing fell in our laps, it really scared the bejesus out of everyone. Heck, it even shook me. My wife, I love her to death, but she wants to know every detail of my day now in hopes I'll tell her the feds are gone. She said the day they leave she'll know we're safe. I assure her we are, but until that day comes my three daughters will have to suffer an overbearing momma bear in the meantime."

"So, you came here to tell me everyone is scared?"

"Of course, not. No. Th— the county has held some meetings since the New Year, and everyone agreed many changes to the department should happen soon."

"Changes? What kind of changes?"

"Um, they're the sort of changes, well—"

"Come on, spit it out already."

"You, Oren. You."

"That right?"

The commissioner reluctantly nodded. Anson sighed and leaned against his front door in a defeated stance.

"Everyone agrees that it's in the county's best interest if you don't seek re-election coming up. We have our eyes set on someone we want to back, who moved up here from downstate. Someone who is more experienced in handling gang behaviors."

"Someone younger, right?

"Oh, no. Age wasn't really—"

"Don't bullshit me."

"Oren, you've been at the helm of the department since I was a kid. Everyone in the county respects you and likes you. We know the great job you've done over the years for us. I mean, if it wasn't for you leading this thing, we'd never know about the criminal activity here. We're in debt to you. I'm sure down the line you'll have a street, or a park named after you."

"A street?" Anson said with unenthused skepticism.

"Absolutely. I'll see to it myself."

"I don't give a flying fuck about a street or a park, David."

"Don't you look forward to retirement? Spending more time with your kids, your grandkids? Why be stuck in the stress?"

"To be honest, my work isn't done just yet."

"Why's that?"

"Cy Ford. He's still out there."

David rolled his eyes and sighed his response, "Oren, that work is being taken care of, I can assure you. Feds and even Homeland Security got that on lockdown. Even the State Police have stepped away from the case. There's no need to get in their way."

"They haven't caught him yet. I damn well know I can help them."

"And the next elected sheriff will assist that. Doesn't matter if you're taking the work home with you with those file copies you're holding there. Your time is running out in office."

Anson smacked his lips on each other and acted as if he didn't know what he was referring to. He lifted the box again, holding them closer.

"Yes," David said. "Jarvi reported to everyone the copies you had."

"That little shit."

"He was just doing his job. Besides, the feds, CBP and HSI were going to strong arm you, and I had to plead with them to let you end your time in office with dignity. I told them I'd have a word with you myself, after you were discharged."

"Here I was thinking you cared about how I was doing."

"Oh, I do, Oren."

"Well, I don't give a shit if you do or don't... And I suppose if I ignore you and seek re-election, you all will make it harder for me, won't ya?"

"A good bet, yeah. The people of this county will not want to back a sheriff who had all of this crime going on under his nose for so long. Save yourself the embarrassment, Oren."

Anson exhaled an elongated sigh and scanned at nothing, while he stood there at a loss. Maybe in his younger years he could spin a good spiel for keeping his job on the fly. But regardless, whether he wanted to believe it or not, he knew he didn't have the patience or fight to drag what he knew was a lost cause. His reluctant nod to David gave the answer that was hanging.

"It's the right thing to do," David said. "Oh, almost forgot, here," the commissioner reached over to the porch's railing and grabbed a Tupperware full of Christmas cookies and handed them to Anson. "My wife wanted me to give you some treats. Not sure if you're on a restricted diet, given your injury, although I'm sure you can sneak a goodie here and there. Those are snickerdoodles and sugar cookies. They're very good. Someone has to take them; I'm eating too many sweets as it is this time of year."

He winked at him and patted his small paunch, while Anson appeared annoyed and less than interested in the cookies. When the commissioner caught on to this, he paused his yarn, straightened himself, and buttoned the undone button of his peacoat to return to the rest of his day.

"I'll see you next week, and we'll get to setting up a formal press conference to announce that you won't seek re-election," David said.

Anson nodded that he understood. There wasn't anything he could say. Everything he placed value in was now ending. He could fight this request and have an arguing match with the dopey county commissioner, but he knew David Saari was nothing more than a mouthpiece for unneeded stress down the line. Say a fed drove there to have a word with him instead, or Deputy Jarvi came by to announce the county's wanting a new sheriff, who's to say they wouldn't be rolling on the ground and throwing punches?

Maybe the county commissioner delivering the tough reality was the best person for the job.

"Take it easy for the week," David said. "My family will continue to pray for your quick recovery."

Anson watched the commissioner leave his property the same way he came in. When he drove away from sight, Anson flung the Tupperware of cookies over the porch in disgust, where it broke, spreading the treats across his frosted front lawn. He then entered his house and slammed his door shut. He tossed the coats and box of files on his couch nearby and advanced to the kitchen.

The house was dark and colorless. It was a home without love that was once full of children and noise, mostly laughter. Anson checked the fridge. He took a whiff of the milk, which had a putrid sour smell. Any food left behind had begun to rot as well, so he took whatever had expired and proceeded to throw it in the trash can near his paint-chipped backdoor. When he finished, he filled a tall glass of water from the sink and guzzled it down. It was the safest thing to consume in the house.

The sleeve of one of the coats that hung on the couch in the living room caught his attention. It wasn't his. It was Ford's, which he used to cover Anson with after the shootout at the post. The soon-to-be retired sheriff just held the blood-stained coat in front of him. His head shook in disgust. The thought of the word *almost* stuck to him like a stink he figured he'd never quite be able to wash away.

He's heard of these sorts of feelings from his retired, or dead, law enforcement buddies in the past. Some of them were lower ranks, but most were detectives. They'd always ramble about the criminals that got away under their watch. Each of them had a story of a case that stayed in their thoughts daily.

Most balked at it being a curse, but Anson knew that's exactly what it was. Like him, they were men and women with respectable career highlights. A few even had medals on the job, and others medals in wartime. Still, though, they could never escape the thoughts of the cases that were left unfinished.

Anson remembered a friend he came up with in the police force, who eventually was promoted to a detective. He remembered his friend would constantly speak of this notable case in Copper Harbor of a three-year-old girl, who was swiped from her parents' home in the middle of the night while they slept. Two years later, her remains were found in Sault Ste. Marie, clear across the state from where her home was. His friend had always said how close he felt he was to solving the homicide and bringing closure to the family of the murdered girl. Over the years when the two friends discussed the case again and again, usually over a brew at a bar or a buddy's retirement party, Anson realized his friend was just spinning his tires. He had been "close" for nearly two decades. Truth was that the trail went cold and so did the case. That detective friend worked hundreds of other cases afterwards. Sent countless bad people to prison, brought relief to many families.

Still, though, the Copper Harbor girl never left him. It consumed him to the point of obsession. Three divorces later, he retired and became a private investigator. He hoped that he could solve the case under his own time, without restrictions. Unfortunately, his friend never did.

Depression reared its ugly head. He was lonely. Pushed everyone away, including Anson. It was a fall day Anson remembered when he received the call from his friend's second ex-wife telling him that he had hung himself in his garage.

Until after he was shot, Anson never understood how a single case could control somebody. He'd be damned if that was his same fate. Maybe, he thought, it was a good thing the case was ripped from his hands. In reality, Ford wasn't a sick man, nor was he someone that posed a threat to society. The only thing that drove Anson to catch him was his own ego, and he understood that. He didn't bury those feelings.

His ego affected many of the relationships in his life. Catching Ford, to him, might've been the icing on the cake. His finest moment to date. He could retire off that final, memorable note. The case will soon be out of his hands, but it wasn't like he would forget what happened. The case in the physical sense is gone but that was it.

From the coat, he looked to the framed picture hanging on the wall directly in front of him of his kids and his grandchildren; that hit him harder than any bullet could. His eyes brimmed when he observed them.

He was scared to turn into his friend — obsessed to the bitter end. Already he had lost so much time with his kids and grandkids. The job had always come first. His ego had always come first. Retirement didn't seem half bad now. He could leave the north for good and finish his days as a grandpa to the people that mattered most. People who would fondly remember him. Being remembered as a good father and a good grandpa sounded just fine. Maybe even admirable.

To the trash can near the backdoor he moved and began to ball the coat up to toss it in; a fitting end to the mess that came to his county. As he threw it inside the can, his hand felt a stiff object through the lining. He grabbed the coat back from the trash and unfolded it and dug in its inner pocket to discover an Alaska postcard. Ford's Alaska postcard. It was slightly water damaged, but not in bad condition. The color was faded and the inscriptions on the back had run a bit but were still readable. Anson examined the card for what seemed like forever before he realized what he was holding. He was quick to place the postcard on the counter near the sink and then searched the jacket for anything else. When he found there was nothing more left in it, he redirected his attention back to the postcard.

"Alaska," he said to himself, as if he was trying to understand the word. "Alaska…"

His mouth slowly turned upright in his absolute clarity of what he'd come across, and a loud laugh slipped out. The more he laughed, the more his stomach hurt. It didn't bother him at all now. His gut laugh echoed through the emptiness of his house, awakening the lonely lull.

XXVII
HOPE, ALASKA - 18 MONTHS LATER

Inside a rustic party store named Simcox Grocery, an early twenties man with a shaggy mullet and a name tag that read *"Ike"* stocked canned goods, mostly soup, on gondola shelving. He was mentally simple, but nonetheless, very friendly and well-liked, on top of being a constant hard worker. Ike had worked at Simcox Grocery since he was fifteen, after the owner's husband became ill, and she needed the help. He was someone that had to have a routine to live a normal life, which made him excruciatingly detailed in every aspect of his job. Every local knew Ike.

A bell above the store's entrance rang when the door slid open. Hearing it, Ike finished restocking what product remained by his side in the aisle and returned to the front to wait on the new business. He watched for the customer that had just entered, only spotting slivers of him through the store's four aisles. It was Ford.

He had a full, well-groomed beard nowadays. A few scars remained from his Krowchuck/Easter conflict. His look appeared even more rugged than before. He wore sandstone Carhartt bib overalls that were tattered at the knees and frayed on the bottoms, steel-toe boots that were heavily used, an Arco Alaska oil company trucker's hat, and a matching Arco Alaska parka with a hood lined in faux fur.

"Good afternoon," Ike greeted him.

Ford gave a reassuring nod to him as he placed a bag of dog treats on the counter, followed by a ten-pound bag of rock salt. Ike rang them up on a vintage metal register.

Seeing the amount on the backside of it, Ford handed him the exact money, a ten-dollar bill.

"Would you like to donate a dollar to the Drug Free America

Foundation?" Ike asked.

He proceeded to point to the paper American flag cutouts that hung across the counter, and the windows from locals who had previously donated — most likely with their purchase of anything in the hometown store. Ford politely nodded again and handed Ike a crisp twenty-dollar bill. In return, Ike slid a donation acknowledgment cutout to him and then bagged his items.

"Nice," Ike said of the twenty. "Thanks!"

Ford took the Sharpie on the counter to write on the cutout.

"Get a day off from the pipelines?" Ike asked. "Must be nice, huh?"

"Sure is."

He printed his name on the donation acknowledgment. It read: "*Sam Bass*"

"Perfect," Ike said. "I'll put it right here."

He then taped it near another cutout, next to his register. "Thank you, Sam. Have a great day!"

Ford nodded and left the store with the items in his arms. When he stepped onto the wooden porch of the store that connected a line of other family-owned and operated businesses, he gazed around the one-trick-pony town. A few vehicles rolled along the dirty salt and snow-covered street, mostly trucks with plows. There were probably a dozen people that roamed Hope's quaint downtown.

Long ago, Hope was called Hope City, when it was established in 1896 as a gold mining camp along the popular Resurrection Creek of the Kenai Peninsula. It wasn't until 1964 when portions of the town were swallowed by the earth and destroyed in the Good Friday earthquake that left the place a far cry from the one-time flourishing community. Present day, Hope consisted of various small storefronts, a tavern, a mechanic shop, and a post office. Not a single piece of franchise America was found for hundreds of miles. It wasn't quite a dying place yet, nor was it thriving in any sense of the word.

Hope was simply a symbol of survival to the people who lived there. They were proud of their hardships, and whatever good came their way they knew was earned, which created a hardened, yet resilient unity.

Next to the store was an alley that sat between Simcox Grocery and Yarney's Supply. Parked in the alley, a team of five dogs hooked to a Zephyr C-48 sled awaited his return. They were Lucy's puppies, now grown. When the lead dog of the pack spotted him, he rose to a ready position, followed by the rest.

Like his former team, Ford prepped them from the moment he could, which was when they were five-months-old. The same with his previous dogs, he started his new bunch on a diet that consisted of more protein and calories than an average domestic dog would eat any given day. Raw meat and Kibble mixed with water was their daily intake. And since he was also a frequent fisherman nowadays, his pups ate like kings. Salmon was their favorite treat, served to them at least a couple of times a week.

Before he ran them in harnesses attached to his sled, he put them through rigorous training, where he'd have them chase his four-wheeler through obstacle courses he'd created across various land. By the time they were a year old and understood his commands and the different meanings of the clicks of his tongue, he attached them to his sled.

He'd bring the dogs on weekend-long camping excursions, challenging them with every test he could think of in the wild, to see if they were able to withstand the worst of circumstances. This included unexpected weather, unimaginable rough terrains, where he strapped various weights to tow on the sled that they would have to pull, and endure, any noises that could startle them and break them from their synchronized run. He'd practice sharp turns, speeding up, slowing down, and hard brakes. Each interval fast and slow.

There were some sled dog breeds who couldn't hack the life. Synonymous to hunting dog breeds, there were those who were deemed untrainable. Ford had seen many of those sorts in his experiences. His team was unique, though. They worked in unison from the get. A well-oiled machine. They trusted each other.

There were two wheel dogs tied to the back of the rest.

He called one Izzy and the other Tom-Tom; an homage to his late friend Tom Two Feathers. Izzy was entirely snow white and extremely fluffy, comparable to a koala bear. She whined more than the rest and couldn't sleep without a toy in her mouth. Tom-Tom was a distinct brown dog with a white mouth and chest, which made him appear as if he were wearing a mask. He was an absolute spaz and had a sort of endless enthusiasm that only ceased when he wore himself to complete exhaustion, normally by sunset.

As for the swing dogs tied ahead of the wheel dogs, Ford named one after Jett, and the other dog he called Eleanor.

Jett's fur had a good mix of black, cocoa brown, and pure white. His eyes were light green, and he had the largest tongue Ford had ever seen. So large that it hung out of his mouth more than in it. His ears were folded at their tips as well, which was odd because the others didn't have the same distinction with their ears. Eleanor resembled a Siberian Husky the most, unlike her other siblings. She had a sleek gray coat that stood straight when encountering anyone but Ford. She wasn't fond of newcomers and was incredibly territorial. If anybody risked nearing the sled, she'd be the first growl heard, complete with a full set of ferocious choppers. A rather nice sled security system for Ford, and a warning for the occasional nosey person.

The leader tied to the front was different. Indescribable. That amused Ford.

There were nights when he'd feed the dogs before turning in, he would just ogle through the kennel at his lead dog with admiration, maybe even a little nostalgia. He was the dog the rest of the siblings gravitated around. None had ever contested him. He was the wolf to their sheep. From the very beginning this dog was the undisputed alpha, there wasn't any question. His coat, more fluffy than flat, was entirely black and he had intimidating golden eyes, just like North had. The only white on him was the tip of his tail and each giant paw, as if he were wearing shin-high socks. Also reminiscent of his father's, these were the unique marks of his Akita mix. He hadn't yet matured enough to become the constant rock North was, however.

On occasion, he tried too hard to impress, pacing the team until their legs burned on trails that rose into hills, or were the thickest with endless snow. He was also overly excited at the sight of bison, elk, deer, or small game anywhere within the range of his nose or ears. Nevertheless, Ford was confident his pup's youthful tendencies would fade into a great leader with age, and that's why he picked him to helm. It was his presence, not just his sled instincts, that made him a solid choice.

He called this dog West, after the setting sun.

Digging into his bag, he gave each dog a bacon treat and brushed his hand along their coats when he did. Lastly, after he fed his lead dog a treat, he bent to his level, where he was showered with a face full of warm saliva, which made him smile.

"Got my six, West?" Ford asked and was answered with a generous lick to the face again.

Ford, now Sam Bass to anyone he'd come across, stepped on the footboards of his sled. When he did, the teams' tails went stiff and straight, ready to run. Two clicks of his tongue and they sprang into action. They spit out of the alley and onto the side of the road, off the main drag. He and his team glided across the majestic land with the same grace as his former team.

Sometime later, miles beyond, Ford peered at a remote log cabin with a large wooden kennel built next to it along a meandering creek that sat on two-hundred acres of dense, unforgiving Alaskan frontier.

It was secluded and rustic. It was serene, and at last, it was his.

www.ingramcontent.com/pod-product-compliance
Lightning Source LLC
LaVergne TN
LVHW040050080526
838202LV00045B/3567